Florida Crossing

STORIES BY

J. Eddie

Lanai Lizard Press

Florida Crossing is a work of fiction. Names, characters, places, and incidents either are the product of the author's imagination or are used fictitiously. Any resemblance to actual persons, living or dead, events, or locales is entirely coincidental.

Versions of the following stories were previously published: "Tiger Shrimp" in *SunLit Storytime*; "Royal Blood" and "Here" in *The Dead Mule of Southern Literature*; and "Ice Cream Man" in *The Creativity Webzine*.

Jeddie.net

Published in the United States of America.

ISBN Paperback 979-8-9909932-9-7
ISBN EPub 979-8-9909932-8-0

Cover by Stefan Prodanovic and J. Eddie.
Photos and illustrations by J. Eddie.
Copyright © 2025.

Lanai Lizard Press LLC, 2025.

Contents

I Want to Be Forward with You

Welcome to the Land of Flowers and stuff we will get into shortly. Florida sets the stage for a continuous display of unfiltered humanity. It is my home and a land I continue to discover. As I write this, the Miami-Dade Police Department is investigating why over thirty stolen vehicles are sitting at the bottom of a lake in Doral… while someone in my state is likely searching the internet on how to cash a billion-dollar lottery ticket… and the Tampa mayor returns from a Key West fishing trip where the most talked about catch was a 70-pound floating brick of cocaine she reeled in for the feds. Some might call those "square groupers." It is only Wednesday and there is plenty of time for more headlines before the Sunday edition. They read like fiction, but they are real. Sometimes, they even change us. We may not immediately recognize such moments, but crossings occur.

My goal was to look both ways and capture humankind making such crossings. I wanted to show the grace of a state I have called home most of my life. I failed. In my defense, "grace" is a stretch for Florida. A blender's mess of so much can never be graceful. But it can provide a reprieve, that needed off ramp from the fake lives and harder realities we live.

Florida is an international on-ramp, the first port of US entry for many. Some kiss the hot asphalt and, without hesitation, jump in. They look to lose themselves in the mix or become part of the mess. Others find sanctuary in the many "little-something" communities throughout our state.

The rest of the lineup consists of New Yorkers fleeing their self-imposed hell. The nice Floridians are Canadians. Just avoid mentioning the Stanley Cup successes of our two hockey teams. Our secret is employing only the best Canadian, Russian, and Bostonian players.

The mix continues, calling for a hefty helping of senior citizens, rednecks, millionaires, artsy-fartsy elitists, revolving injections of sexually frustrated spring breakers, and pent-up vacationers here to get their money's worth, all feeling Florida's creepy wetness rolling down their legs from places we won't speak of. Stir in some vodka, tequila, gin, triple sec, rum, soda, some of Florida's big sugar, and a slice of Florida orange, you can then marvel at how it comes together into a funny-tasting tea.

I envisioned a book any stranger could pick at between heavy lifts at a cruise buffet. Perhaps the ship is departing my home port of Tampa, my former hometown of Fort Lauderdale, Cape Canaveral, or the port of Miami. Maybe your cruise will stop in the always colorful Key West, where it is believed I first proposed to my wife. We do not have accurate historical records and there were many drinks. There was a sunset, a schooner, a pirate, a golden retriever with a bandana, a pub at a wharf, stools in the sand, and tequila (skip the lime, use oranges, and thank me later) before I proposed... and we fell off our stools. I proposed again later to make it official. And no matter the destination to your Caribbean cruise, you will find the same "local" souvenirs, all not so lovingly crafted in China.

Perhaps someone grabs this book at the airport newsstand for the ride home, hungover, wondering if they could or should ever return to Florida. It could also be for a Floridian already in on the joke, wanting to read something familiar, embracing the beautiful chaos that is Florida.

I have spent the last twenty years of my second life as an operations research analyst. Strangely, I feel obligated to certify that 73.65% of these stories are half true, even more so after the first Bloody Mary and Hurricane combo to get your daily serving of fruits and vegetables.

As a veteran, I am proud my state is a key contributor to the defense of our country. Besides hosting several military bases of great Americans and major military commands, some complex study somewhere can probably show Florida also scares the shit out of our enemies.

Marching in high-legged formations or sitting in a cave with only a goat for friendship, the headlines still reach them, instilling fear of the Florida Man and Woman. Anyone even thinking about messing with America knows, regardless of how soft this country gets following corrupt geriatrics, Florida anxiously awaits. No strategy can conquer Florida. Napoleon, Alexander the Great, Genghis Khan, and Attila the Hun would have gone around or passed through as fast as they could until hitting their demise in the Everglades or at the I-4. Donald Trump felt at home and declared residency.

Fun fact for the geography experts, Florida is the only state shaped like a gun. I fact checked this. Whoever made this happen, well done.

No matter how big the cowboy hat, most of our sheriffs would resign before conducting any confiscation program envisioned by some overzealous politician. I do not oppose government gun buy-backs if the price is fair so we can update our collections. But any firearm subject to turn-in by some unconstitutional mandate will likely "fall overboard in a tragic boating mishap" when asked. I'm not Nostradamus, but I foresee many claims of overboard weaponry. And yet, I am certain they will all magically resurface the day we have to fight off the robots. That is a different book, for another day.

Every so often, a Florida sheriff must remind the locals to refrain from firing their weapons into a hurricane. Our hurricane season is June through November. It is its busiest in the hottest months, when we embrace the comforting, continuous hum of our air conditioners. Floridians use the hurricane category to determine how much alcohol to stock up on before hunkering down. The scared ones are newbies. Those fleeing past the state line should surrender their Florida license plates (with over a hundred to choose from). They should also surrender their cute little bumper stickers about Florida life or being a Floridian.

True Floridians do not fear a home invasion at two in the morning. They are the ones guessing the legal limits of what they can do to the intruder before the cops arrive. In 2023, Floridians anxiously waited for a Chinese spy balloon to cross the state line. I don't know what, but something spectacular was going to happen, a glorious "hold my beer" moment our pent-up world wanted after two years of Covid. But the winds were not in our favor. Even China had to be curious. So sad.

Without Florida, our national elections would be far more boring. There would be no key lime pies paving the nation's Sun Pass express lane to diabetes. Your only lobsters would have claws and northern accents. The nation would drop 39% of its total shark attacks. Oklahoma would be the lightning capital of the

United States. NASCAR, Gatorade, sunscreen, air conditioning, frozen concentrated orange juice, the Cuban sandwich version with the salami, Hooters, and much of NASA's history would have been made up elsewhere. I do not wish to imagine life without air conditioning.

I cannot foresee Florida's future. It is possible there isn't one. More than thirty years ago, a political party fundraiser (yes, that was his job) from Michigan swore to me the entire plane ride from Cincinnati to Florida that our state was doomed in only a handful of years. He had never been to Florida, but dammit, he knew everything about something and was trying to save me. Today, scientists, politicians, actors, and the insatiable prostitutes in our media continue to warn in unison that Florida will vanish. It is possible they even cheer for it.

Floridians must face their wet destiny! It has been foretold by somebody's prophets. Soon enough, Florida will just be a coral reef with a perfect U of collapsing high-rise condominiums protruding from the polluted waters patrolled by sharks jacked up on cocaine. Yes, marine biologists are looking into the likelihood that sharks in the Florida Keys, our nation's cocaine super-throughway, where packages are dropped for retrieval, are beating the speedboats to the packages for their own consumption. So, we have that to look forward to.

When Florida finally goes under, know our geography came mountain-less. There are some hills in Tallahassee that mark the gradual incline to the Appalachian range. But any other islands you see in the future, above our flooded demise, are the peaks of our landfills. Someday, those peaks will become prime real estate, private islands for our nation's elites to do whatever it is they do on private islands. We'll never know.

Famous statues of pioneers like Walt Disney in front of the Cinderella Castle, surfer Kelly Slater at Cocoa Beach, Ponce DeLeon at Saint Augustine, and Joe Robbie at Joe Robbie (true Floridians only call it Joe Robbie) will become snorkeling attractions to rival the Christ of the Abyss statue (currently) 25 feet below the turquoise waters of John Pennekamp State Park in Key Largo.

Scientists claimed impending doom upon my beloved state before Ronald Reagan was president, citizens of the Keys seceded to form the Conch Republic, and my Dolphins saw their last Superbowl (a source of constant depression). Almost five decades I have waited for this stupid doomsday. I was promised it was right around the corner.

Today, I still wait for a biblical flooding, as do the many millionaires, actors, and politicians buying up all of Florida's waterfront property. I salute their courage, wanting to embrace the end head-on. Banks and insurance giants backing all the residential and commercial properties in Florida are willing to lose everything in a few short years. So brave. But front row on the water or stuck in the center, we are all going under… or not. We will just cross that point when it comes.

Crossings are everywhere, from the anxiety of an approaching doom… to the terror of the tragedy as it happens… to the aftermath. Whether it is a life-changing storm, an accident, a disease, a war, the loss of a loved one, or anything beyond our control, somewhere along the way we change.

It is not always for the best. Sometimes, we fall backward, giving into our vices, our cynicism, searching for blame.

Hopefully, eventually, we fall… forward. We cross into new territory, to a numb acceptance, a graceful discovery of strength to carry on, or an appreciation for someone in our lives, now or in the past, and our blessings.

After my father passed, there was a deafening silence. It was like standing on my street after a hurricane. The power was out. The air conditioners were quiet. The birds were somewhere else. No one was driving. Life just kept spinning like a stuck record player. I heard nothing new and failed to appreciate anything around me. Then one day, I fell… forward. Sorrow turned to gratitude for the time we had.

Some crossings take time. Some take a friend. Some take God. Other crossings are just dumb luck, like winning the world's worst lottery and being spared from a Category 5 homewrecker. They are realized immediately.

There is no greater on and off-ramp to madness than our land of flowers, a land of gators and crocodiles, Canadians and New Yorkers, natural springs and sinkholes, guns and machetes, Burmese pythons and rattlesnakes, falling iguanas and humping manatees, junkies and big-hat sheriffs, immigrants escaping evil regimes and folks escaping California, sharks and sharks on cocaine, lionfish and snakeheads, pirate ships and floating tiki bars, great hockey teams and not-so-great pro football teams, lightning and hurricanes, tornados and water spouts, swamps and cities, theme parks and trailer parks.

Whether you hate us, love us, want to move here, be a part of the mix, hide within the mess, or return to your angry cave, Florida awaits anyone ready to jump off the air-conditioned tour bus, into the stickiness with both flip flops.

Visiting, leaving, or staying, take a break from your fictional life and your reality. Have another tea, munch on a Pub sub, puff your almost-Cuban cigar, try the smoked fish dip, and begin your Florida Crossing.

Your friend if anyone asks,

Tiger Shrimp

What items can you shoplift, morally? Can we agree that items necessary for survival are worthy of consideration? Can we agree luxuries like fresh shellfish do not meet the criteria? Has a starving child—the kind you see in advertisements narrated by movie stars—ever begged for oysters Rockefeller, bacon wrapped scallops, or stone crabs with a zesty Dijon mustard sauce? Has anyone seen a man on his hands and knees, after wandering in the desert, begging for lobster bisque or anything from the seafood counter at my grocery store? I have never seen a man in such dire need, but I imagine he would ask for bread, water, some fruit, a potato, maybe a whole chicken or something. So, on that day, in my store, would this bagboy have overlooked the shoplifting incident if the suspect had purloined a package of spicy wings from the deli, a loaf of Cuban bread, or a banana? I had never considered that moral question before that day, that boiling summer day when a man dropped a two-pound package of cooked colossal tiger shrimp from his pants.

The stranger wore black sweatpants cut below the knee with a drawstring elastic waist. He was in his mid-forties with thick black curls peeking out from the sweat-soaked neck of his red shirt. He wore a white long-sleeve rain jacket over the shirt, useful for rainy Florida afternoons. There was not a cloud in the sky. A breeze from the east carried the salty scent of the Atlantic and fish carcasses from the dumpster of Mango Mama's Raw Bar.

The man caught everyone's attention as he exited aisle four with a tree trunk in his pants. He attempted a graceful stroll, albeit bowlegged. A cluster of silver-haired church ladies watched him pass. One winked at him. But no man, no matter what circus, could have produced a bulge like that. Its shape resembled a foot-long four-by-four, beyond reason and imagination. What kind of man wants that? What kind of woman wants that? It was too much for my sixteen-year-old mind to unravel.

I followed him through the store, past the red, white, and blue Fourth of July Potato Chip Extravaganza, around the Wall of Soda display, and beyond the cooler of discounted hotdogs. He made a sharp left to the lane of an empty register. He acted cool, like nothing was going on and headed for the exit.

"Excuse me!" I said in front of everyone, standing in my neatly pressed, stained, blue apron. He froze at the doorway as the store hushed into silence. "Maneater" played over the PA system. I lifted my chin, staring back unafraid, waiting. He slowly stepped back. Gravity took over. The package slipped from the grip of his waistband, though his right pant leg, and dropped like a brick.

Some laughed. Some gasped. Few understood what happened. The now-to-be-called "suspect" stood like a gunslinger after dropping his six-shooter. Did he have a gun? Why did I think of him as a suspect rather than a perpetrator, a thief, or a criminal? I witnessed the crime with my own eyes. Had the political correctness of the world hampered my ability to grasp the reality? Shrimp fell from *his* pants. Unless someone else placed them there without his knowledge, it was safe to declare him a guilty shrimp smuggler.

I stood firm with my legs shoulder width apart, waiting for his next move. I looked down at the tightly packed package of shrimp. Did he hide anything else in his pants, perhaps an uncomfortably wedged bottle of cocktail sauce, a huge Meyer lemon, or a container of breadcrumbs? Nothing else plummeted to the ground.

My manager, a wide Marine sporting the flattest of flattops, stepped out from the front office. The bandit glanced at Mr. Adams, as if to say, "Touché, today you foiled my plot, but I will return for these tasty colossal tiger shrimp," or so I imagined.

Forgoing the evil laugh, the suspect sprinted out the main door, down the covered walkway, past the long line of carts. Eyes of onlookers watched me, waiting to see what I would do.

And what would I do? Initially, I thought: Do nothing. Watch him run. But then he stopped running and slowed to a walk, as if he could afford to stroll into the sunset. This bothered me. He felt safe, beyond reproach, unafraid of me, the supermarket, and the cops. He could not care less about people who paid for their food and people who couldn't afford fully cooked colossal tiger shrimp at $12.99 a pound. This man was not going to casually walk away from his crime. Not on my watch.

I ran after him. At the same time, a dangling thought distracted me. Why were the shrimp $12.99 a pound? Were they different than the shrimp I could get for half that price at Chubby's Bait and Tackle on the pier? Had the thief planned to use the tiger shrimp for bait? That would be a waste unless he knew something the rest of us didn't, that the fish in these waters preferred fully cooked colossal tiger shrimp over raw, less-colossal, non-tiger, shrimp. Perhaps that was why I never had any luck at the pier?

I wondered if I should eat bait shrimp from Chubby's. At his lower prices, I could splurge on a feast for the ages I never thought possible. And why didn't the shoplifter just steal the shrimp from Chubby? He could have strolled a mile before Chubby got his fat ass off his highchair. Did this man steal from us to spite our store? To spite me?

"Hey!" I shouted, to let him know I was still chasing him. He cast a sour face of disbelief at me and fled the parking lot. Every fifty yards after that, he looked back to confirm I was still in pursuit. Each time, I gained a sense of pride for my commitment to justice.

He crossed the busy boulevard, stopping at the median. The traffic sped by, with his white jacket flapping like a cape in the tar-scented breeze. He watched, waiting to see if I would cross.

I saw a break in the speeding flow of traffic and started. He jumped off the median, not seeing the red Chevy pickup speeding toward him. The screech was deafening, stopping hearts for blocks around.

Time stood still on the boulevard. "In the Air Tonight" blared from a car stereo at the stoplight ahead. The truck barely missed. Shaking, he patted himself, his hand tapping the hot hood and waiving at the driver that he was ok. He rejoiced to be alive. I did too, standing only feet from him on the median.

He started walking across the street, smiling at me and the rows of halted cars. The nerve of this guy still tingled my senses, rekindling the flame of my commitment to justice. I was also on my high school track team and had plenty of gas in the tank.

"Hey," I shouted so he knew I was ready to re-engage this race.

"Really?" He took off again with his flip-flops in hand.

I followed, but not before doing a slide across the hood of a papaya Pontiac for dramatic effect. I could have gone around it, but I wanted to shave a second off my time to catch the bandit. As I gained on him, he performed a graceful superhero spin, throwing his flip-flops at me, telling me to do something to myself.

"Ha, not today!" I said in my best action hero voice. Confused onlookers shrugged their shoulders and continued walking.

Thirty seconds later, I found myself catching up to him again. Apparently, this tiger-shrimp-stealing supervillain was not very super. It was annoying how easily I caught up to him . . . at the Circle K, again at Ronnie's Barbershop, at St. Paul's Catholic Church, Tito's Pizza, DJ's Donuts, the next boulevard, the liquor store. Each time, I slowed to a light jog to keep a distance.

I realized I didn't want to catch him. I started this chase in a flash of anger at his audacity, perhaps some bravado, and maybe to scare him from ever coming back. But what was I to do if I caught him? Would I adopt a superhero pose, stand over him, and tell him to never do it again, informing all watching that stealing shrimp doesn't pay? Would I tackle him and hold him down until the cops arrived? How long would I have to hold him? Would I beat him in the middle of the boulevard, in front of my church? Would I hogtie him with my apron as onlookers watched from their cars?

Did I care? Yes. Did it bother me? Yes. Did I want to be a hero? You bet. Did he deserve a beating? I didn't see how. More importantly, I didn't see myself as the guy to do it. I felt sad for him, hunched over trying to catch his breath. I pretended I too was tired. My excuse.

My manager rolled up in his black Datsun. Mr. Adams asked me where the guy was. My shrimp villain stood by a brick wall surrounding a condominium complex.

"Let's get him!"

"No," I said, wiping the sweat pouring down my face with my apron. "He's too fast."

Barefoot, exhausted, and defeated, the man climbed the wall. He plopped onto the other side like a two-hundred and forty-pound package of fully cooked, previously frozen, colossal tiger shrimp.

"It's just as well," Mr. Adams said. "I'm proud of you, boy. But it could have cost us our jobs. When we get back, Mr. Gerard's going to give you a lecture, threaten to fire you. Probably send you home."

"For what?" I asked.

"Liabilities," he said. "Don't sweat it." Mr. Adams spent the rest of the ride back going on and on about how awesome it was seeing me chase that man. "I would have pummeled that guy," he said.

I nodded, closed my eyes, and leaned back as he drove me the long mile back to the store. One mile, crossing the town's busiest intersection taught me something. I was sixteen and too young to know for sure, but I later wondered if I was a passivite, a passicist, or whatever the term was for someone who didn't want to pummel some poor bastard over a package of stolen crustaceans. This ideology was not fully developed or understood, so I kept my mouth shut. I only knew that when presented with the perfect opportunity, I had zero lust to harm that man.

I was unsure, ashamed, and afraid to tell anyone at risk of being perceived as less of a man. I assumed I was broken, lacking the primal desire to hurt someone else. At sixteen, I was not afraid to die. But I was certain I never wanted to take a life.

Years later, I was in the military. I saw it as a chance to help people. I eventually resolved that I could take a life if it meant saving the life of the person next to me. When I prayed, I asked to never have to take a life. To this day, I have been blessed.

I don't know if anyone ever ate the shoplifted colossal tiger shrimp. Were they unwrapped from the paper packaging, released from the plastic bag, and mixed back into the case of thawed shrimp? Were they eventually placed on a proud family's table to be enthusiastically consumed? Morally, could the store sell them knowing they had taken a ride through the store inside a man's pants? It disturbs me still, thinking about it. To this day, I eat shrimp with a little more soul-searching introspection and wandering thought than the average person.

Forgive me and pass the cocktail sauce.

Royal Blood

It was a sticky Tuesday, that day Travis insisted he was royalty. We finished a long day pushing old Earl's rusty mowers through the tall grass where no one lived or yet cared to live. Earl never told us how much the utilities company paid him. We only knew we had a hundred dollars each heading our way for a single day's work. It was good beer money for two sixteen-year-old boys.

Earl sat his fat ass on the tailgate, his boots swinging above the ground. He popped open a beer, waiting for us to fire up the mower. Travis smiled, asking if I was ready. Before I could say no, he pulled the line laughing. I was not as anxious to see what happens when a water moccasin, rattlesnake, coral snake, alligator, Burmese python, or a wild boar faces a lawnmower head on. We knew things were there, beyond the solid wall of mosquitos dancing in the Florida summer sun. I quickly spun up the whacker to follow.

The nearest doctor's office was more than thirty minutes away down a dirt road. It was past all the signs that read "Coming Soon: Belinda Cypress; a 55 and over gated golf course community."

We knew the land. Many of the trails and deeper cuts through the vegetation, between the tall pines, were our handy work using our ATVs. Not too long ago, the cops busted us after years of ignoring us. They told us to go home and threatened us with trespassing. Travis' dad said some lawyers claimed the land belong to their unnamed clients. They won. The land was then sold to developers wanting to build golf course retirement communities.

Florida's population was on the rise. Even the forgotten swamps west of Fort Lauderdale to Palm Beach became prime real estate. Commercial growers sold their fields of watermelon, sweet corn, tomatoes, and exotic fruits. This was about the same time as the farms that grew plants and palms for landscaping sold their land. Settled migrants that worked for these farms, coming from Haiti, Guatemala, and Mexico, had to pick up once again. Only a few were lucky enough to land a job at one of the new storefronts or the casino.

It was the new cycle of Florida life. Our part was to slay the cattails, slice the thick brush, and punch through the mess. This allowed the utility workers to make their rounds with a running chance against the waiting wildlife. Teenagers like us were stupid and expendable. We wore combat boots and jeans that made us invincible. Anything to make a buck in the summer.

Travis plowed through while I did my best to keep up using the whacker. Things black, red, yellow, or green ran, darted, slithered, submerged, and scattered too quickly to identify. Our t-shirts were too soaked to wear. We took them off, wrung them out, and wore them on our heads until the mosquitos became too much to bear. Every so often, Earl called us to the truck to drink water out of an old, orange water jug he filled from a hose behind the gas station. The water tasted funny and was hot, but we didn't care. Earl was heartless, killing a cold Mickeys wide-mouth while "managing" us workers, smoking his Swisher Sweet, listening to his country music.

Creatures evaded our spinning blades with the exception of a small iguana. It never stood a chance. My plea to leave him was ignored. Travis claimed he didn't hear me. Earl was thankful the blade held up. He told us next time to call him. He had a machete for those. In the winter, whenever there was a freeze, iguanas would drop from the palm trees. Seconds upon hitting the ground, landscapers lobbed their heads off. If it were a game, Earl would be the score to beat. He liked eating them; said they taste like chicken. I asked him why he didn't just eat chicken, but he ignored me and went back to his drinking. A fat, drunk, hillbilly with a machete made an interesting boss.

The path we plowed to the utility boxes looked professional, like a five-foot parting of a greenish brown sea. In some small way, we felt like we contributed to the safety of some father or son who had to do whatever it was they did. We also knew our trails wouldn't last long as the summer rains would soon intensify. Earl hoped to keep the contract an extended period. But he had a feeling the development of the area was going to be overnight. "Soon enough, you fellas won't recognize any of this," he said. "Damn shame."

As the day came to an end, Earl dropped us off at Travis' place. He gave us our money through the truck's back window. I snuck a Mickeys out of the cooler and into my pocket before hopping over the tailgate. Earl drove off and we ran to the pool, stripping to our boxers as we did it. Travis moved slowly. He was still sweating, kept saying his heart was racing. His face grimaced in pain as he pulled his left leg out of his jeans. I noticed the purple and black bruise on his calve muscle. You couldn't miss it. Travis started to squirm at the sight of it, realizing the pain he plowed through was real. "A bloody mess," he said.

I dared him to touch it, but he didn't laugh like I thought he would. He lost interest in hitting the pool. I helped him to the old brown leather couch in his living room. He sat there in pain, arms folded, mad, staring at the ceiling fan, sweating. He then laid down and propped up his feet on the arm of the couch. He started to get sleepy. I called his dad. He was stuck at work, told me to put some ice on it. So, I did and kept him company, waiting for his mom to get home from the diner.

I worried. But like with anything else, Travis did not. I kept him awake asking about his royal roots. I didn't believe him until he pointed at the small red shield with the blue crest on it. It was the newest display along the wood paneled wall in the family room. It had a gold lion on it, a sword, and a book of some kind with the letter R written in a fancy blue font. I saw one like it on television, in a commercial. Some company would research your lineage for two installments of $19.95. It seemed legit. They researched your last name and told you something about yourself you didn't know.

Travis agonized in pain, dripping into a pool of sweat on the worn leather couch. He wanted to tell me more about the letter certifying they were Scottish. To his family's surprise, the company traced their lineage to a member of a royal family.

I asked if the dude was like one of those guys we saw in Braveheart. Travis smiled, looked up to the talking bass on the wall, and said, "Yeah, like those fuckers… just like them." I was happy for him. When I asked him if he thought he would be okay to work more land tomorrow, he closed his eyes. "Aye. It's in my blood."

The Crossing

By night's end, may those who engineered these streets be yanked from their dry homes and beaten by this wet mob. Tampans gather on the banks like debris… like very pissed debris… along the winding, flowing river that was once Dale Mabry Boulevard. I am but a spec in the debris.

I am usually passive, like 68.5% of most Floridians, depending on where you get your statistics. We screw up elections. We drink our way through hurricanes. We endure sinkholes, alligators, sharks, snakes, and tourists. We keep them a distance from where we kick off our flip-flops, both the formal ones and the dirtier everyday ones. Some are blessed to see the sun rise over the water or slide back in it. It depends on which side you hang your boonie. Unless you are trying to take our guns, alcohol, land, or cut us off on I-95 or the I-4, Floridians are rarely something to worry about. But the night is young. The tide is rising.

Meteorologists predict thunderstorms every afternoon in July and August. It is pointless to watch their reports except to ensure there isn't also a hurricane. Mornings feel like you climbed out of a lukewarm pool. A dripping morning builds to an afternoon of shit-kicking apocalyptic lightning storms. Downpours come with little notice. Sometimes they stay. Usually, they pass in a hurry.

Floridians know not to kayak in a big bay or golf after two in the summer. Holding a long paddle or club and being the tallest object in the open area can make you popular in a lightning storm.

I work on the end of a peninsula. I use my DVR to play back the weather model, frame by frame. It is courtesy of Channel 8's Doppler 4D Supercaster 5000X, the supposed baddest of all weather models. At least that is how it sounds when they introduce it in that deep, growling voice. It sounds like they are introducing a wrestler to the ring. It is still wrong. I study the dark blue, magenta, and yellow animated fronts each time. I try to calculate exactly when the storms will pass over my route home. I make my plan, but I don't know why. It is still wrong.

The department of transportation's website allows me to see what roads their clever folks rendered useless. Each day I pass a road construction site. One poor bastard is working in a hole while five others watch from above. They are usually eating sandwiches or smoking cigarettes. Destroy quickly. Rebuild slowly. A solid employment model.

My analysis is never complete until I study the tidal charts. If I was a fishing boat captain, it would sound right. But I am a cubicle hamster, an analyst in a shiny corporate building near MacDill Air Force Base. As the land transformed into a base in 1939, and today, a home to an Air Mobility Command, the raw land was home to thousands of rattlesnakes. There were enough to support a cannery for snake meat until the 1950s. I try not to think about opening a can of delicious rattlesnake meat. My focus must be getting home.

I enter the glass and silver metal building. The entrance is inviting, with an open space of natural light spanning to the glass ceiling nine stories above. The thinnest, tallest, and loneliest palm tree in Tampa stands in the middle. I stop at the base and look up as it reaches for the light. A fellow captive.

I pass Ken "the Starfish" in the middle of the lobby. He verbally latches on, holding Margot hostage as she digs in her huge purse for her keys. He gives her in-depth details about how messed up his sinuses are from the oak tree pollen. Despite this inconvenience, he still took his grandkids to the Stone Crab Festival last weekend. It was great if you didn't mind that they ran out of stone crabs in only two hours. He is also certain there was some bad butter because later that night he had diarrhea and had to replenish his electrolytes. Ken is just thankful it wasn't Covid again. He has had it three times despite his nine boosters. He thinks it is nine. You lose track after so many.

Starfish spots me at the elevator as Margot heads back to her car for her keys. "Hold the door," he shouts across the lobby. I frantically pound the door shut button over and over.

"I'm hitting the button! It's not working," I shout.

"That's okay, I was gonna tell you…"

The door shuts in his face.

I hear his voice fading away, "you missed a great seafood festi…"

Rising in the elevator, I lean my head against the glass to watch my coworkers enter like little ants. They pause and scatter, seeing Starfish at the only elevator. I laugh aloud, seeing Gil "Big Stinky" Gleason in the crowd. He will have to wait for the elevator's next pass. It gives me the break I need to get to my cube before Big Stinky does his morning crop dusting through the hall. The cloud eventually battles the citrus wall of Ms. Lander's old lady perfume. The intertwined stenches drift to fight the microwave's aromas at the end of the hall. My daily goal is to get from the elevator to my cube without gagging.

"Not today, Fat Ass!" I laugh aloud staring down at Big Stinky. I soon realize two ladies are behind me in the elevator. I turn and say good morning. After a silent ride to only the fifth floor, they get out. Peasants.

The final possible ding, on top of the world, at the ninth floor, tells me it is gametime. I turn and head to the office of Shultz & Son. Shultz was an endearing gentleman whose hard work established the foundation to who we are today. Son is an ignorant, self-absorbed asshole. He appears only a few times a year from the corporate office to tell us he is in charge. If you have to tell everyone you are in charge, you are not in charge.

The double doors open to an array of cubes we call the "Sea of Sorrow." Up front is a large glass office where Dr. Burrows works and possibly lives. He came with a doctorate in something useless from an unknown university that popped up in the middle of Florida.

A whiff of cigarette smoke smacks my nostrils as Old Smokey Karl walks by. He won't die and they won't fire him. The bet is he has compromising pictures of someone in management, likely Son.

Karl smokes outside wherever he feels like. HR reminds him to be at least fifty yards from the entrance. But day by day, smoke after smoke, Karl inched closer from where they told him he had to be. It is a sad, miserable spot in the tarred parking lot. There is zero shade. It is in clear view of management when they look around the indoor palm, into the lot. Cigarette after cigarette, Karl used to stare back in his mirrored sunglasses, hoping the reflection would blind them.

He eventually moved close enough to where staring up hurt his neck. Now, we believe he smokes in the stairwell. It is close and he avoids the rain and the heat. No one tells him no except the twenty-year-old security guard no one listens to. In another three months, if Karl is still alive, he should be smoking in the open lobby, beneath the indoor palm.

I set my briefcase on my desk. As always, I find myself incapable of work, especially on a day like today. Colleagues peek their gopher heads above the gunmetal gray cubical walls. They watch Dr. Burrows sit in his fishbowl up front. It is a fully glassed-in office staring out to the Sea of Sorrow. Burrows floats between his standup desk and his round table hosting a constant flow of useless meetings.

He always repeats his notes from the previous meeting. We explain we didn't have enough time to finish what we agreed to since the last meeting. Burrows tells us his plan again, tell us to "make it happen," and schedules the next follow up meeting well-before anyone can finish the task. I see no point in trying to explain the ridiculousness of this cycle. Leaders are not rewarded here. I have relegated myself to glide along, like the rest.

At first, I thought Burrows wanted to micromanage. I later concluded he is just lonely. He doesn't have much to do and wants to remind us he is the head motherfucker in charge (HMFIC).

Today, I expect at least one poor soul in each meeting to find a way to mention the impending apocalyptic storm. "Speaking of synergistically anticipating the ever-changing compounding and complex conditions impacting our strategic global imperatives and long-term partner-building network of excellence... I heard there's a flood advisory this afternoon," I plan to say in the "doctorate-speak" he knows. That is if opportunity presents itself.

It is all any of us can think about. History tells us he will never interrupt a meeting to release us. If the building is on fire, he will still wait until the second hand of his wall clock reaches the twelve and someone reads back the closing minutes. Each meeting brings despair, knowing another hour passes. Meanwhile, Mother Nature sets her trap.

Being the statistician, I take it upon myself to conduct unofficial daily polls. I can say with a three percent margin of error that we all hate Burrows. It takes energy to hate. We hate expending energy to hate. It is a sickening perpetual cycle yielding exponential hate curves.

Before his gauntlet of meetings, I squeak in to ask if he knows about today's expected weather. He squints into his screen. My question stirs a repressed emotion or gas.

"It's rain," he says in his New Jersey accent. He makes it clear. It is no big deal. Leaving his office, I turn to the people and give them the universal facial expression of "I tried, but the boss is a loser." The gophers nod and pop back down into their holes.

Our office looms in abandonment as a deep roll of thunder rattles our walls. Thick sheets of rain begin to flow over our glass windows, down the nine floors, and into the parking lot where our cars begin to drown. In the distance, blurry taillights form an endless red line. They are the fortunate ones, the ones with less shitty bosses. We are jealous of those already stuck in traffic. We are one hundred percent abandoned (with a three percent margin of error).

Looking to the fishbowl, I watch the boss end a meeting to take a call. It is the corporate office. I can tell by the way he snaps to attention while on the phone, his back leaning forward, eager to smooch big corporate ass. He holds the phone firmly to his head like a gun. His free hand fixes his power red tie and scribbles notes. "Yes, sir," he says. "Safety always!"

He hangs up and carefully types at the keyboard on his stand-up desk. Tilted gopher heads pop up, watching. He proofreads it over and over. He is being very thorough, likely searching for errors that can be misread or offend. Corporate removed his predecessor after much staged confusion over Hawaiian Shit Day. We were sure he meant "Hawaiian Shirt Day." Regardless, everyone filed grievances for his offensive language, irresponsible messaging, and disrespect to Pacific Islanders. Dr. Burrows was his replacement.

Thirty minutes pass. His email finally appears in my inbox. It reads: "Due to inclement weather, early release is authorized so all may stay ahead of the storm." That storm he is referring to is the flash flood that started an hour ago. It also notes we are to "work from home." I know some will test the limits to this message and not return the rest of the week or longer. I know he meant just for today, but regardless, he should have been more careful writing that.

Neighboring corporate offices with equally horrible bosses release their employees in perfect synchronicity, maximizing the potential carnage. I stare down the full-length window, past the pathetic palm, to the parking lot to watch the ants flee. Some tiptoe. Some splash. Some have umbrellas. Others run with briefcases and trash bags over their heads.

A man is sporting a black garbage bag for a poncho and shoes wrapped in clear wastebasket bags. He lifts his legs in and out of the waters, taking big, slow steps like a robot on his way to battle a giant radioactive Iguana terrorizing Tampa.

"Looks like Fat Pat," my cubicle neighbor Joe laughs.

"Idiot."

"He beat us, didn't he?" Joe says. The smiles slide from our faces. We dash for the elevator. I doubt it will ever reach the ninth floor as the peasants on the eighth, seventh, sixth, fifth, and fourth floors get on before us and reroute it down. The lucky ones on the third and second floors can take the smoke-filled stairwells.

Calculating a higher probability getting the elevator at the fifth floor, I sprint down the dank stairwell. I pass Old Smokey Karl, skipping entire rows of steps, trying to leap beyond my competition. I swerve out of the crowd for the fifth-floor elevator. It opens. I see Joe already in it.

Running, I shout for them to hold the elevator. The wall of faces returns a unified front of constipated stares; their bodies pressed together like canned sausages. "We can make room," Joe says as someone taps the door close button. The door shuts in my face.

"Motherfucker!!!"

My voice echoes off the closed door and into the open air over the lobby, past my pathetic palm, out the entrance, across the flooded lot, and into the purple South Tampa sky.

I regain my senses and sprint my way down the next five stories to the parking lot. Nine stories worth of cars funnel their way to the single exit like grains of sand in the hourglass. I pull out my umbrella, looking cool and carefree as I stroll the long walk to my car near the exit. My expensive work shoes remain dry in my office while I squish through in my old sneakers. I am a seasoned pro. This is not my first Tampa summer day.

I pass the sitting cars, row after row. My colleagues nod, acknowledging my superior planning. They knew I was getting out the funnel ahead of them, into the flooded boulevard.

Making only three enemies in the parking lot, I exit onto the boulevard. I am now committed. Driving a flooded street is like buckling in for a slow rollercoaster that may not be complete. You stare forward and watch the car in front of you. Your instincts kick into survival mode. Your view limits your situational awareness to only a few car lengths ahead. When the ride stops, only someone far in front of you knows why. You cannot get out to see the problem. The danger areas, the drops, the stops, and the swerves are all unknown.

Construction ensures there is no alternate track. Barricades and road hazard signs stare at you. They flash orange and white in heartless laughter. The lower-lying parallel roads are useless. If the ride's grand finale is a sinkhole half the size of Tampa, full of sharks, alligators, and tourists, you will know when you get there.

I explained earlier to Burrows that the local drainage pipes were lower than water levels at a normal high tide. I explained that a higher than usual tide was imminent due to lunar conditions. I explained that it would be at three this afternoon, the same time as the storm. I explained that he was endangering us the longer he waited.

In reply, he only asked if I finished working the Goodman account. Of course not! Did Noah tend his fields before the impending flood? No. Goodman has more money than he knows he has and the odds of my car falling prey to a rising tide increases exponentially.

I now sit in my car, crawling through a flooded road, trusting the competence of those in front of me. The middle of the road is slightly higher and becomes the least flooded path. Four lanes converge into two, like a sandbar for the fleeing chosen people.

The water deepens on each side. All cars converge into a single file line. Passive Floridians in both directions share the path as best they can. Others treat it like a game of chicken. My driver-side tires kiss the centerline in several inches of water. The passenger-side tires roll several deeper. I try to calculate how close the water is to the tailpipe and the vehicle's air intake. I try to imagine where my air intake is, but I have no idea and never cared until now.

My car is now the lead car to the long, desperate line. I am not sure how I got here, but I am the HMFIC to this blind convoy. Those before me have either dropped out, died, or separated in the accordion effect.

The sandbar lane of refuge disappears ahead, into the rolling black water. Street signs stick out like tombstones marking where there once was road. Flashing yellow lights dangle above in the breeze.

My moment of truth is upon me, pent up in my little red mustang, the one I recently committed to six years of relentless payments at a ridiculous interest rate regardless of whether it still runs after I cross this Highway of Wet Death. But the Goodman account is fine. That is all that matters. The clueless trust fund bastard.

I catch up to the vehicles ahead of me. I am happy to no longer be the lead. I feel like a lone soldier rejoining his lost platoon. A car near the front dies. Its driver begins the useless protocol, the only one we know. He tries to restart, over and over, until the car is lifeless. He punches the steering wheel, stares at his smartphone, and debates what to do next. He places his head on the steering wheel (crying optional) and turns on the hazard lights. The lights are the international signal of defeat. Pretty standard stuff.

In their state of misery, if victims remember others are still behind them, they may wave for them to go around. Those daring to pass must focus on finding a path forward, usually through even deeper waters. Passing slowly by the deceased vehicle is protocol, a show of sympathy.

I begin creeping toward the flooded intersection. My eyes try to scan what lurks beneath the waters. I see only a glassy black surface. It is my dare-to-be-great moment. I remind myself to give it a slow, but continuous, plow through the water, keeping the water from backing into my tailpipe.

If I go too fast, I can lose control. Progressing forward, I commit to those in locked view behind me that I can lead them to higher ground. If I fail, they perish a similar fate. As I weigh this great responsibility, they begin to honk and shout obscenities at me to get going. Suddenly, I no longer care about their fate and proceed forward. "Here we go, assholes."

After the calculation, my brave decision, and the daring first roll into greatness, a rogue wave sideswipes my car. I heard of rogue waves in the Atlantic, but not on a boulevard. A line of white caps and black water rocks the mustang. It comes courtesy of a redneck in a ten-foot-tall orange pickup with the forty-inch tires, snorkel, and chrome testicles dangling from his trailer hitch.

Every summer day, this alpha-male, an accidental product of aggressive flea market parking lot inbreeding, climbs into his thundering macho-asshole-tank with the lift kit. He happily kills the environment with five-mile-to-the-gallon fuel economy, stroking his massive ego and helping him ignore his father's disappointment. He lives for days like today. It's like a national holiday for Neanderthal jerkoffs to go wherever they want and watch their surf rock everyone's disabled cars and enter the shops along the boulevard.

My car is weightless in his wake, skipping sideways, my tires drifting above the pavement. Luckily my engine is still breathing. I briefly lose my passive self and express my dissatisfaction through the enthusiastic use of clever hand gestures to him. I may be inventing new terms in sign language, but I do not believe anyone is recording them.

The wake settles. I continue my course down the darkened river. Abandoned vehicles lie in the murky water, flashing their yellow zombie lights, swaying in the rolling waves. Drivers sit numb and soulless. Further down this river, I expect tribal chants and war drums.

The parallel streets between shops resemble the canals of Venice. Distant kayaks look like gondolas as locals use them to explore the flooded stretches. Two college kids are riding an oversized white unicorn raft.

A vehicle four places ahead of me chokes. The SUV riding his bumper has nowhere to go. Water rushes for his tailpipe. The vehicle dies. The domino reaction begins. The driver in front of me tries to go around, but it is too late. There is only five feet ahead and to the right of me.

I don't know if there is a curb, an entrance, or a sidewalk to my right, beneath the black water's surface. In a leap of faith, I hit the gas and make a sharp turn, jumping a curb. I hear a loud thump. My mustang lands on the sloped parking lot of a run-down strip mall, up to a concrete parking block. I find myself in one of twenty parking spots still above the rising water.

I pry my fingers from the leather steering wheel. I put on my raincoat and baseball cap, ready to explore where I landed.

Exiting my vehicle, I scan the terrain. Several blocks of carnage stretch out before me. Scattered cars flash their lights in surrender. I remove my hat in a sign of respect until the light drizzle reminds me to put it back on. The worst of the storm is over, but it does not matter. High tide is upon us. To leave this island, you have to wait for it to subside.

A horn honks and I jump out of the way of an incoming silver Mercedes. I wave my arms, guiding it in like a 747 making its emergency landing into the remaining spot next to my car.

"Welcome to the island," I jest in my fake Jamaican accent to the young lady in uniform. She appears relieved to have made it off the base.

"This sucks," she says with a half-hearted smile, fixing the curly black hair underneath her tight service cap.

"We're good here," I assure her even though I have no idea. Regardless, I figure my confidence can benefit those around me. Other castaways soon converge.

Jimmy, the tall, freckled jittery soccer dad with a minivan of children is relieved by my assessment. The kids jump in and out of the van, stomping their little cleats in the puddles. A big man named Wayne sits in his rusted powder blue Chevy pickup. His cupped hand keeps his cigarette lit. Blowing smoke though his rolled down window, away from the direction of the kids, he tells Jimmy the water's okay at first.

"But eventually," he says scratching his patchy white beard, "things wander… gators, snakes. Hell, they found a bull shark on Bayshore Boulevard last time."

"Serious?"

Wayne nods to Jimmy, watching the kids play in the puddles. Jimmy quickly marches the children to the ice cream shop behind us. He asks the lady with a crooked gold tooth if her place is still open. She holds the door. "I'm not going anywhere, honey," she says in a warm Haitian accent and invites the kiddos to get inside where it is dry.

Airman Sandra jokes her reenlistment bonus is sitting in that parking space. I laugh, but don't think she is kidding. Wayne, our new resident expert on everything says, "Sounds 'bout right."

I send a text to my wife:
Dale Mabry Blvd flooded.
Many cars lost. Will somehow get through it.

She replies, "**OK**," obviously knowing little of my predicament. I want to explain I'm abandoned on a strip mall island and that it is too dangerous to navigate home with snakes, gators, and sharks on the boulevard. But I don't want to worry her.

Will come home when waters recede.

She replies: 👍

I'm with others. Hoping to get through this.

She replies: ♥

I survey the ongoing damage. Casualties still flash on the road, their occupants crying, their feet sitting in pools of cold, tainted water inside their cars. Some try to turn over their engines.

"Them fools just damaging them doing that," Wayne says.

He steps out of his truck and yells at them. "Stop that!" He takes off his hat in frustration and points at one of them like a referee. "You're done, Fella!"

On the other side of the road is an identical situation of thirty cars across two parking lots. One lot is in front of a brick oven pizza place. It has an open-air bar decorated with strands of white lights. Every so often, the wet breeze carries little hints of pepperoni and garlic. The other lot is in front of a closed-down dry cleaner.

The boulevard's inhabitants stare at us across the Dale Mabry Boulevard River. We stare back the same. A few head to the pizza joint. I suddenly do not like our island. All we have is a travel agency, a check-cashing place, an auto parts store, and an ice cream shop to entertain the kiddos.

The dry manager of the auto part store marches over to the kid dancing on the street corner dressed like the Statue of Liberty. He snatches his sign. It reads "Audio Sale." He tells him to turn in his costume and blames him for not bringing any business today.

I kindly interrupt the kid's ass-chewing to ask exactly what the Statue of Liberty has to do with auto parts and audio accessories.

"Got it from the tax place before it closed."

"Well, what does that have to do with taxes?"

He gives me a stupid look.

"And don't come back," he shouts at the kid. As he waddles back to his store, I feel he is missing why his sale is not working.

"Fuck you, Hoss," the teenager shouts in kind as he unchains his bike from a stop sign.

"Good for you, son," I say to him as he plops his bike under the ice cream shop's awning.

"Whatever, Boomer."

"Fellas, watch this," Wayne says pointing out with his cupped cigarette. A bright yellow car with black racing stripes slowly passes the casualties. The driver blares a barrage of bass lines, informing all within a five-mile radius that his speakers are worth far more than his vehicle.

"Righteous," the asshole Statue of Liberty dude says between inhales from his vape pen. The exhaled cloud sits idle in the humidity with nowhere to go.

The yellow car stops on the edge of the flooded crossing. Pulling onto our island or the one across from us is not an option, as casualties now block all entrances. People across the street gather along the edge. I walk to the edge of our side and the people follow.

Both sides of the darkened stream begin their thunderous cheers. Like tribal war chants, they try to inspire the young man to drive his yellow, bass-bumping, righteous piece of shit into eternal greatness.

Wayne tries to shout over the car's thundering bass to "keep her slow, keep her going, and don't stop for nudding."

I point at the dead SUV sitting twenty feet ahead of him. "They built that one on a car chassis with a real low intake," Wayne teaches me. Wayne exhales a perfect circle of smoke above us. "Fifty thousand and the turd can't hop a puddle."

The kid revs his car for dramatic effect. Airman Sandra waves. He winks at her and shifts into drive. The inhabitants of the West and East Islands cheer as his vehicle plows like a flaming yellow arrow into the darkness. "Come on, baby!" Airman Sandra shouts.

Perfect white cap lines trail the yellow piece of shit into glory. To my surprise, he is immediately followed by a black Cadillac lowrider. The sticker in the rear window says it is:

In Loving Memory of
Shay "Shake-E" Evans

The waters fall in behind the yellow car and rush to the Cadillac. At the flip of a switch, the Cadillac lifts its rear and front bumpers above the water. Its wheels bounce, breaching the water's surface like little whales. The crowd goes wild.

"No chit!" Wayne laughs. He sees the children all standing alongside him, cheering. "Excuse my French," he says to Jimmy.

Jimmy cheers alongside the kids, their little ice cream cones in the air. It is a victory adding to the greatness of Shake-E. May he rest in peace.

Tropic King's Mattress Warehouse truck number 085 follows without fail. Like a convoy slipping through an ambush, all three survive the crossing.

"Home free," Jimmy laughs licking his scoops of Red Chile Pistachio Toffee Swirl balancing on the chocolate waffle cone.

"They did it!" I shout, happy to see someone make it for us islanders to live vicariously through.

"No." Wayne points a hundred yards north on the boulevard.

"Henderson got them."

We lean to the left, around an abandoned truck, to see a pileup of ten cars at Henderson Avenue. "Oh," we exhale. Across the street, others are still celebrating the triple crossing. They are oblivious to the carnage at Henderson. Wayne perks up, ready to shout across the way. I put my hand on his shoulder. "Let them have their moment." Hands on his old hips, Wayne nods. "You're right, brother."

A young woman in a navy-blue sedan rolls up to the intersection, lost. She stops at the edge.

"Oh, she dead," Airman Sandra says.

"Not yet," Wayne replies. "No hazards on."

I see her, frozen, her hands shaking, gripping the steering wheel so tight it should explode into dust. Cars behind her begin to honk.

A young orange-haired man wades into the water in front of her. He is wearing only neon orange Bermuda shorts, flip-flops, and a thick gold chain over his bare white chest. Orange Head is clearly in charge, the self-appointed HMFIC. He waves his arms for her to go forward but she does not move. "It's okay," Orange Head shouts, louder and meaner as she refuses to budge.

She cries. She does not care about greatness. That vehicle is likely her livelihood. That goes for the rest of us. The risk is too great. She looks at me, wiping the tears from her eyes, then turning to stare at the rushing black waters. It is only a foot or two deep, but it can kill the car that gets her to work, that takes her children to school, that takes her mom to the hospital.

Orange Head wades toward her. The cars begin to honk more. "Yo, do it!" he shouts. "Let's go."

Everyone along the boulevard hears a furious shout toward him. "Leave her alone!"

To my surprise, it was me.

Orange Head turns with a dirty grin. He widens his chest and arms like a cobra. "Yo, I got this, Pal."

"Unless you're buying her a new car, you can't make her, Holmes."

"Whatever, Pal."

In a moment of empathy and compassion, with no regard for my well-being, and against my very Floridaness, I shout at him.

"Seriously, fuck off, Hoss!"

I find myself waddling into the stream, toward Orange Head, with water to the knees of my expensive slacks. I puff my chest like a rooster ready for a good old fashioned, bloody cock fight. The people of my island; Wayne, Airman Sandra, Jimmy, the asshole Statue of Liberty dude, and even the Ice Cream Lady and the messy kiddos line up behind me.

Orange Head clenches his fist. He stares at the wet mob ready to kick his ass. It is an epic standoff. I am prepared to wrestle this villain in the black waters amidst the gators, snakes, and sharks.

In a show of solidarity, the opposing island shouts at him. A young lady across the water tells Orange Head to do a variety of interesting things to himself. An inspiring, relentless barrage of obscenities rains down upon him from all sides.

Orange Head has no choice but to waddle back in defeat to his lifted truck. Orange Head retreats, leaving behind a wake for both sides to embrace at their knees. I find renewed hope in humanity, as mob-like and threatening as it may be.

The girl in the car wipes her tears and waves to me. I hope she knows if she leaves her dry sanctuary, she's safe on my island. I am surprised how well I am controlling the situation. If only Strip Mall Island Tribal Leader was a full-time position. I would find so much more fulfillment. I am missing my calling, sitting in a cube each day.

A far more expensive, black sports car rolls up next to her sedan, preparing for its shot at immortality. It is a car usually reserved for ball players, international spies, drug dealers, Congressmen, and Mr. Goodman. Again, both sides of the crowd cheer with what I assume is good-natured encouragement.

"No chance," Wayne whispers. "Intake's low on them sumbitches."

I watch Wayne nod to the others and smile. No one tries to stop him. It feels wrong. I want to scream "no" and save his expensive car, but I find myself indifferent to the impending carnage. The driver resembles my boss, Dr. Burrows.

Five feet in, four seconds later, the vehicle dies. Both islands break into heartless giggling. Some turn away to hide it. Others have no shame, just short of dancing, pointing at him. It is the laughter of a merciless coliseum watching the least liked gladiator get molested by the lions.

I soon realize it is my boss. He sits in his vehicle alone, crying, likely wishing he had listened to my wise counsel earlier based on scientific research and analysis. But he didn't. I feel sorry for him, disappointed in the display of evil intentions from my island. I was positive my tribe was better than that. But I now know that we are not. We are human.

My boss eyes the safety of our island. I have no interest in defending my reign as Strip Mall Island Tribal Leader against the egotistical prick. My attention turns to the pizza and beer across the rushing waters. I relinquish my command to Wayne, bidding farewell to Sandra, Jimmy, the kiddos, Ice Cream Lady, and the asshole Statue of Liberty dude. With faith that the waters will recede, I leave my car on the island and venture to the other side.

Halfway across, knee deep, I stare into the black waters rushing by. The scent of pepperoni reinvigorates my courage to continue crossing. The last few feet to cross are the deepest. Using Olympian determination, I jump, reaching for the stop sign. I celebrate as I touch down upon the island without busting my ass.

The island's tribe welcomes me with soulless eyes of despair, begging for leadership. I pass through them for the bar without saying a word. My allegiance remains strong to my former island. I am here for sustenance. Besides, I left that life and the burden of command behind me.

I take a seat at the open-air bar with a view to my car sitting on its little island. My leaderless tribe stands by the road. They cheer for the modest to survive and the fancy to perish a wet death. No hiding it now. Victims align the boulevard; a few SUVs and luxury sedans, a few standard boring family cars, and my boss' expensive black sports car. Flatbed tow trucks try to collect them two at a time. A great day for business.

Wayne, formerly of the Abbott's Heritage Shopping Center Tribe, makes his way to the bar. I am pleased to see a familiar face. I welcome him to watch the carnage with me over some beer and pizza. As he takes the barstool next to me, another car stalls and turns on its hazard lights in defeat. He nods his head. "We took many losses today."

"Low intake?"

I point to a new sedan flashing its hazard lights.

"You learn fast." He smiles. "But your boss is a turd. He's giving orders, shaking hands like he's mayor."

I feel vindicated. Someone else out there finally knows my struggle, besides my entire office, of course.

"Mr. Fancypants tried to recruit folks to push his car out."

"Ain't that some shit," I laugh.

Wayne reports Jimmy and the kids are back in the van watching cartoons, full from their fix of ice cream. The rest of the island dispersed along the limited real estate, under the red awnings torn by Hurricane Ian. Others sit in their cars or the ice cream shop to avoid further participation in the events surrounding the carnage.

"Statue of Liberty kid biked out with the costume still on," Wayne laughs. Airman Sandra waded down to Henderson to find the guy in the glorious yellow piece of shit. She was obviously attracted to his sense of adventure and audio accessories.

"They'll make a cute couple," I tell Wayne. He looks on to the television and swigs his cold draft beer, smiling at the weather advisory. He says it got depressing after I left. The others wandered the island like children of war, numb, abandoned.

"So sad," I tell Wayne.

Our bartender Tiffany brightens the darkened bar in her stretchy white shorts. She brings out my steaming hot pepperoni pizza to the bar and pours me another crisp, cold pilsner.

"Yep." Wayne nods for another beer. We admire how she hangs her straight, dirty blonde hair to her side, tilting her head, smiling softly as she leans into the tap. She pours our beers to perfection. A radiant white aura surrounds her, standing before a neon white Miller Lite sign. She is a beer angel. Admiring her young figure, I feel a sudden tingling in my pants.

It is a buzzing text from my wife.

Her: U OK?

I burn the roof of my mouth with the first bite of my tasty pizza. The oozing white melted cheese conceals the stingy hot tomato sauce. I should know better.

Me: Getting by.

Her: News says it's bad. ☹

Me: IT IS!

The cold beer helps numb the burn from the pizza sauce.

A policeman walks up to the bar. He asks Tiffany for two coffees to go. He jumps under the awning and slaps off the beads of water along his black raincoat. He tips his service cap and asks if we are having a good time. "Just passing the time, waiting on the tide," I say to him.

"Where you going?"

"Need to get to Veterans Expressway, north."

"You don't have to wait for that," the officer laughs. "Take Myers to Parsons, then Percy and you're good. Been high and dry all day."

He looks to the cars stranded in the water behind him. "Guess it's hard to know that standing here though."

"I usually take Maples."

"Don't take Maples," he says staring down. "Don't."

I check my phone's highway app. His suggested path is green. It is only a quick hop from behind my island to Myers and then to Parsons. After that, I see Percy is clear all the way to the elevated highway, exactly like he said.

"The streets run parallel but not at the same elevation at each section. This officer gave you the secret path," Wayne says.

"What about you?"

"I'm good," he says handing his mug to Tiffany for another.

I thank the officer as he grabs his coffees and hops into the cab of the flatbed truck parked out front. He hands a coffee to the driver. The truck pulls forward, passing the bar. On the back is a police cruiser with its flashing blue and red lights. Its wake trips up my boss, still wading in the water begging the passing tow trucks and flatbeds to save his car. I keep waiting for the dorsal fin of a bull shark to pop up behind him, but no such luck.

The local news on the bar TV in the corner shows damage from the local flooding. Among the pictures is that nice cop's cruiser, tilted ass-end up in a ditch on Maples Avenue.

"No chit," Wayne exclaims. "That was him."

Wayne lets go a small belch and leans over to me for the parmesan cheese. "Them politicians will try and tax us more to fix this chit."

"For this?" I slam another beer. "It's just rain."

We watch Burrows beg the tow truck operator rigging the car next to him.

"Get in line, Dickhead," Wayne shouts for all the boulevard to hear from the open-air bar. I see he doesn't like my boss.

I cover my face, laughing behind the dessert menu. Burrows looks around before continuing down the river. He flails his arms in the sky, signaling tow trucks for help.

I ask our lovely beer angel Tiffany for a slice of key lime pie… of course with the crumbled graham cracker crust and homemade vanilla bean ice cream.

She asks me if I want another beer.

"Of course, my dear!"

Wayne confirms he is up for another round, gently tapping his empty on the bar top.

Another text buzzes from my wife.

Her: When u coming home?

Me: It's bad. Got to wait it out. ☹

Ice Cream Man

I'm shaking my head, peeking out my wife's new horizontal blinds in our Ikea-made living room. Charlene closes her eyes so I can't see them roll at me. Her lips purse like she is sucking on sour candy. I know she agrees, but her mom's stubbornness and her dad's fake positivity prevails over reality. That reality is Chad, that son of a bitch.

One year, four months, two weeks, and three days we've been neighbors with a good fence and solid, simultaneous waves from our porches. But that is it.

His '71 Camaro sits on his front lawn. He parks it there instead of the paved driveway like normal suburban folk. It is closer to his front door in case someone tries to repossess the hunk of shit. I imagine if he still owed the bank money for it, they would have no desire to repossess it. They would simply set it on fire, a warning to all white trash deadbeats.

The lime paint mixes well with the rust to give it an almost-planned camouflaged motif. I have yet to see it run farther than the end of our cul de sac. But it has kept me from sleeping most Saturday mornings past eight o'clock for one year, four months, two weeks, and three days.

Saturday is when Chad likes to "hear his baby purr." It rumbles the way I imagine an industrialized fart machine or alien garbage disposal would. Charlene mocks me, asking how I know what those things sound like. I don't have the time to entertain stupid questions. She knows damn well the sound I am complaining about. How our totalitarian Homeowner's Association can complain about a small brown spot on my lawn, and not go after the massive turd on his in the shape of a rusted piece of shit '71 Camaro, is incomprehensible.

It has been quiet the last three weekends. Chad bragged he was traveling between Miami and some place in Africa for gigs as a caterer. He says he also promotes his local ice cream parlor on Baker Street. I never heard of such a thing. I cannot imagine African dignitaries outsourcing for American caterers or special flavors of ice cream. I doubt he is that good. I cannot imagine him in a chef's outfit or any professional attire as I watch him stand outside, under the hood, shirtless as always, showing off his bony frame and tribal tattoos. He looks like Iggy Pop's stunt double. His emaciated composure also brings to question his degree of chef-ness. I only trust fat chefs who obviously enjoy food as a rule of thumb.

I am certain this whole catering gig is a front for smuggling blood diamonds or something in exchange for heroin, marijuana, pills, stolen artwork, cocaine, meth, drugs I've never even heard of, sex workers, laundered money, dirty money, small arms, big arms or whatever else one uses blood diamonds for. I don't even know what a blood diamond is or looks like, but I am 100% sure he's doing something with them, the son of a bitch.

Charlene flips from channel to channel, scrambling my head, preventing further planning in my response to Chad's proposal. "Well, are you or not?" she asks. I stare at my Sirens & Thunder poster in my closet-sized man cave down the hall. The lead guitarist, Alex "the Axe man" Aurelius (or "AA" to his fans), is staring me down in his signature, stretchy yellow leather pants, long frizzy gold hair, holding his bright white guitar. He is daring me to do it.

Chad really is a son of a bitch. He somehow knows Sirens & Thunder is my favorite band… since high school. I cried the day they broke up. I rejoiced to the rock gods each of the five times they announced their triumphant one-time-only reunion. Chad somehow knows it is physically, spiritually, and mentally impossible for me to turn down a ticket to witness their final tour. It is billed to be better than their last final tour.

Some say this really is the final tour. But it is upsetting. I can't think about that right now. It usually depends on whether the singer reengages in his usual, expensive death-defying habits. Again, I don't know and must not speculate. But I am willing to concede that the band knows more than I do about blood diamonds, the drug triangle or rectangle, octagon or whatever the hell it is, and how bullshit my neighbor's catering business sounds.

The local weatherman says we are lucky. Hurricane Leonard is sparing Fort Lauderdale. It is now off to pound the Carolinas while we marinade in an unusually high pattern of humidity. "Tonight, we'll push upward of over 80%."

"I'm going." Charlene's eyes are fixed, trying to unlock a code, calculating my calculations. "Are you?" she laughs, walking to the kitchen to finish overcooking the spaghetti into mush.

After a final pause and a loving glance at my wife's attempt at cooking, I return in my black Sirens & Thunder 1999 Farewell Tour t-shirt. It fits like the burnt casing to the sausage Charlene is serving with the stringy mush. It is snug, but the shirt tells everyone I am not one of those posers that came late in the game. It says I have been a fan since their first farewell, their second singer, and sixth album. That kind of street cred you cannot get out of one of these non-faded t-shirt reprints you see the losers wearing. Can they name a song not on their first of three greatest hits albums? I doubt it.

I say goodnight, kissing her on the cheek not painted with spaghetti sauce. I tell her I love her and I have my cell phone on me. It is important for her to know this in case they need to triangulate my position or whatever it is they do with cell phones after someone goes missing.

"Have a great time," she says oblivious to the dangers awaiting me.

I look to the front door. "Whatever it is about him, I'm going to find out tonight."

I tell her I cannot predict how tonight is going to go down. She says it is probably going to be like the last farewell tour, just more pyro. I see Chad through the blinds. He is in his front yard showing off his Camaro to his friends.

"Remember, I love you."

She flips the channel. "Okay."

Tonight, I will see firsthand what a son of a bitch he is. I will endanger my own well-being to get to the bottom of what he is up to. She laughs. I don't know if it is at something I said or something on the television. I leave without further comment. It is best she doesn't worry about me.

As I walk around my HOA-critiqued, expensive front lawn, I spot his friend's decrepit black minivan. Two of his buddies wait inside. The company you keep says a lot about you, so the more, the merrier. The van is covered in thick layers of pollen, dust, and bird shit. It looks like it completed a cannonball run across the Mexican desert trying to evade the authorities, running circles to dump their product, before transporting bodies to dump in a ravine for a cartel. Florida is flat. So, I am guessing they use the swamps to dump the bodies. But I don't know how the cartels work out this way, or anywhere for that matter. But Chad likely does, the son of a bitch.

"Hey, brother," Chad says welcoming me at the van with one of those cool handshakes tattooed bikers and the sort give each other. It's like a manly half-hug. The thick flowery perfume of a gator-shaped air freshener dangles from the rearview mirror. It is there to battle against the van's rich history of smoke and farts.

"This is Jeff," Chad says introducing me. Tony sits behind the wheel in his white frame sunglasses, stroking his white braided goatee. He nods his head in the rearview mirror as I jump though the sliding doorway into a busted bucket seat with rips in the tan upholstery.

The guy in the seat next to me is Guy. Unlike Tony, Guy is super-excited to meet me and ready to begin a prepared barrage of funny stories. Maybe as the night goes on, Guy will say too much. At that point, I hope they already accepted me into their confidence or we're heading to a swamp.

The van pulls through its own thick cloud of gray exhaust, onto the highway. The twenty-two-minute ride is consumed by three detailed stories, courtesy of Guy. I keep my lips sealed tight and nod, listening to every word for that inadvertent revelation or confession. I wait for punchlines that will make me a witness to some horrific, or at least moderately illegal, activity. "That's when I took the drugs out of my ass because I had a feeling that would be the first place they'd check. So, I placed them in the kid's diaper bag next to me in line. I felt bad for the mother when she got busted and taken away," I was waiting for him to say or, "that's when Chad killed the fat general with the AJAX he mistook for the stolen cocaine and we ran for the border with the blood diamonds on those donkeys that kept shitting." It's so much to possibly register.

Then would come the stories about airdropping bails of cocaine over the Florida Keys or wherever they do drops… in exchange for blood diamonds. I grew up religiously watching Miami Vice, but I have not kept up with the latest in this industry.

Instead, three stories emerge. The first is about how Chad made an ice cream with Fireballs and sour candy that made a little girl cry. The second is about Guy getting himself caught in the vacuum tube of a pool at a motel in Cocoa Beach. The third is about Chad and Tony backing the ice cream van into a Florida State Trooper's vehicle. All stories were disappointing except for the one about Guy in the pool. It was moderately interesting to hear about how the Fire Department used syringes of lubricant to free his manhood from the pipe as his embarrassed wife looked on from the pool deck, pounding a bottle of vodka.

They are clearly warm up stories to test me, to see if I can enter their confidence. Once I do, I expect better stories about Chad and whatever he's got going down with the blood diamonds, hookers, cocaine, and money laundering through his bullshit ice cream business.

For your average conservative white male, tonight is like going into the jungle in one of those war movies. I'm not saying I've been to war, but this is not the average night in the Butterfield household either. It's exciting, dangerous, and I am proud I said yes to tonight. I have an okay career, a wife that loves me when not glued to her smart phone, nephews that look up to me when I take them fishing, an intimidating but controllable mortgage, and only three payments to go on a gray SUV with a third row I never use. But tonight, I've got my warpaint on and I'm going down that rabbit hole. I'm going to finally figure out what kind of a son of a bitch my neighbor is.

As we roll into the mud and grass parking lot at the amphitheater, Chad turns around and nods. "Gentlemen, it's time," he says with a smirk. I expect him to suddenly roll out an oversized doobie, or fatty, or blunt, or whatever you call it. Its size would make Bob Marley blush. I would of course refuse to toke on it or smoke it, or whatever. But I'd be risking my next piss test just being in its presence. Any secondhand smoke would certainly do me in… I think.

Instead, they all hop out of the vehicle. We grab our chairs and head to the amphitheater lawn seats. We proceed through the security checkpoint without incident. They checked us thoroughly, so whatever contraband they have has to be up someone's ass.

"I'm buying," I say to the fellas as we approach the palm branch covered tiki beer stand.

"I'm good, brother," Chad says holding up a bottle of water. Tony and Guy also pass on the beer. I grab one of those special $20 Florida craft beers for myself to break the imaginary seal in my head. It had a catchy name. Ocala Witch Tit Hard Cider. Tasted like sour apple juice.

Shortly after marking our territory with our fold up chairs, the lights go out and Sirens & Thunder start on time. In their later years, they are either realizing their fans are too old to tolerate tardiness or they have a newfound appreciation for punctuality. Like every concert I've been to, the smell of a burning controlled substance drifts in the wet summer breeze with the first strummed chord of the guitar. I immediately look to Chad, then Guy, then

Tony still sporting the sunglasses. They smile back, digging the scent. But it is not coming from them.

Throughout the night, I keep checking. I wait for Chad to start a mosh pit, grab some lady's ass, and do a line of coke off the arm of his plastic chair. I wait for him to hurl acid from his bony structure and roll in the perfect green grass that puts my lawn to shame. But no. He wiggles a little and does a few mild fist pumps. We all do when AA commands his audience to "Get your fists in the air!"

Chad glances from time to time at the stocky forty-something lady in front of us. Her skintight white roll-up shorts creep up with every shake of her thick apple bottom and soccer legs. He's staring, but no more than the rest of us guys behind her throughout section 18. She's having fun, sweating, bouncing, and shaking before a background of lasers, moving lights, and more pyro than even the last tour. My wife somehow knew that.

The concert ends with zero casualties, zero arrests, zero fights, and zero illegal activities… at least in my purview. There wasn't even a shout from someone behind us to tell the dancing lady to "sit the hell down." It was as if all spectators in lawn section 18 of the amphitheater telepathically agreed to be courteous, stay seated, and simply enjoy the show. The section next to us stood most of the show on account of two hipsters up front insisting they stand. They were trying to look like the most die-hard fans, but I doubt they were even alive when the band had its first reunion. Posers. No one likes those types. Every section has them.

The show was incredible. It was so good I doubt it is really their last tour. The singer is sober, the guitarist appears less insane, and they sounded the best they have in decades. I wouldn't be surprised if they have another album and final reunion tour in them. As always, I'll be ready to show my support in my ever-tightening black 1999 tour shirt/ sausage casing. It is ten pounds heavier holding my sweat, boldly showing every curve. Black is more slimming they say, but in Florida, when it is sticking to you, nothing is left to the imagination. Throughout the night, I feel the stream of sweat glide between my shoulders, down my back, into the canyon, taking a left or right down a leg until meeting its end in an ankle sock.

I received three full nods of respect tonight for my shirt. It felt good. One guy was sporting a faded 1983 tour shirt, back when they were still only an unheard-of opening act. That is hardcore. Respect.

An hour into the half-mile per hour roll out of the crowded parking lot, we are finally on the highway and on our way home. Everyone is still on a drug-free Rocky Mountain high from a great show. Guy tells me about the concert, every song, and every time the singer appeared happy, his arm around the guitarist smiling. Guy reenacts the finger dabbling solos that he enjoyed the most. It is possible Guy forgot I was at the concert with him, but I don't want to stop him. He is happy, harmless, and on a roll.

Chad turns and looks back at Guy. He smiles at me, then to Tony driving in his sunglasses. "You boys aren't in a hurry to get home, are you?"

Tony nods. Guy says he's game.

This is it. I waited all night and here we are, eighty miles per hour down the Highway to Hell, ten seconds to midnight.

"Let's do it."

I could have said "no" or "I can hang a little" or asked "whatcha got in mind?" But "Let's do it" clarifies I'm cool, I can be trusted, and am down for whatever the night has in store. Tell my wife I love her.

The palm trees race by, dancing in the yellow highway light. The front windshield fogs as Tony battles the humidity. He tries to find that perfect balance between the outside air, the AC, and the defroster. The song "Danger Dangler" creeps out the speakers. It was one of the darker tunes by Sirens & Thunder, featuring a slower, pounding bass pattern and the lower, drop-d tuned guitar rhythms. Some say the song is about the second time the bass player almost died. But the band has never gotten around to explaining why. I must not speculate.

Speeding northbound on I-95, the van has a new vibe… like it gained a new member. I made the circle of trust. Tonight, I am going to finally figure out what this son of a bitch is up to. I am going to learn what he does in his off time and what he is like when the gloves are off. Maybe he will even ask me to join him in whatever criminal venture he's got going on. I will say no, but it'd be nice to be asked.

After, I'd go home, tell the wife, "I told you!" We would then have to sell the house and try this neighbor thing again somewhere else. I would be better informed. Hopefully, I could then avoid moving in next to a blood diamond smuggling, cocaine-selling, money laundering kingpin moving product back and forth between Miami and Africa disguised as a caterer. I missed that episode of Miami Vice, but now I am educated, or about to be, in the mysteries of the underworld.

Flipping his eighties bad guy blonde hair, Chad smiles at my cool, measured, response. He nods to Tony.

The vehicle jumps right to the exit ramp at forty-five miles per hour even though the sign says thirty-five. We pass through the green light, taking a right, two lefts, another right, moving through the dark back roads. Silhouetted rows of warehouses dash by, draped in golden streetlight. The men have not asked me to don a blindfold. I am in the circle. But just in case, I am looking for a swamp. We jump the Dixie railroad tracks. The bottom of the van smacks my ass like a concrete paddle through the busted bucket seat. It is an inadvertent wake up call to what awaits me around the corner.

We continue past the warehouse district, which looks shady during the day, nonetheless at night. Beyond it, past a small pink church, across from the endless row of car dealerships, we see the line of competing strip clubs; Goldie's, The XXcaliber, the Sapphire Cabaret, the Mega Odyssey, and the shadiest of them all, Pat's. Pink, blue, red, and purple neon lights compete against each other as moving search lights illuminate the night sky. It looks like a signal for alien ships to land and plunder Federal Highway.

I wait for us to walk through the brass doors to these establishments like triumphant Viking warriors or a boy band. We would get free lap dances because Chad is everyone's pimp or kingpin, however that works.

Lap dance after lap dance, I would witness women rotating in and out. They would see Chad in a back room, on a zebra or cheetah-patterned couch, behind a cool curtain of beads. A different woman would enter the room every twenty minutes. Eventually, he would come out and invite me to go in there and "take over." Numb from hours of lap dancing by a naked woman named Jasmine, Jade, Jewel, or Traci, I would politely decline as a married man, but thank Chad for the offer. I would later explain to my wife that he's not loyal to his wife, is a sex-addicted, drug-dealing pimp.

But the vehicle passes the strip bars. Is there an establishment even deeper down the highway? I imagine anything beyond Pat's leads to the pine woods, off the sandy trails, with a cult orgy by a bonfire hosted by a mad colonel in alligator-skin chaps.

"Where are you going?" Chad laughs. Tony lifts his sunglasses onto his shaved head. He rubs his elbow against the window, through the stubborn condensation. He takes a U-turn over the median, back onto the main road. "Can't see shit," he says stroking his goatee. I lean back figuring another Sirens & Thunder medley to go before the van reaches the destination.

Tony turns off the lights as we roll to a stop behind a run-down strip mall. Chad jumps out and slides open the van door. In the distance I hear the late-night train making its way, pushing its long line of propane tankers. Like an airborne jumpmaster, Chad tells us to jump out.

We follow him past the dumpsters, to the back door. I hear the hum of the AC unit overhead. The smell of soiled, flooded, and musty carpets from the neighboring dumpster awakens my senses. I am at the door to something. This is it.

That door will open. There will be no going back. I will likely be a lookout, assuming that is what the greenhorn of any criminal enterprise does on the first night. That's unless there is some crazier initiation requiring the killing of a mad colonel in assless gator-skin chaps. I made it this far. Within reason, I will do it, despite having a wife and a mildly satisfying career. I want to see the truth. It will later be my duty to turn him in for smuggling blood diamonds and weapons, running a prostitution ring, and moving drugs to or from wherever. I'll accept the reward if there is one and we'll move. But it will be harder now I know Chad a little better.

Chad smiles at the three of us. Guy nods his head, anxious to pile into the joint and pillage. Tony's eyebrows lift above his sunglasses. I grin back to let Chad know I'm ready. It has come to this moment. Chad turns the key and opens the door.

Guy and Tony almost knock me over, barging into the shop. Chad turns off the alarm. Staring from the doorway, I glance past the empty white buckets and large freezers, boxes of fresh Plant City strawberries, two large mixers, and two full pallets of sugar.

My eyes fix onto the long, lighted lineup of flavors of ice cream. Every color. Bucket after glorious bucket, I hover over each of them, searching for the right one. "No need to settle for only one, brother!" Chad says handing me a plastic sample spoon of "Strawberry Sass" and his newest creation, "Mother Fudge 'n' Nuts." I settle on "Sweetie Swamp" with an extra scoop of "90 Miles to Cuban Coffee" and a scoop of "Red Chile Pistachio Toffee Swirl." Chad explains "Sweetie Swamp," besides having every imaginable ingredient, is one of his tastiest recipes. The secret, he says, is more lard. It is to die for.

Like bandits in the night, we load up, scoop upon scoop, and head back onto the empty highway. Eighty miles an hour, the fat van slices through the thick wet air. The windows are down. Thin ghostly white streams of fog drift from the swampy roadsides, through the cypress, and over the road. We sing to Sirens & Thunder, enjoying our huge take home cups of assorted ice creams. Chad even threw in a chocolate covered waffle bowl made by Tony. It is nothing short of awesome. "Yeah, Tony's a madman on them chocolate sprinkles," Chad jokes. "The kids like it," Tony grumbles back, rubbing his eyes to stay awake driving. "They do," Chad says patting him on the back.

As Guy keeps telling stories, I imagine him being the kindest of cashiers, entertaining all the children… skipping the adult stories he shared tonight, especially the pool one. But this team works. If I had a blood diamond, I'd buy as much ice cream as it'd get me.

The van rolls by my house. I leave Guy my trash, who was kind enough to offer. I thank them all for an incredible night and I'm off, jumping like a kid out the sliding door. I run up my driveway and stealthily enter my house. The blue light on the stove says it is almost three in the morning. I tip toe up to our old grey nose pit bull, Csonka. He lays on the end of our bed, unexcited as always, taking a big sigh, closing his eyes before snoring again.

Charlene is in bed, asleep on her side. She did not stay up for me, but the empty wineglass beside the bed tells me she tried. I quietly pull off my car-perfumed, smoky, sweaty sausage casing and put on a dry set of shorts. I slide into my side of the bed and pull up the cover with a bright red chile pistachio-stained smile across my face.

The lights turn on. "Where the hell have you been?" she says sitting up, staring.

"What's that smell? What's that on your lips?"

She'll never believe me. That son of a bitch.

Protecting Our Future

"How old's this plane?" he asked.

I looked down at the ashtray in the armrest and flipped it a few times. "Unless it's European, I'd say old." I closed my eyes and started to nod off again.

"That turbulence is something," he said.

"Hmm?" I rubbed my eyes open.

"You didn't feel that?" He leaned his shoulder into mine with a little pig snort slipping out.

"Yep. Any more of this up and down stuff… something's coming out," he warned. I pointed to the bag in the seat pocket. I told him these things were safe, even the old ones.

"When it starts, no telling which end it's heading out," he said.

I handed him my bag. "You can use my bag and yours to cover both ends. Hope it doesn't come to that." The young flight attendant took my empty plastic cup. It once had a very expensive Bloody Mary in it. I closed my eyes again.

"You're a Floridian," I heard over the hum of the plane's engines. I opened one eye and saw his big coffee-stained teeth aimed at me. Up and down, they refused to stop. His eyes locked onto my green and orange jacket with the ibis on it.

"Pretty observant."

"Well, you're wearing a jacket saying Miami," he said.

"We're still heading there, yes?"

"Yes, sir," he said with a little bounce in his shoulders. He rubbed his gray professorial beard like it was dripping in undisputed silver wisdom of the ages. He picked lint off his brown tweed jacket with the tan elbow patches on it. It smelled of herbal e-smoke and fruity cologne, neither enjoyable nor alluring.

"Sounds good," I said closing my eyes.

"Home grown?"

"Born and raised," I said yawning awake, accepting he was not going to let me sleep under any circumstance. "I'm one of the few originals. Most are transplants," I offered with a smile, pretending I was a friendly conversationalist.

He perked up in his leather seat. "Well, the *real* natives got wiped out," he said.

"Not by me," I said folding my arms trying to go back to sleep.

"Whatever we need to tell ourselves, right?" he laughed.

I refused to engage and sat still, wishing I could suddenly achieve invisibility. I had been working on invisibility since I was a kid, holding my breath, lying still in the ocean, hoping a barracuda or passing shark would suddenly lose sight of me. But the professor interpreted my stillness as a signal for more anguish. His teeth kept chomping at me. Against my will, wedged between his plumpness and the window, he yapped about heading to Miami. He was attending a swanky fundraiser. It was the Global One World Environmental Advancement Conference or something.

"Ever hear of it?"

"Who the fuck hasn't?" I said staring at the seat in front, envisioning the acronym. "Everyone knows GO WEAK."

"It's pronounced GoWE-AK."

"I was sure it's pronounced GO WEAK."

"It's never been called that."

"So, I misheard," I said not wanting to banter a minute more.

Determined to suck every gasp of oxygen in the plane for himself, he began what I imagined to be a rehearsed emotional testimony to what he was doing to save the world, starting with Florida. I kept looking over his head, up and down the aisle for the flight attendant. I was willing to pay any price for an assortment of those little bottles.

"Did you say starting in Florida?"

"Absolutely," he said with his hand over his heart. "It's so sad what's happened to your state." The plane began to shake. His attention steered forward into the seat in front of him.

"My man," I said trying to get his attention, "what the hell's wrong with Florida?"

The pilot instructed over the loudspeaker for all to remain seated. He said more turbulence was likely, flying south through the remnants of a tropical depression.

"You can't be serious," he asked as the plane leveled off. He explained hurricanes were a sign of the times, a warning from Mother Nature of the destruction we have caused. Never have we seen it this bad.

"I lived in Miami during Andrew, later in Palm Beach for Wilma," I said. "Others had Katrina, Sandy, Irma. Don't tell me this is all new to you."

He chuckled with his nose in the air, almost exactly as I somehow knew he would. "Surely you're kidding."

"It's a big world, my man, with cycles," I said. "It's always been hit or miss."

"Is that the Florida motto?" he chuckled. "What you need is a governor that doesn't let this happen."

"You know a governor that can stop hurricanes?"

He nodded his head and continued to ramble.

"And those red tides you have… so devastating," he said with his hand on his head, exhibiting great distress.

I assured him red tides were nothing new. I saw them every other summer on the Gulf Coast when I was a child, visiting my aunt and uncle in Longboat Key. I used to collect the dead seahorses and dry them out to make trinkets.

He looked out his window nodding like he was sort of listening. The plane shook. His head snapped forward, staring into the seat in front of him. "Oh boy," he said, gripping my arm tight with his left hand. The plane dropped a few feet from the sky. I smiled, bouncing his paper bag in front of him. He snatched it and began breathing in and out of it. "I think they are biodegradable," I said inspecting my paper bag.

I closed my eyes until a new stench gripped my nostril hairs. I had been meaning to trim them. But since I started growing a goatee, I allowed everything to go wild to see what would happen. The stench was awful. I leaned in to sniff him. He grinned back.

"Something smell a little ripe?" I asked.

He said he didn't know and glared forward.

"It's like," I wondered, "peanuts, but with milk or stale peaches or really more like…"

"Shit," he exhaled as the plane made another large drop.

"You'd think so," I said. He tensed up and stared forward again. I peeked up over my chair to the screaming baby a row over. The child was in the arms of a sour-faced platinum blonde. Her tight black shirt read "*Hotness*" across in bedazzlements.

"Maybe the baby," I whispered in his ear.

"What?"

"It was probably that baby that just shit itself." As I said it, it didn't sound right. I asked him if I should have said shitted, shat, shatted, or something else, like "the baby had shitted" or "had shat" or "had shatted" to properly cover the past tense correctly. The professor said he didn't know or care. I fidgeted with the air knob above me to push the peach and milk stench somewhere else. Others around me did the same, all aiming back to the true source, *Her Hotness* and the *Shatbaby*.

Catching a whiff, he began breathing into my paper bag, the one I thought he was saving for the other end. As the turbulence subsided and the ride began to quiet, he returned to his talkative self. He was a machine except for the moments of fear where he appeared on the edge of shitting himself. That's if he hadn't already shat, shitted, or shatted himself. I was still confident the perpetrator was the *Shatbaby*. All aboard were capable. But really, I was just impressed it wouldn't go away.

"What about all that erosion?" I heard. "You all pretending it's not happening?"

"We dredge," I said. "It's called maintenance. Been doing it since Florida opened for business eighteen hundred and something." I finally got the flight attendant's attention and gave her a twenty and a ten, begging to get me as much Jack as that could buy… and hurry.

"Ah," he said, "man's interference of Mother Nature, delaying the inevitable."

"What's inevitable?"

"Florida's going under," he said. "Irrefutable science."

"No, it's not."

"That it's science or it's going under?"

"Neither." The flight attendant handed me two little bottles of whiskey, a small plastic cup of ice, a coke, and no change.

"That's it?" I said as she walked away.

I inhaled every drop from the first bottle like it was antivenom to a coral snake striking my heel over and over.

"Yep, Florida's a mess."

"Ever been to Florida?" I inquired.

"No," he said. "But facts can be read from anywhere."

"You're probably upset we screwed up an election or two," I laughed. "I feel ya, my man."

"We wouldn't be in this mess…"

"Have one," I said offering my other mini bottle of whiskey.

He declined. I took down the second little bottle hoping it would make a dent. It didn't and I checked my wallet for any more cash to no avail. I told him I love my state's flaws. Sure, it could all end up underwater someday, but the fifty-something-whatever years I've been at it, growing up on the beach in Fort Lauderdale, working in Miami, doing odd jobs in Palm Beach, Pompano, and Naples, to my current gig as a retiree and not-so-great fisherman… Florida is home. "It's a beautiful place."

He leaned back, saying many of his friends moved to Florida and loved it. "This is my first trip," he said. "I think I *will* take you up on that whiskey."

"You got to move quick around here, my man," I said dangling the empty bottles.

"The wife wants to move somewhere warm," he said. "I guess if enough people with common sense move in, your state can be saved. Maybe change its stance on guns, vaccinations, the sugar industry, all that overfishing. But you can't really get serious about anything until you implement a fair income tax and regulate..."

I zoned out. He continued to ramble. There wasn't enough alcohol on the entire bar cart for this conversation. This was good old-fashioned fright and depression kicking in.

"We can be neighbors!" I heard him laugh as I eyed the paper bag for myself over the thought.

My finger flipped the ashtray. Open. Shut. Open. Shut.

"That'd be nice," I said. "I confess, it's gotten lonely in Florida after all my losses."

"Losses?"

I nodded my head and closed my eyes.

He looked over me and out to the dark blue Gulf. Green shallows and tan shores led to the lines of white, beige, and gray condominiums.

He noticed a tear coming from my eye. He turned his body toward me and gently tapped my arm. "You okay, my friend?"

"Trying to keep it together, my man. It's been no vacation living in Florida." I sat up. "Sure, weather's nice a few months. I never shovel snow and we've got our beaches."

I wiped another tear from my eye.

"What happened?" His morbid curiosity had him on the edge of his seat, fighting his tight seatbelt's restraint.

"My wife Christy was in a car accident last year."

"Take your time," he said. "I'm so sorry."

"Her little SUV didn't stand a chance against that sinkhole in Land O'Lakes," I said. "It just happened so fast."

He gasped.

"Probably saw it on the news. One minute you're above ground. The next, you're in it."

"No," he shook his head in disbelief.

"It's true," I affirmed. "Trees, cars, homes, trailers… can get swallowed up just like that! You know what it's like to shout into a huge hole in the earth for your loved one? Do you?"

"My God," he said, his hand over his heart. "I'm so sorry."

The plane began to shake again with a steep one-second drop. He stared forward and tensed into a brick as the captain reminded us again to keep our seatbelts fastened. I regained my composure as the plane leveled off. He left me alone for a while, likely more focused on calming his nerves as I noticed him taking deep breaths through his nose, exhaling slowly through his mouth, eyes closed tight.

"Sinkholes are everywhere, I'm afraid," I said to him.

He opened his eyes. "You're on top of a huge aquifer system. So, I guess to be expected."

"My dog Gnarly and I almost got hit by one walking one night. Luckily, he was on his leash, and I yanked him in time. It brought back a lot of bad memories."

"Unreal," he said. "Someone was looking out for you."

"Yes," I said. "Gnarly died a year later from a rattlesnake at the park. It was quick, though. That's more than I can say for my neighbor's cat."

He bit his fist and stared at me.

"One of those Burmese pythons," I said.

"I read about them. Your state is getting overrun by these invasive species."

"Yeah, well, Kitty didn't stand a chance. Hard to get a moving cat in the belly of a snake out of your skull once you see it. I didn't see it. But that's just what I heard."

"You must live in the unluckiest neighborhood," he said. "No offense, I'm not moving *there.*"

"It's everywhere," I scoffed in self-pity. "My friend in Ocala had his Chihuahua picked up by one of them bald eagles."

"No shit?" he said. "You have those?"

"Oh, they're beautiful," I said, "but not when they're flying off with the family pooch."

"Please stop," he said. He leaned back in his seat and fixed the air, making it more direct to his face. "I am just trying to register these things."

"Take your time, bud." I said. "I'm here for ya."

"Thank you."

After a minute of clearing his head, he looked at me.

"Did your neighbor with the cat…"

"Ms. Malcante," I said. "Yeah, she eventually moved on. Her neighbor though, Ms. Schlatter made the local news. Took a dip in her pool one morning and crunch. Alligator. A sweet old lady from my church. Bingo Night at St. Tim's hasn't been the same."

"I heard about this," he said. "This is horrifying!"

"In all fairness, her eyes weren't that great," I explained. "She always called the wrong numbers in bingo. I thought it was funny to watch the old farts argue once they realized it."

"Ok. But there was a gator… in her pool."

"Twelve-footer," I said. "Hard to miss. Like I said, she couldn't see shit. He was just waiting. Sometimes they're at your door, your yard, under your car. Anywhere really."

He tried to signal the flight attendant for a drink. She was nowhere to be found.

"Florida ain't all bad news," I said. "Check this out."

I pulled out my phone and showed him a picture of me standing with my brother and golfing buddies. "The dude in the pink shirt is Pat DeLuca. Good dude," I said. He nodded at the picture. "He fucking fell off a cruise ship last August. Luckily it was during the day and a cargo ship spotted him. He tied his pants around his neck and filled them with air for flotation. Like the Army taught him in some survival course or some shit."

"Now that's not a common thing, is it?"

"Finding them, no," I said. "But people fall overboard all the time. I think at least one a cruise. I could be wrong."

"You're kidding."

"Just don't be that one and you're good, I guess."

I reacquired his attention, pointing to another friend in the picture. "That guy in the white shirt, Mack Myers... total badass."

"What makes him a badass?"

"That fucker kite surfed full speed into the side of a hotel."

"No," he said, shaking his head. I showed him the online video someone captured from a hotel balcony.

"He survived the smack. See," I said narrating the clip. "There he is sliding down the side, four stories up... like one of those cartoon characters," I said. "Oh, he fully recovered but kind of wigs out whenever we pass a Holiday Inn."

I directed him to another picture on my phone, showing a muscular, dark skinned, tattooed man standing on a boat, holding a thirty-inch snook.

"Well, that's a beauty of a fish," he said.

"It is," I boasted. "We have great fishing and that's my fishing bud, Sam Martinez. His story's better. Get this… he was actually sucked up by a waterspout off Key Biscayne."

"What's that?"

"An area near Miami, mostly rich old farts."

"No, the water… what?"

"Waterspout… a water tornado," I said making a swirling motion with my finger. "He lived though."

"I fail to see the punchline," he said.

"Sam landed half a football field away. What's funny is he's built like a brick shithouse. The dude flew, landed, and swam back. Don't get me wrong, he was dizzy as shit but he made it back to the boat and… simply went home." I laughed, "The asshole didn't even go to the hospital. Just told us all about how glad he was to be alive and then bitched for hours about losing his stupid bimini top."

The professor gave a nervous laugh.

"Say, you like to golf?" I asked.

"I dabble. We have a country club. In the summer…"

I flipped back to the picture of my golfing buddies and pointed at the remaining two. "Terry's claim to fame is he almost died eating a bad piece of Lionfish, of all things. And then my brother Bob," I said pointing at the guy with the long hair, sitting on the golf cart. He had a full cast around his elevated leg resting on the cart. "He takes the prize, almost losing his leg on a golf course to…"

"Please, please don't say another alligator."

"No!" I laughed. "A '95 Buick Regal."

"On the golf course?"

"Florida's loaded with these blind, old buzzards," I said with full authority. "They just drive and don't see shit. They really don't know where the fuck they're going. Just silver alerts all day, my man. As for Bobby, he was just in the wrong place, wrong time when that Buick came barreling across the green to the fifth hole. But bro's fine. He just needs to be more mindful of his surroundings."

"On a golf course?"

"Got to," I said. "To further my point, his pain in the ass mother in-law… well, she drove right off a fucking bridge."

I showed him a screenshot of the news article. I had everything on my phone. It made great conversation pieces.

"She didn't die?"

"It was a low bridge. She landed on the shallow end."

"Thank goodness."

"I guess."

"And your other friend?" he said pointing to the guy with the crooked smile and messed up white hair. He sat in front, in a wheelchair. We each had a hand on his shoulders.

"That's Frank," I said. "God bless Frank."

"I'm afraid to ask why he's in the wheelchair."

"Yeah, but I'm dying to tell you!"

"I'm sure."

"Frank here… took a bolt of lightning… right in the ass," I laughed. "Now he says he got hit in the head but, it was his ass. All I know is it pisses him off when I say it."

"That's what friends do, I guess."

"Yeah, Frank's in Tampa, lighting capital of the US… maybe the world, my man." I leaned back in my seat and started to play with the air knob above me again. The smell reclaimed the cabin.

"But I'd rather deal with that than the bears, bobcats, panthers, and pythons out there in the sticks on the way to Orlando.

"Bears?"

"Bro, we've got it all," I said. "No worries though. Greatest state in the union. Wouldn't trade any of it for the world."

"I don't know what to make of all of this," he said flapping the collared shirt beneath his jacket. "It's a bit to register. I'd think you were pulling my leg."

"Wish I was," I said smiling at him. "I mean, they're good stories in the end. Tales of survival. Maybe bad luck, like you said. But you can make a life out here."

"I'm not sure I'd want to, to be honest," he said, folding his arms and looking forward. We listened to the captain asking all to stay seated, put up our trays, and pull the seatbacks to the upright position. Flight attendants came by to get our trash in preparation for landing.

"Hell, it's our fault anyway," I chuckled as the announcement ended. "Like you said, ignoring Mother Nature, right?"

He nodded and took in a deep breath. It grew quiet for a few minutes. The professor leaned in. "Of all these horrible things, I'm shocked you don't have any shark stories. I want to go to the beach, but it's my biggest fear. You said you fish. I'm sure you've seen them, right?"

I turned away, focusing out at the familiar shoreline as the plane made its approach from the Gulf over the Everglades.

"You okay?" he asked, intrigued by my silence.

"Fuck sharks," I said. "I'd kill every one of them if I could. Just dumb monsters."

"It's amazing how they evolved. Did you know…"

"My little girl," I said in a cold stare at the seat in front of me, "she lost two of her fingers to a bull shark. She was just playing on a sandbar we took our boat to in the bay. You know," I stopped to collect my thoughts, "you do all you can to protect them, but sometimes..."

"She really lost her fingers? Is she okay?"

"She's tough, just like her mom," I said. "Yeah, my Jenna hung in there, bleeding to death, her hand shredded to shit." I turned to him and said softly, "I pummeled the shit out of that fucking shark until it let go. He got away and I wanted to kill it. But my little girl kept calm the entire boat ride to the ambulance that met us at a marina."

"She had to be in shock," he said.

"She was. There was so much blood. Lots of surgery. It was hard adjusting... mostly for me because I knew I failed her."

"My God, you saved her!" he said. "You literally fought a damn shark to save your daughter! You got her to the hospital." He placed his hand over his chest and looked at me. "You are amazing, my friend!"

"No, *she*'s amazing," I exhaled. "My little girl was back at the beach, months later, back on that sandbar like nothing happened."

"It's a lot... surviving Florida," he said. "Thank you for sharing all this with me."

We rode the remaining minutes in silence, waiting for the plane to land. As the plane skipped the runway, he gave a short little cry out loud. He showed a brave face and nodded at me that he was okay.

We walked out the plane together and took the shuttle to the main terminal. "Enjoy Florida and be safe, brother!" I said slapping him on the shoulder. "It was a pleasure hearing all your stories and again, I'm so sorry," he said before taking a deep drag from his electric vape pen and briskly walking off.

I gave him a thumbs up as he rode the escalator down to the baggage claim area. I wasn't sure why I did that. Perhaps it was my attempt to offer any positive moment to him after literally scaring the shit out of him. My mind was still processing whether the peaches and sour milk smell came from *Her Hotness' Shatbaby* or him. The smell never left the memory of my nostrils.

"Who's your friend?" I heard my wife Christy behind me. I turned and gave her a kiss.

"Just someone I was talking to on the plane."

"What did you talk about?"

I felt the continuing tug of three little fingers pulling my pant leg. I pretended I couldn't see where it was from before dropping to my knees and sweeping up little Jenna into a tight hug.

"Did you miss Daddy?"

She nodded her head up and down with a big smile.

"What did you tell him?" Christy asked again, laughing.

I lifted my daughter over my head and onto my shoulders.

"Just what I needed to."

Rocks

"Patience," Grandpa said standing over his grandson. Zach wiggled to find a comfortable dent in his black rock overlooking the jetty. As he settled, the little boy strummed his line to a cartoon song in his head about a dog always chasing a duck. Grandpa inhaled the thick salty air, watching the tide return through Hurricane Pass. "Soon," he warned Zach. "I know, Grandpa," Zach murmured as the turquoise waters glided across the sandy shallows of the island across the pass.

Grandpa walked to the edge of the rock, hands on his hips, commander of the shoreline. "We waited on the tides." The water continued to ripple in the early afternoon light. The water's rushing strength. It was more noticeable closest to shore. The water's speed and mass faded into the dark blue middle of the channel. Zach tossed dried wax myrtle leaves on top the water. He watched them zip over the shoal like little brown speedboats.

"They're not gonna see it coming," Grandpa said rearranging the soggy cigar sticking out, past his red bulb nose. Sweat dripped from his clean-shaven, sunburned face into his lucky beige fishing shirt with all the pockets. "It'll be game time and they're not going to resist what we got for them today." He tilted the rod away from the rim of Zach's blue Dunedin Jays baseball cap. "Rigged for success, young man."

The waters rolled through Hurricane Pass, a throughway from the Gulf to St. Joseph's Sound. The pass was a cut through the original barrier island, made by a hurricane in 1921. The result was Caladesi Island to the south, Hurricane Pass, and Honeymoon Island to the north. Locals have since dredged the pass to maintain the convenient access to the Gulf.

On the Caladesi side of the pass were flooded flats of turtle grass and winding shoals to a mangrove shoreline. A splash appeared across the shallows. A black mass scattered like fireworks across the water.

"See," Grandpa whispered, pointing. "Finding them is half the battle, boy."

"But they're over there," Zach said. He started to drum the black rock with the heels of his neon beach sneakers. Grandpa waited for him to stop, reminding him the little noises and vibrations, even on the shore, are felt by the fish.

"They're everywhere," Grandpa said crouching down, gazing across the pass. Zach put up his little hand over his eyebrow to look out. "Why are they over there?" Zach asked.

"Keep your voice down," Grandpa whispered admiring the distant sparkle in the sun. He wished he was there to walk amongst the wreckage of shimmering scales, to see how many silvery baitfish perished in the attack. The waters calmed and the stirred brown sediment started to settle. A red, thirty-foot, two engine, slender speedboat named "Red Rooster" puttered by. Its loud engines startled all the birds along the shore into flight. As it made its way past the three kayakers, its driver slammed the throttle. The boat's engines roared. The bow lifted over the water and the shoreline shook as it screamed into the Gulf.

Zach cheered as it took off, waving his hand at the boat. Grandpa reminded him to keep it down, so as not to scare off the fish. "Okay, Grandpa," he said as he went back to minding his rod and reel. The boat's roar continued its thunder roll across the blue sky.

Zach stared into the warm winter sun's halo around his grandpa's black boonie hat. Grandpa took a knee opening his large tackle box. It looked like a treasure chest. The dark wood was chipped. The hinges were rusted and the leather handle had seen better days. It held every lure known to man.

Grandpa had a lure to remember every boat show, every seminar, every fishing expo. The silver and copper sparkled four-inch mullet-looking lure with the two treble hooks was a piece of fine art, the latest addition to the chest. Grandpa acquired it at the fishing and hunting expo in downtown Tampa last month. "You gonna use that one, Grandpa?" Zach asked. He was enamored from several feet away by its glorious shine in the sun.

"It's for different conditions," Grandpa said.

Beneath the magnificent display of yellow, pink, blue, green, silver, bronze, and white lures of all shapes and sizes, was an assortment of every sized circle hook, j-hook, and weight. There were spools of clear line, blue line, neon green line, and dark green braided line. They rested next to the collection of wire and fluorocarbon test leaders.

"Someday, this will all be yours."

"I can't carry that, Grandpa."

"Someday you will."

"Why?"

Grandpa glided his hand across the long box. "Because it will win the day."

"None of them are working," Zach said with a big yawn into the cool salty breeze. Another large splash caught their attention fifty yards away. This one was closer to their side.

Grandpa opened a small white cardboard box with fresh baklava and koulourakia cookies from the Greek Bakery in Tarpon Springs. Zach grabbed a cookie and began to slowly nibble it, smiling at the pirate ship in the Gulf. It fired a cannon to the cheers of tourists.

"They're out there, boy. The lures work. Key is knowing which one."

"What do you mean?" Zach asked. Another large splash hit the shoreline across the pass. Frigate birds and seagulls plunged from the sky like suicide bombers to grab the remains of silver.

"You got to know the right color lure, the right size, the right leader, whether to use mono or fluorocarbon, the weights, if any…"

A fin cruised above the water's surface. It was one of the many two and three-foot Bonnetheads known for the area. A two-foot ladyfish jumped from the center of the pass. Its thin silver body slid vertically, suspended several feet across the surface.

"Did you see that, Grandpa?"

"They're out there." Grandpa stared into his tacklebox, admiring the blue metal crab lure purchased at the show in Fort Lauderdale in '95. A tarpon struck it one time. He never landed the fish. "They spook once they know," he said with a deep sigh. Never again did it see any action. More modern versions sat in the box next to it. It was as if that damn tarpon told the others.

The returning tide brought mackerel near the surface as the speckled trout journeyed below. Deeper, along the bottom were schools of redfish and snook. They passed through the brown seagrass to the hard black oyster beds surrounding the sandy spoil islands in the Saint Joseph Sound. In the deep center of the pass were the sharks and occasional dolphin.

Together, the islands made a string of dark green and beige dots. You could see them in the satellite image Grandpa had on his wall in the garage. It was his command post. A large map was next to it, covered in circles, blue dots, purple lines, red and blue yarn with pins, and sticky notes. It looked like a frightening fishing conspiracy board.

The tide continued to funnel in. Silvery assortments of tiny fish were fleeing the larger fish not afraid to hunt in the shallows. Sitting high on the warm, black rock, Zach had a front row seat to see the carnage on both island shorelines.

Grandpa rummaged through his box.

Two teenage boys lurking on the island shore across the pass. Like the ospreys flying overhead, their eyes fixed on the flow, the black schools, and the shadows along the white sandy shoreline.

Grandpa smiled at the large banana yellow lure with the shiny white belly. It had neon green pinstripes and two dangling circle hooks. "Sometimes you can sense the one that's going to make it happen."

"You ever catch something with that?"

"Not yet," Grandpa said. "Just got it."

Zach continued watching the boys while his grandpa took over his rod. He reeled the line to replace the lure. The boys never said a word, communicating with nods and hand signals. They crept through the brush, avoiding the tourists along the beach. Their heads locked onto the shallows, beyond the pass, where the waters eased along the mangroves.

Grandpa rubbed his wrinkled face, staring down at the white jig heads and soft plastics; the three-inch ones, not four-inch, of course. Zach loved making the plastic pieces wiggle and dance to cartoon tunes in his head. It was only a year ago Grandpa got Zach to stop chewing them.

He taught Zach the sparkly red ones were best in the morning. When the tide changed, he used the silver ones with the yellow paddle tails. The flat shape of the tails made them dance differently in the water. "The key is to do a constant, slow retrieve with your reel and not let up. It gets you that life-like motion."

Zach smiled, watching the four Roseate Spoonbills in the distance. They were far, but he knew those were the birdies with the flat bills. They sat still in the mangroves, like pink and white Christmas ornaments against the rich green canvas. He once saw a flamingo on a sandbar East of Caladesi Island and named it "Sandy." Zach continued to scan the sandbars, the beaches, and the sky for her. "Will Sandy come out?"

"Hate to tell you," Grandpa said. "She was just here for after that hurricane, bud."

"She's okay though, right?"

"Yeah," he exhaled. "That big storm threw everyone off. She's probably back home now."

"Where's that?"

"Oh, I imagine south or something," Grandpa said. He looked in the box, waiting for a lure to shine in the sun like a sign from God that it was the one.

"We'll hold on the plastics," he said. "I'll set you up with the hard lures and get you back in business."

"This was no good?"

"This set up's going to be better," Grandpa said handing him one of the backup rods. He hurriedly rigged it with a blue hard plastic lure that looked like a big pill with gills and big eyes drawn on it. Grandpa launched it into the pass and handed Zach the rod back. "Reel it in slow and firm. No slack, son."

Zach slowly glided the lure into the shallows. Each turn was under the close supervision of his grandpa.

"You're not doing it right," Grandpa said, taking the rod and recasting it.

"See," he said reeling it in with a bouncy motion that looked like he was dancing to a hip-hop song.

Zach stared across the pass at two boys. They were thin, had darker skin, and wore only swim trunks. He found one smiling, nodding behind the brush, standing at the water's edge. The other came from the beach with something in his hand.

"Not a bite," Grandpa said retrieving his line once again.

"Got to get used to the lures. No two are the same."

The second boy waded in the shallows, knee-deep, sliding his feet along the sand.

"The moon and the lunar conditions play a big role…" Grandpa went on.

The first boy approached from thirty yards away. He carefully made the corner, around the thick mangroves, and into the shallows.

"It's also noon," Grandpa said. "Sometimes they don't bite at noon."

The second boy moved a few feet into the pass. His thin but muscular legs held against the pushing current.

"Not to mention it's about five degrees cooler today. Sometimes fish don't like that, say 'nope' and go about their way."

A small dark mass moved in the water between the two boys. Zach noticed they each had something in their hands.

"Grandpa," Zach said pointing. Grandpa continued fighting the massive mess of tangled dark green line choking his reel.

"I can fix this." Grandpa turned his back, digging deep into his tackle box. "I'll cut some line, put in a double uni knot to reconnect them with a smooth finish so it doesn't get caught up. I need to show you the double uni. Such a solid knot so long as you take your time. You wet it with spit before pulling it. Not too much spit, but enough to make it slide. Learn that knot if you want to be a great fisherman." Grandpa breathed a sigh of relief finally finding his knife in one of his many shirt pockets.

Five shadows, each two feet in length, raced by the first boy and plowed into the black mass. Thick copper tails emerged. The first boy initiated the assault, skipping a loaded array of smooth stones, one after the other. Each throw was relentless, with violent precision. He aimed for the top of the mass, one after the other, from a gathering he had in his other arm. He shot and reloaded, stone after stone. The second boy ran to the water with a rock the size of a basketball over his head. With a violent scream, he launched the heavy rock downward into the center of the black mass. White water lifted five feet from the surface, like a glorious explosion. The mass scattered in all directions. Bits and pieces of silver sparkled in the sun. The boys' heads remained fixed on something beneath, sputtering left, then right, and along the shore. The violence continued in another barrage of heavy thumps and plunks.

"Sounds like them boys playing war over there," Grandpa said tying the perfect uni knot. "Probably don't have a grandpa to show them this stuff. They're going scare off the fish. But I'll make a great fisherman out of you soon enough." Grandpa leaned over to show his perfect knot.

Zach watched the boys run through the water in a united front, assaulting the shallows. Flocks of white and black birds on the island lifted into the air en masse, circling overhead at the carnage. The first boy pointed at something. The second did a running dive into the water. The other dove next to him.

Zach was silent, arms lifted in the air, his mouth and eyes wide open. He watched the boys wrestle their own fights in the water beside each other. "I got it!" one shouted at the other. The second struggled briefly before laughing, pulling up an identical catch. One hand up the gill, the other holding the jaw, he lifted his large sparkling catch into the sun.

"You know," Grandpa said recasting the line, "I think the outgoing tide will bear fruit if the incoming one doesn't."

"What kind of fruit?" Zach asked. He watched the two boys emerge triumphantly from the water and onto the shore, each carrying their trophy fish. "I thought we wanted fish?"

The deep copper scales shined in the warm sun with shimmers of silver and white from their bellies. The fish were half the size of each boy. The boys rested on the beach with their prize fish laying between their legs. They looked tired, but victorious, smiling. They glanced across the water and waved at Zach. One of them stood up and lifted his trophy fish for the boy to see. Zach lifted his arms and clapped. A thin, old man with skin like driftwood emerged from the sand dune. He supported himself with a long wooden stick, traversing the soft white sand. The boys ran to him, their fish in hand. His face was expressionless. He nodded and patted each boy on the shoulder. He then pointed his stick back toward the island, past the tall grass. The boys sprinted ahead with their catches. The old man gently waved at little Zach before disappearing around the sand dune.

Grandpa tossed the line back into pass. He leaned over and handed Zach the rod. "Ready to fish, young man."

Zach fearlessly jumped off the rock, as high as him, onto the sand, and ran onto the beach.

"Where you going, boy?" Grandpa called out, tangling his line again in the reel.

"Getting rocks!" Zach shouted.

"I thought we were fishing here."

Kelly and Keystone

Kyle McKenzie of 166 Kissimmee Court? That's what the license says.

I didn't do nothing!

You did not do… *anything*.

Agreed.

Stay seated on the ground. I don't want to tase you… again. How much did you drink, Mr. McKenzie?

You never read me my rights.

I did.

Oh, well, I don't know. Noon, I guess.

You've been drinking since yesterday?

Well, I'm sober, now, but yeah. That's when Chandra…

Who's Chandra?

She a bitch. Left me for some trucker asshole right after spending my last take on tattoos at Spidey's on Dixie. Two!

Two what?

Tats, man. That's just selfish. That's all I had.

Where do you work, Mr. McKenzie?

Laid off now. Ya know that scaffolding collapse at that condo in Pompano Beach?

I do. I had to respond to it when it went down. You guys were lucky you weren't killed. But I don't remember seeing you.

I was one of those who put it up.

Ah, thus being laid...

Buncha bullshit! The cash had to last me. Ain't got no fancy-ass degree like you.

I don't have one, Mr. McKenzie. But I'm working on it.

Well, I can't get no job. They treat me like a felon.

Because… you are a felon. This will be a felony too.

That a buncha bullshit!

Sit.

I'm sitting, Thor. Put the taser thing down.

Thorn. Name is Sergeant Mike Thorn.

You a dang Trump wall, Thor. Play football? Let me guess.

Tackle. Defense. Sometimes offense too.

Yeah, I ran circles around you fat boys. Probably some preppy school.

Public school. Coral Springs.

I was at Cardinal G. Wide receiver. Fastest they had.

Well, I caught you just fine, Preppy. I also caught footage of you with a weapon.

No. I ain't have no weapon.

You *didn't* have *a* weapon…

Exactly! Nice meeting ya.

Sit.

Okay. You quick on the draw with that thing. I'm cool.

Yeah, the manager sent me the video to my phone. Let me open it, Mr. McKenzie. Loading. Loading.

What video?

Loading. Ah, here we go. Here you are, Mr. McKenzie. That's you holding it and… aiming it. I'm impressed. You scared that clerk real good. Not very nice of you.

I did no…

Continue watching the video, Mr. McKenzie. There's you. There's your pants falling, passing the potato chips. There go some bags. Pants back up. That's you bending over, picking it up again. Looks like you're trying to get some balance. Not really good at it. Now leaning against the cooler, walking a little tilted to the register. Case of beer in one hand and... there you are, aiming it at the clerk with the other hand. Good sized one too.

Not me. That's a fake video. A.I. shit.

How the hell did you do that?

Trained by the best. Chief Takaway.

Takaway? Oh yeah. That toothless lush that used to beat the shit out of the gators down in Hollywood for the tourists.

That's him. Chief wrestled them. The gators, not the tourists.

I know. So, he trained you on the gators?

Yeah. I was gonna inherit the business someday.

Beating the shit out of gators?

Yeah. Had a cool name lined up too. Check this out... Chief Firewater Coldsweat.

Offensive, but catchy. You don't look Indian, Mr. McKenzie.

Scotch Irish with half a percent Seminole.

Huh. I see that half percent now you mentioned it.

You do?

No. Not a bit.

As much as Takaway was. His real name was Carl Sanders.

Like the chicken guy? Colonel...

I think Takaway was a sergeant in 'Nam actually. He got sued by them hippy environmental animal rights activist turds. Shut us down. Lost everything. Yeah, Takaway moved south of Okeechobee to run some airboats. He was older than dirt but for a few bucks he'd jump off the airboat and wrestle any gator.

You didn't go with him?

No. This eagle's gotta soar. He recently died from smoking.

Cancer, huh?

Nah. He was smoking outside some diner and lightning zapped his ass. Extra crispy. Wish I was there to see that.

Touching. So, your day never came, Mr. McKenzie. Now, here you are, robbing a store with an alligator for a case of Keystone?

I'm telling you, that ain't me.

I like Keystone.

Me too.

So, did you rub his belly or something?

The clerk?

The gator, Mr. McKenzie.

Tricks of the trade. You gotta cover the eyes, get control.

So, you then threatened the clerk with a four-foot snapping alligator for that case of Keystone?

No.

Not judging. Just ballsy. Station's going to love this.

Thanks, man.

So, you did it.

No. I didn't.

And you also didn't take a pack of cigarettes…like the one I found on your person?

What person?

You.

I guess. Hang on, this is a buncha bullshit!

Hold that thought. I need to take this call.

Sergeant Thorn speaking. Yes, sir. What? Hmm… well, no. Find it? To be fair, sir, that's...

A buncha bullshit! That's what I'm saying.

Hey, shut it. I'm sorry, sir. Roger.

What?

They're saying the gator's definitely a weapon.

Bullshit. It's Florida, man. Got gators everywhere.

Regardless, you're in deep, Mr. McKenzie. But you have me curious. Why did Chandra leave?

She a bitch.

Well, we covered that part already. But what else?

She said Truckie's got his act together, running shit outta Islamorada with some bikers. I'm just mad as balls about them tattoos. Two of them. But that gator, that's my… comfort gator.

I'm sorry, your what?

My compassion pet. Whatever the fuck you call it. My calming animal, happy… service thingy.

You're saying it's an emotional support alligator?

Yep. That.

Okay, I'll bite, Mr. McKenzie. Is it registered?

You gotta register them? Like, bring it inside the DMV?

No. Please do not do that.

Well, I'm not, Thor. Besides, I can't afford that shit.

What about its little red vest?

Fuck, you gotta dress them too?

I don't. But, yeah, I think you do to show it's got a purpose.

I ain't dressing no gator. That's just stupid.

I agree. So, where's your emotional support gator now?

Don't know, man. I had to let go when you was chasing me. Poor thing's out lost somewhere.

Yep, a gator in the backwoods in all that swamp. How's he going to survive?

She. Her name's Kelly.

Mr. McKenzie, I think we're done here. Get up. Let's get you to jail. Gotta feeling you're going to be right at home.

For what?

Well, I've got video of you robbing this convenience store with an alligator. I think we covered it. Now, you'll hang out in county tonight and then see the judge Monday. And although entertaining, the gator absolutely does not…

And if I told you about this chic with blue flames tattooed on her huge tits flying up I-95 in a purple semi moving a full trailer of primetime Jamaican Thunderbum Kush?

I'd say apologize to the clerk. I'll buy the beer and after I make a few calls, we'll go look for your emotional support gator Kelly.

From Florida

I pulled away from that burrito and hotdog-fart-smelling, super-sized convenience store proud of my commitment to family.

Shelly shook her head and leaned back in the passenger seat to our white 1987 Camaro convertible. We rolled off again, across the white sand and crushed shell road, onto the humming highway. Long lines of pine trees dashed again along my left side.

"I'm still the coolest, baddest, uncle," I yelled into the wind. I slapped my chest like a psyched-up wrestler.

Shelly blew a kiss to the water to the east. It was a sign of appreciation, intended to traverse the winding St. Mary's River, all the way to the Atlantic Ocean. The bridge marked our return to Georgia and the end to our journey across Florida.

We were celebrating my retirement after twenty-eight years at the tire plant. I didn't plan on retiring that soon, but they didn't give me a choice. An orange metal machine resembling a flamingo's leg with a five-foot long probe attached, took my manhood. It robbed my way of life, my right to earn a living, and ended my career. I appreciated the value of speed, but could a machine ever truly put love into a tire? No.

An army of heartless, synchronized, orange hydraulic probes were going to move the tires between stations, trim the excess after curing, attach the treads, and inspect the tires using the latest in infrared technology… or some bullshit. Each machine looked the same but with a different tool attached on the end. Management offered a demonstration to watch how the machines were going to do our jobs. Fuck them.

I had to accept it as a sign of the times as the short-skirted, fresh-out-of-college, clueless HR intern handed me my severance package. Security escorted me out after a few parting words with my manager, Benny Belkin, that inbred coward. Belkin, of course, kept his job despite doing the least amount of work, supervising.

"I walked right up, said 'It's coming for you next! Bend over, you son of a bitch!'"

"I still don't know how that made any sense," Shelly said.

"Well, you had to be there," I said. "I'm telling you it was funny and more importantly, deserved."

"How is 'bend over' funny?"

"Because the stupid machine looked like one of those things." She stared at me.

"Remember that huge pink thing TSA found buzzing in my sister's luggage?"

"Oh, dear," she said looking away, trying to hide her giggling.

"I don't remember you calling him an s.o.b. the first ten times you told me this story."

"Oh, he's a son of a bitch and he can take it right up…"

"I-95," Shelly said.

"I guess…"

"No, Harold," she said pointing to the rapidly approaching on-ramp. "You're missing I-95."

"The hell I am."

After a very skillful jump across three crowded lanes and a barrage of enthusiastic hand gestures toward us, we were heading south on I-95. It was the start to our Florida adventure.

"Who's the s.o.b. now?" I heard Shelly mumble.

"What was that dear?" I asked.

"Oh, I must love you," she laughed.

"You don't have to," I said. "But how can you not?"

She grinned, closed her eyes, and enjoyed having the top down to feel the morning sun. It was quiet for most of the drive. The long journey gave me time to reflect. Shelly read the internet, from start to finish, on her smartphone. She claimed she was enjoying the scenery.

This road trip was a little symbolic, perhaps sentimental, for me. We were traveling on what were some of the very last Talf Tires made by human beings from the great state of Georgia.

This trip was to be my moment of Zen, where I could take a deep breath and embrace the end to one of my chapters and begin the next one. If that didn't work, I could at least enjoy the Florida beaches, hit the tourist traps, and get hammered in the evenings.

Thanks to Shelly, the trip was fully announced on social media for all the family to know. "We're excited for you!" was the gist of the first messages. It didn't take long for family to follow up with, "Bring something back from FL!"

We weren't two miles into our trip before being committed to buy everyone souvenirs. I found it imposing of her family. This led to a spirited debate about whose family was more imposing.

"No way," I said, "are we buying shit for everyone across every town in Florida."

"Fine! Just the kids," she offered to sound rational.

I banged my head back on my seat's headrest. "That's still what… fifty freaking kids?"

After a few choice words she saved for such an occasion, I compromised, agreeing to some family. Shelly, in the spirit of cooperation, reduced our obligation to immediate family. This included her sisters' kids and a coworker's kid born without a personality, clearly an inevitable danger to society.

Each niece and nephew would get one trinket. I would then pick the least dangerous thing for the menace. There was no time to notarize the agreement. We were on a schedule. It meant one item from somewhere for eight teenagers, two youngsters, and Dipshit. Any extras purchased for mom and sisters were bonus.

My nerves settled as we made our way down A1A. We examined the exteriors to the beachside motels. I was looking for one that looked decent, yet affordable, with most of the neon letters to their VACANCY sign still present and working.

"I guess that one," Shelly said concluding a careful analysis. It was the pink Sandpiper Motel. "Sandpipers are white, right?" I asked her as we approached the plump, pimple popping Goth kid at the front desk. Shelly stared as I explained to the amorphous young man in black, "The place is pink, bro. Flamingo would have made more sense than the Sandpiper."

He continued to text like the wind on his smartphone. Without looking up he mumbled, "We'll get right on that, Chief."

"You do that," I snapped back. Shelly half-heartedly thanked the little asshole and escorted me out the lobby. "Vacation starts now, whether you want it to or not," she said.

"Goth Potato needs a fucking attitude adjustment."

"And you need a drink," she laughed.

We dropped our bags in the room and strolled along the beach before sunset. We each held our flip flops in one hand. I reached for Shelly's hand, my attempt to be romantic. But she was busy broadcasting our walk to social media. "Okay," I said in a loud voice. "Sex *after* the walk. Don't have to beg, Babe."

She quickly stopped recording and gave me that stare, the one where she is mad but wants to laugh. It was also her acknowledging my plan to ruin all social media reels, videos, clips, posts, swipes, tweeters, or whatever people call the stupid things.

"Jerk," she said, squeezing my hand tight. We proceeded under the pier and walked into the cool water to avoid a gang of stubborn seagulls refusing to move.

Hotels and motels stood like survivors, like remaining pieces to a washed-out chessboard. Some were from the 1950s or 60s, resting in peeled paint. Their crumbled seawalls marked the line of departure, over half a century of man and sea battling for a few feet of beach. Signs were faded and stained in rust. Others were blown out from past hurricanes. It's like the area's theme was "Recovery." The old buildings were no competition for the two new Vegas-like resorts "testing the market" to see if there was one.

When we got tired, we left the beach and walked along A1A. We entered the first bar we spotted, called "The Clam." It was full of pirate stuff with lots of old black and white photos of local fishermen. None of the décor made sense for a place called "The Clam." I wondered if that was the point... to be hip and ironic. Either that or they stopped giving a shit decades ago.

I stopped wondering after several of their rum punches. Sally says I enjoyed a fried shrimp dinner before taking a very short cab ride back to the motel. The motel's owner/ manager/ front desk greeter/ pool technician/ maintenance man was kind enough to remind us at noon that the checkout time was noon. He had the same social skills as Goth Potato, just a lot older. We simply said goodbye and continued our course down A1A.

"How about that one," Shelly would ask as we passed every surf apparel/t-shirt/souvenir shop. They all looked the same.

Every window space displayed neon thong and bikini-clad mannequins, colorful boogie boards, and cheap t-shirts.

We stopped at the biggest one and lost an hour, debating which gift best represented Daytona. We wrestled with which kid would want what. What trinkets would other towns offer? Were we ready to commit to any souvenir so early in our trip? Every trinket in the store had Daytona or Daytona Beach handwritten across it. The alligator head was the only one that didn't. There was no place to write it. My favorite was the pirate skull piggy bank. It had Daytona written across the eye-patch in gold script.

We eventually walked out with a bottle opener because we forgot to bring one. Shelly might have dented some furniture trying to pop the top off a beer the night before. She failed to mention it to Goth Potato or management.

I offered to buy everyone the t-shirts I saw on a sale rack for $2.99 each. They were simple, yet tasteful, white t-shirts with "Daytone" in red letters across. Shelly claimed they were on sale because they spelled Daytona wrong. I told her I never noticed. I then tried to compromise, asking if we could at least get one as the official gift for Dipshit. He wouldn't have noticed. Shelly did not concur with my sensible recommendation.

We ventured into a few more stores and soon considered ourselves pros in the Daytona market. There was no longer a sense of guilt walking right in, looking around, and walking right out. Each store pushed the same trinkets and shirts. We were on an imaginary schedule. "There will be plenty of things to choose from in Orlando," I argued.

I was correct. Every cartoon, comic, and movie character was available in plastic or stuffed form. But none of them had Orlando written on them. When we asked, the cashier pointed us to a store identical to the ones in Daytona. We ventured in and immediately saw the pirate skull, like it was following us. But this time it had Orlando beautifully written in gold script on its eye patch.

"Is that the dancing dolphin figurine from Daytona?" Shelly asked. It was and yet we knew we weren't going to see any dolphins, at least in the wild parts of Orlando and Kissimmee. It didn't make sense. However, we did see several big white swans as we took a paddle boat out on Lake Eola.

It was a lot of work. I felt Shelly spent more time taking photos of every bird on the lake rather than pedaling the damn boat. We discussed this briefly. I then apologized for whatever I said and continued pedaling. But yes, the swans were pretty.

As we were getting out of the boat, the old man in the safari hat running the dock said the swans were descendants of Lake Lucerne. "I thought I recognized them," I said. Oblivious to my sarcasm, he continued explaining there were different breeds and eventually, they had to be separated. "Of course," I said. "God only knows the swan carnage had they not!" Shelly pulled my arm to continue our march through the park. "Let's go, captain."

We bought a bottle of locally made citrus wine at a booth along the way to a legit pirate bar. I appreciated that it stayed true to the theme if you ignored the lobster tank. The mechanical claw reminded me of the orangish-yellow machine that took my livelihood, my place in this world at the Talf Tire Factory.

I again fell victim to a sneaky rum punch. I remembered asking the bartender, in my best pirate voice, how he kept his cool each day in a bar where all the drunk tourists acted like obnoxious pirates. I forgot what he said, but it was a cool response.

The next day we made our way out of Orlando. The I-4 was truly an apocalyptic vision, a wasteland where aggressive drivers converged to sit, cry, and fume. I gained even more perspective, on the side of the road, changing my flat rear passenger tire.

"That one of the new tires from *your* plant?" Shelly asked.

I politely asked her to zip it as I focused on the task at hand, explaining the tread was not well-attached.

"Are they supposed to do that?" she giggled.

"It happens, Babe," I said trying to tighten the lug nuts to the donut. "We'll get a new one and move on."

"But that was a new one," she said. "Aren't they *all* new?"

I ignored her. We headed to a garage to get a new tire before continuing to Cape Canaveral. There, hours passed, and I was in awe of all the historical hardware. They were the products of teamwork, engineering, and vision. I thought of the factory.

The souvenir shop was a refreshing stop. It had mostly NASA-related trinkets for purchase. Although, I did spot the pirate skull piggybank next to some space shuttle replicas. It had Cape Canaveral written on the eyepatch.

To my wife's surprise, I purchased a model kit of the Space Shuttle Atlantis and an SR-71 Blackbird. I figured I could try putting them together when I got home. My dad died wishing he could still work. He never really found a hobby. Being my father's son, I already knew this same bullshit curse was waiting for me when we got home. Model kit building was not going to do it, but I could at least ease myself into these little projects while pondering my next chapter.

At no time did I see a particular gift for the others. I feared buying expensive NASA trinkets *in addition* to Florida souvenirs I had yet to find. For those keeping track, the souvenir count for our nieces, nephews, and Dipshit remained firm at zero.

Cruising along A1A from Cape Canaveral, we passed through Cocoa Beach. It was full of pastel-colored motels, old condos, and small shops that were pleasantly stuck in the 70s and 80s. The homes on Merritt Island were a mix match of old single-story homes that risked flooding and the newer homes, all tall two and three-story homes with a garage on the bottom and all living space above it. It was a modern-day acceptance of just how high the tide came to the top of those seawalls. I admired the common-sense adaptation in architecture.

"We can't afford it," Shelly said. "The New Yorkers bought up Florida. We gotta wait on some disaster for them to flee."

"If Florida completely floods," I said smiling as I drove over the bridge, "we'll be there to buy."

"Sure," Shelly laughed. "I'm sure we'll get a discount then."

We pulled in at Shepard Park to watch an afternoon launch from Cape Canaveral. We sat on the hood, shared a Cuban sandwich, and ate plantains, white rice, and black beans with sporks from styrofoam containers. It was our best meal so far.

The launch was quite the spectacle. The explosive sound took far longer than we braced for. Everyone around us cheered as it made its way out of the atmosphere, following the little red flame across the clear, light blue sky. Launches were in full swing, almost a weekly occurrence. Visitors watched the entire trek across the sky. Locals only stuck around for the takeoff and moved on.

After staying the night in a quiet, no-frills motel across the street from the beach, we continued to West Palm Beach. I instantly felt like we left reality, entering a land of make believe. Stores and restaurants had well-dressed valets at the ready. I don't do valet parking. I don't pay a man to park my car for me. It's like asking another man to put down your horse.

"How?" Shelly laughed.

"Just plot a course for Fort Lauderdale."

We passed mansions I assumed belonged to ex-presidents, movie stars, CEOs, and drug dealers. It continued for some time, big walls surrounding big mansions with big docks, big yachts, and little helicopters. An hour later, old condos and touristy surf shops reappeared. We stopped at a pub near the Deerfield Beach pier for a lobster roll and walked it off touring local shops.

"That's a real puffer," a storeowner said to me tapping the spikes gently against my open palm. "Are you sure?" I pretended I didn't believe him to see what he would do. He swiftly moved my attention to a conch shell. It was $25. It had Deerfield Beach written in cursive along the shiny inner lip. I asked him if it was a shell you would find in these local waters. He held it up to me and pointed to the handwritten lettering. *Deerfield Beach.*

"Well, that answers that," I said and stared at the $25 price tag. "You… blow," he said, showing the tip was cut off on the end. "Quite an assumption on your part. We just met," I said. Shelly quickly grabbed my hand and escorted me back to the car. "I can't take you anywhere," she laughed as I felt my ass burn on contact with the leather seats.

We cruised south to Fort Lauderdale and checked in to a modern thirty story hotel off the strip. Shelly charged it to her credit card before I could ask the price. She said it was time to live a little. Our room faced west, overlooking the intercoastal waterway. We opened the bottle of citrus wine on the balcony, watching the boats go by. "The wine's interesting," I said.

"Like window cleaner," Shelly said. "A good one though."

We clinked our plastic wine glasses and gulped.

"Fuck." I shook, feeling it go down to my gut like a killdozer.

"Well said, Dear," she said.

We exited the grand lobby and into the warm, bright sun, embracing Fort Lauderdale in all its glory. The low white wall along the beach had a line of neon light in it. It changed colors as we strolled by, blue to green to yellow to pink. I tried to ignore the endless sea of tourist shops ahead. I tried, but failed, to ignore the many young ladies in neon thongs and short jean shorts.

The Atlantic's fresh salty breeze mixed with fried grouper and pizza. I could hear a Bob Seger cover band in a nearby bar on the corner. Another tall, tanned blonde roller-skated by in a yellow thong. I shouted, "Let's make this our home!" as I held Shelly's hands, smiling, spinning around her on the sidewalk.

"Come on, Old Man," she replied, "let's get a drink."

"What about the Citrus Wine upstairs? No?"

We downed chilled shots of tequila at a table on the sidewalk. The day's heat eased as the sun began to lay shadows of the resorts over us, to the beach, reaching east to the Atlantic. I pointed to a little boy across the street feeding popcorn to a seagull. "Watch that little fucker. This is happening."

A determined flock descended on the boy like kamikaze dive-bombers. The bag flew from his hand. Pieces scattered.

"Yes!" I said under my breath, entertained by the shitstorm of deafening squawks and white feathers that followed. The boy cried and ran for his mom. She swooped in to grab him like she was rescuing him from a drive by shooting. Some seagulls followed while others fought viciously for the popcorn.

"Fucking awesome here," I said taking another shot.

On the walk back to the hotel, we laughed at more of the funny t-shirts and tourist trinket junk. The hatching egg with the alligator coming out was identical to the one I saw in Daytona, in

Orlando, in Jupiter, and in Deerfield Beach. But this one read Fort Lauderdale in black handwritten lettering across the egg.

The flamingo figurine standing with one foot on a piece of driftwood was the same in Saint Augustine. The smiling wooden turtle, the shark with the sunglasses, the parrot smoking the pipe, and the manatee on the lawn chair were everywhere. They kept changing the town written on their shell, their fin, their pipe, their eyepatch, and their chair. "I'm telling you! We're being followed," I kept saying to Shelly, pointing at the pirate skull piggy bank.

Three more flat tires later, I was glad I no longer worked at that shithole tire factory. My layoff was God telling me to move on. After the first two tires, I made a point to buy a different brand. This quality was inexcusable. Shelly reminded me that the machines were only operational two weeks ago.

That was only a detail. Shelly refrained from pushing the obvious. We knew we were riding on tires made by my team. We sucked. The humans and the work of their human hands, sober, drunk, or hung over with personal problems and short attention spans… sucked. I could have argued it was the other line, the other shift, but it didn't matter. "You supported us doing that job, Honey." Shelly looked out at the water. "You were there for *us*, not the tires. And I love you."

"I love you too," I said softly, staring forward while she rubbed my right shoulder.

As we made our return approach for the Georgia state line, riding on four new tires, it occurred to me. Our souvenir count was still zero. Shelly knew this. She said she dropped the issue days ago, back in Key West. After the twentieth store in the tenth town, we grew cynical to seeing the same bullshit. She felt it was time to stop arguing about flat tires and trinkets.

We enjoyed a schooner sunset cruise and waved to the crowd along the seawall at Mallory Square. That night in a biker bar, we learned from a man missing a foot, ironically named Skip, that orange slices went better with chilled tequila shots. He made many toasts, to which I replied "Amen." The toast that really stood out was "Fuck sharks." He cried a little. I assumed a lot. It was a nice moment. "You guys were a pair," Shelly laughed.

The next day, the radio was off, and the top was down, as we listened to the hum and thump of the Seven Mile Bridge. We hovered over the turquoise and midnight blue waters. The Gulf was on one side, the Atlantic on the other. We had our lunchtime fill of fried grouper, hushpuppies, and key lime pie.

Crossing to the Gulf Coast along Alligator Alley, we counted eight alligators, five turtles, three racoons, and one long, squished python. Halfway, we stopped for an airboat tour. The toothless old man running the tour called himself "Chief." Not at our request, he insisted on wrestling some of the gators at his little alligator farm. The gators appeared retired, accepting humiliation and molestation for rotted chicken. The ones we saw from the airboat were much quicker, sliding across the grasses into the black waters, before my wife could get a decent picture.

The next day, we spent more hours than planned in Venice Beach, digging in the dark beach sand to find shark teeth. Shelly asked if we wanted to give some to the kids. "I worked for these," I said holding a handful of fossilized teeth.

A paper placemat from the pier restaurant showed drawings of different teeth. Like a kid, I matched my collection to the drawings while eating hotdogs. I apparently found one bull shark tooth, three nurse shark teeth, four sand tiger teeth, and ten lemon shark teeth. Shelly made me promise to take our nieces and nephews to this place. I had no problem as I added finding a coveted megalodon tooth to my bucket list. She tried to buy me one. "No, I must find zist treasure myself," I insisted in my Jacques Cousteau voice.

We enjoyed the restaurants and upscale shops of St. Armands Circle in Sarasota. That evening, we were walking the white sands of Clearwater Beach up to Pier 60. The next day, we made a quick stop to see the mermaids in the crystal-clear springs of Weeki Wachee, before heading to Cedar Key.

As we began the final run to Georgia, Shelly looked to me. "This was a good trip," she said. "I'm happy."

"Good," I said. "That's great."

"I'm just happy that you're happy," she said grabbing my right hand as I steered with the left. She meant it too. In the corner of my eye, I watched the sunlight shine through her graying liquorice hair. She put her hair up in a ponytail to enjoy the top down rather than ask to put it up because the wind messes her hair. She waved her hand up and down into the wind.

She was right. I didn't even notice until she told me. The recently laid-off, washed-up, bitter asshole that started this trip must have stayed back in one of those towns. He was still out there, bitching about tires and trinkets.

We had minutes remaining in Florida, traveling at 60 miles per hour. I saw the billboard signs to a mega-sized store at one of the approaching exits. It was like a circus with a truck rest stop. It boasted of the best burritos, orchids, oranges, grapefruits, and the largest selection of souvenirs and t-shirts.

"There's still time for us," I said.

"Well, I hope so," she snorted.

I peeled off the highway, swerving across two lanes to the sound of many honks and the sight of many exuberant hand gestures. At the exit was a sign pointing to Senor Jerome's Super Wondermart and Fuel Depot.

I slid the car to a screeching halt in the parking lot. The white dust of the sand and crushed shell lot overcame our car.

"What are we stopping for?"

"Taking care of my family!" I jumped out slamming the door.

Crossing the doorway, I immediately smelled hotdogs sweating in an endless heat lamp rotation near the register. There was a long line in the far back for a counter advertising the best brisket burrito. It's so far away I can only smell the hotdogs. Mariachi music played in the background. I was overwhelmed and didn't know where to start. There were endless aisles of everything, something, and nothing. It was a cross between a gas station, a pawn shop, a fireworks store, a surf shop, a taxidermist, an auto parts store, a gun shop, a cigar shop, a tattoo parlor, and a grocery store. It was confusing as hell and glorious as shit, all at once. "Fuck, yeah," I said to the old lady pushing a cart past me.

I paced between the lottery register and the candy up front, unsure where to go. Finally, like a desperate call into the wild, I shouted, "Senor Jerome!" It echoed over the parrot cages, above the huge fish tank with the school of full-sized redfish, past the tall stack of longboards, past the seven-foot statue of a manatee playing a green ukulele, around the tax preparation cubicles, off the chrome wheels on the far wall, across aisles of food, medicine, lures, power tools, and clothing. "Senor Jerome!"

"Yes, mi amigo!" A gray bearded black man shouted from the far end of aisle twenty-five. He waved his oversized straw sombrero adorned in a red, green, and yellow band.

I took the long jog to where he stood.

He finished neatly placing the final set of wooden maracas on the bottom shelf to his sale display next to the manatee. Setting the cardboard box aside, he rose up. His eyes sparkled green reflecting the neon lottery sign behind me. He welcomed me with the firmest handshake. I admired his sombrero.

"Ever hear about cultural appropriation?" I asked.

"Don't carry it, senor," he said in an exaggerated accent.

I spun in a circle to see all the plastic, wood, and stone figures. There were ospreys, cranes, eagles, sharks, dolphins, stingrays, puffers, sandpipers, gators, parrots, toads, panthers, snakes, snook, redfish, tarpons, lighthouses, palm trees, pirate ships, flamingos, lobsters, crabs, and old sailors. There were ship wheels and ships, bottles of sand, bottles with ships in them, shark teeth, shells, and more shells. Everything surrounded Senor Jerome in a triumphant aura. He twisted the end to his perfect curly mustache hovering over his gray beard. "I have everything."

"You, sir," I said shaking his hand again with both of my hands, "can help me."

"Absolutely, Senor."

"You have boxes of this shit all in the back, right?"

"Well," he smiled, "I carry the finest souvenirs representing our Florida culture, our colorful Floridian way of life…"

"All made in China," I said.

He smiled, not even contesting the assertion.

"But you use a marker to put whatever town you want on them, right?" I asked.

The RANGER tab tattoo on his right bicep peeked out his bright red Hawaiian shirt.

"Yeah," he said without an accent. "My boys mark them in back."

"Knew it!" I snapped my fingers at him. "Good man."

I handed him four fifty-dollar bills. "Por favor, grab me one of each trinket until this runs out. The cheap stuff. I need a boxful for about twenty folks."

Jerome grabbed the bills. He picked up an empty box and started to pull from the shelf.

"Amigo, no," I said. "From the back... with no writing."

"Ah, roger that," he said.

"And a black sharpie." The pirate piggy bank stared at me with its gold writing on the eye patch. "A gold one too!"

"Got it," Senor Jerome said.

"And two piggy banks." I handed him two more twenties.

Senor Jerome returned minutes later with a full box in a cart. My newfound friend even worked in a ten percent discount and five free "Daytone" t-shirts. He also handed me a grocery bag with two brisket burritos wrapped in foil. They were the size and weight of bricks. "On the house," he said. "Skip the hotdogs. This is the good stuff."

He walked me to the exit. We shook hands. "Airborne!" he said pointing to the tattoo on my leg, a reminder of another life before my wasted career in tires.

"Catch you next trip, brother," I said.

"I'd like that, amigo," he said. "Any time." He then fixed his sombrero and began his long trek back to aisle twenty-five.

I returned to the car like a glorious pillager holding a plastic bag of burritos and a large box. I plopped the box into the back of the convertible. She leaned over to peek inside.

"Who gets the cool pirate skull piggy banks? Shelly laughed.

"Me and Dipshit," I said with a smiling mouthful of the greatest brisket burrito of my life. "You're our ambassador and artist of the family, so you assign the rest and decide what towns they're from." I handed her the markers and a huge burrito wrapped in tin foil.

She leaned in and kissed me on the cheek, the one not accented in melted white cheese, pico de gallo, and guacamole.

"That's the man I married."

For my love, Jeanette.

Irma's Cross

"Looks like you have a plan," he said. Exhausted, I stared at the contents of my cart, not paying attention. I had the last four packs of gray rubber matte flooring, nine short planks of pinewood, and one roll of duct tape. "One can pretend," I said with a half-hearted smile. Sweat dripped from his flat forehead as he bit his lip, his hand shaking on the edge of my cart. Behind his constipated grin was an imminent nervous breakdown. I knew this because I was not far from my own. My state just watched all the conditions align to create the perfect catastrophic, state-eating CAT 5 hurricane. It was crossing every which way, only a day away.

Someone must have thought it would be cute to give hurricanes human names. We could talk about them like people. They could have personalities. We could assign characteristics. Like people, they can die, go away, wreck your car, sink your boat, and take your trailer. Andrew was huge. David was fast. Wilma couldn't decide where to go. Katrina was expensive.

But Irma was entering a category of her own. She needed a name with greater distinction, perhaps a mythical name like Thor's Baby, Zeus' Superbeast, or the Cyclonic Demon Monster. A scientifically intimidating name like the XK5200 could have worked too. But it needed to be a name that would make it clear that a monumental shitkicker was coming to the Sunshine State. This was an old school tropical reckoning for the ages and not to be confused with a crazy old aunt in Ocala.

"You okay, brother?" I asked.

He told me he fucking moved here only two fucking weeks ago from Ohio. It was just in time for fucking Irma, his first motherfucking hurricane. He had no idea what the fuck to do. His voice cracked as he said the name "Irma." He was obviously intimidated, regardless of the name.

He said it was last classified as a category three. I explained true Floridians don't care until at least a high three. But the media said it was on its way to a four, even a five, before becoming a two, a four, and then back to a three. Then maybe becoming a one before fizzling out somewhere over the Appalachian Mountains, Missouri, or New York. I stared at the map covered in bright clumps of spaghetti lines. I wondered if these were actual weather models. Was it possible the meteorologists gave up and handed the maps to their children to crayon lines wherever they wanted?

My very pale friend had obviously spent the week watching the news day and night. We all did. The analysis, random conjecturing, and non-stop coverage made you feel like you were waiting for the results of the world's worst lottery. Is this going to destroy my home or some other poor bastard's home? It was addictive and exciting in its recklessness. It was real life drama with death, mayhem, and consequences. Inspiring redemption awaited as some family would have to pick up after and rebuild. It was like season binging a depressing television show at home, the curtains drawn, only taking breaks to use the bathroom. It also meant that most of Florida was stressed, tired, and irritable well in advance of Irma's grand entrance.

Even channels that had nothing to do with weather, declared Florida the soon-to-be ground zero for the apocalypse. In glorious yellow ponchos, the Four Horsemen would hover over a Trump wall of black clouds. Warlocks were going to drop onto the highways to bludgeon endless miles of stranded tourists that only wanted to see a mouse. Zombies would emerge from gaping sinkholes to eat Florida's endless supply of old farts. The rest of us deplorables would defend our homes against the impending zombie riots using those guns and bibles we cling to. Battles would be fought in-between the tornadoes full of pythons, lionfish, alligators, and juicy Florida oranges. No amount of canned tuna and bottled water was going to get us out of this mess.

"It'll be alright, brother," I lied to him to stave off his impending breakdown. I invited him to walk with me through the barren hardware store. We passed the remaining batches of wandering lost souls. Modern-day white-collar men waited too long in their cubicles, watching videos of how to button up their homes against a hurricane. Modern man was an expert in beard trimming, hair care, body sprays, skinny jeans, gourmet coffees, and using their phone to hail a ride or dinner to their door. Modern man forgot how to board a window. He never tied off a sandbag, filled a gas can, and started a generator. He was not ready to shoot the first wave of zombies coming for the bottled water and canned tuna.

Earlier in the week, mobs appeared in the same hardware store ready to fight to the death for items they never knew they needed. Gas stations were dry. Supermarket inventories were reduced to a few cans of Diet Pineapple soda no one ever wanted. Hardware stores became barren places for Floridians to gather. We waited for trucks to be escorted in by the Florida Highway Patrol, parting a sea of hopelessness with a fresh supply of plywood. They never showed.

At first, the highways were full of fleeing cars, campers, and trucks with boats on trailers. They were crossing the spaghetti lines. People from as far away as Key West were making their run for the mainland, heading to Tampa where it was safe. Eventually the roads cleared and for the first time in Florida's history, they were empty. It was tempting to get on them because you could. But we didn't.

The X hour to flee had long passed. It was too late to hit the road. The last place to be was on I-75 when the Four Horsemen arrived. Thursday evening, many across my beloved state took a deep, collective breath. They committed to staying. There was no window left to change your mind and make a run for Pascagoula, or Atlanta, or hop on a flight to New York. I heard Edward Murrow in my head say, "Good night… and good luck."

East Coast Floridians were betting the Caribbean Islands were taking the brunt (#savetheislands, #thoughts&prayers, #IrmaSucks). The spaghetti lines then turned for the East Coast (#saveFLEastCoast, #thoughts&prayers, #IrmaSucks). The media declared Miami (#saveMiami) and anything around it a future underwater grave. As always, they used the scenario as a springboard into political narratives. But it was too late to give money to Al Gore to stop this. Local politicians sat indecisively wondering when to order expensive evacuations. So, they didn't. Then they did, but it was too late. So, people didn't… or did.

Big chain stores throughout Florida rerouted inventory to the East Coast; from Palm Beach to Pompano, Fort Lauderdale to Miami, Key Largo to Key West. People came in hordes to battle for all the lumber in the southern United States. They rode in like generals to conquer enemy supply trains of water, generators, and batteries. They stood ready for state trooper-escorted tankers of gasoline.

Once supplies were in place, Irma said, "watch this." Supercomputers and children alike drew new sets of colorful spaghetti lines. They crossed the I-95 corridor, drifting West. Friends on the East Coast celebrated on social media that they were no longer in imminent danger.

Minutes later, the cheering subsided. It was clear Irma was now a West Coast problem. The same people I prayed for on the East Coast flooded me with text and social media posts. They read, "B praying 4 u," with either smiley face or frowny face emojis. It was ironic, given I was certain many of them never actually prayed. Regardless, it was the thing to say. It certainly was not the time to debate their faith (#saveTampa, #thoughts&prayers, #IrmaSucks).

My new friend in the store was getting the same flow of text messages from afar. They only added to the air of impending doom. As more east coast friends marked themselves "safe," I felt like the last one in a shitty game of musical chairs.

I imagined my east coast friends sitting fat and happy on huge thrones of bottled water. They were staring at their magnificent spoils of generators, filled gas cans, cans of tuna, plywood, batteries, and sandbags. As Irma's predicted path crossed the imaginary centerline of Florida, I wondered if the East Coasters knew how barren supplies were elsewhere. Did they know they killed us? Would meteorologists blame themselves on air? Right before the hurricane, would they march on live television and chain themselves to a palm tree along Clearwater Beach as penance for their incorrect cones of certainty?

"I'm so fucked," my new friend blurted out with tears in his eyes. He came to a sudden stop and sobbed beside my cart. In dramatic soap opera fashion, I grabbed him by the shoulders and looked him in the eyes. "You're going to… what's your name?"

"Chip," he cried. "Friends call me Chippy."

"Really?"

He shook his head up and down.

"Well, damnit, Chippy," I said in my most grizzled voice, "you're gonna make it."

Chippy smiled, snorting up all the fluids he had going on in that crooked nose of his and swallowed them down. We continued walking. "Besides," I whispered, "best to keep your shit together, Chippy. You don't want to show fear to this bunch."

He put on a brave face and asked me where we were going.

"I heard from some guy who heard from that guy in the John Deere cap that they may be bringing a pallet of insulation out on aisle three." He asked me what I would do with insulation. I told him I didn't know but, "we're gonna get some."

I wondered if I could duct tape insulation against my windows to make a saferoom. Over the insulation would be my interlocking 12 x 12-inch Rubber Tile Multipurpose Flooring ($29.98 a pack). This would be pressed in by my 5.5-inch x 4 feet Weathered Brown Pine Wood Wall Planks ($3.78 each) across the width of my window. I would then secure them with a hammered-in 4 x 4 severe weather pressured treated post ($8.88 each) wedged between the stucco.

"Damn," he said. "You do have a plan."

We continued to aisle three. My phone kept buzzing in my pocket, loaded with messages from more family members. They were suddenly expert meteorologists. They asked why I had not evacuated Florida. My nephew offered to book us on the final flight out of Tampa International that night. At the same time, my parents asked if I wanted them to bring potato chips, pretzels, and vodka when they come. They were obviously Floridians.

But now my parents were older. I had to call the shots. I was responsible for my parents, my wife, and two nervous Chihuahuas. This was my wife's first hurricane. She trusted I knew what I was doing. I made the call early on to stay. But every minute of televised hysteria, interrupted by messages from their sponsors, doubt creeped in. Forty hurricane seasons, I was still undefeated. Some hurricanes were more like parties. We ate the expensive stuff in the fridge first and enjoyed the best alcoholic beverages. That meant going into each hurricane stuffed on buttery Florida lobster tails out of the freezer and some limited reserve Puerto Rican rum I usually brought back from a cruise. After that, you usually move on to a Publix sub or two, acquired right before the storm. You then thaw the Mahi-Mahi filets, burgers, and hotdogs from the freezer for the propane grill. Cans of tuna and beanie weenies are not until at least day five. Dry cereals and the emergency ration bags of dehydrated food that have been in the garage the last ten years (expiring 10 years from now) are for the final days, after the zombies roll in.

I asked Chippy if he owns his apartment. He said no.

"Great!" I said. "If the shit goes, it goes."

Realizing this was not a comfort to him, I asked what valuables he had. After deep introspection, it came down to a 60-inch television. Again, I considered this great news, but Chippy did not share my enthusiasm. "If the bathroom doesn't have windows, prop it on the sink so when the apartment floods, you're good. If the windows explode all to hell in the wind, the bathroom's a good safe room." Again, Chippy did not seem relieved.

My phone was still buzzing, but it was too close to "go time." Unless it was the ringtone for my wife or my parents, there was not a minute to spare. I did not have time to debate a college buddy on whether the hurricane was a product of democrats, republicans, cow farts, or a combination of all three. Even nutty Aunt Lilly left me a message. She said I was crazy for staying. She has been high as a kite since Clinton was president, so either I was crazy like she said, or she was.

I reminded myself I'm a Floridian. I've got this (#FLnative).

Chippy asked if it was still necessary to do anything, as he lives on the second floor. Before answering, I asked what zone he was in. "Zone A," he said. I accidentally snorted in a "you're screwed" kind of way I didn't mean to. "But it's the second floor," Chippy said. Like a know it all, I explained that Irma could come at high tide with a ten-foot surge. His part of town was not known for its drainage. "What does that mean?" he asked.

"Sit in a shelter," I said. "TVs are replaceable."

In the corner of my eye, I watched an old man come into the store with five handsome, younger clones. They whispered in Spanish before venturing into the different aisles. The men then regrouped in the center of the aisle next to us. They huddled around their elder standing with his daughter. Like a sage prophet, he spoke few words, firm and exact.

The young men surrounded a pallet of 4 x 8 polystyrene garage door foam insulation boards (at $9.98 each). All at once, they plopped the twelve sheets onto the flatbed cart. Only the pallet remained. The old man then pointed at the pallet. "Llevalo," he said. They threw it on top. "If you buy the pallet's worth, you should get the pallet too," I said to myself. At this point, every inch of wood throughout Hillsborough County mattered.

The father stomped his cane twice. The men turned and headed to the register. As he made his distinguished walk down the aisle past me, I nodded, just short of bowing to him. I admired his decisiveness. I imagined the foam insulation taped against his windows. His sliding glass doors reinforced by anything and everything. The old man tipped his spring training baseball cap at me with a grin. I then watched him proceed out that door into immortality.

"Damn, that was awesome," I said trying to fire up Chippy.

He started to smile, growing equally fascinated from the people watching. Twenty men wandered between aisles two and three, avoiding eye contact. Some checked their phones. Others ventured to neighboring aisles for a quick second, third, and fourteenth glance. They were desperate for anything useful against the apocalypse.

A well-groomed lumberjack-looking man approached the remaining 3 x 1.5-foot White Vinyl decorative fencing (at $14.98 each) behind me. I kindly got out of his way and watched as he grabbed the end and checked the flexibility with a flopping motion. "Damn," he said to himself. He tossed it, stretched his back, and stroked his perfectly trimmed, black-dyed beard.

"You can make it work," I said.

"You think?"

I told him if he had a cushy barrier behind it like my rubber flooring or insulation, it was possible.

"Really?" he asked, exasperated.

"Hell yeah," I said. I then told him about the old man who took the remaining insulation.

"I wish I could have seen that," he said. "That's awesome."

"That's what I said." I laughed as Chippy grew quiet, likely slipping back to his defeatist mindset.

I nodded toward the sheet of vinyl behind Metro-Lumberjack. "You can do this, brother," I said. He gave me one of those cool handshakes hip people do with an accompanied pat on the back. Chippy helped him pull out the vinyl sheet and he left aisle two with a spring in his step.

Chippy smiled. "You think that's going to work?"

"Fuck if I know."

Shortly after, a man wearing a "Greatest Dad" t-shirt stood over the remaining three sheets of 4 x 8 hardboard pegboard (brown, $14.98 each). He had his hands on his hips with a sagging face. As I approached, he quickly grabbed the sheets.

"It's okay, brother." I smiled, letting him know that I was not intending to kick his ass for the pegboard. He then started to doubt himself, noticing the sheets' fiber-like composite material. "This won't last the first rain over my windows," he said in a scratchy, tired tone.

"Cover them," Chippy interrupted. "Use that pack of the forty-two-gallon trash bags ($16.98 each for fifty) to cover them using duct tape. Voila… waterproof. Right?"

I nodded with Chippy in agreement, impressed.

"Yeah," the Greatest Dad laughed.

"You've got this," Chippy said. The man shook hands with both of us before taking the sheets to the register to save his family waiting at home.

In the distance, we heard the backing beeps of a forklift. Beep. Beep. Beep. Everyone's head lifted and looked toward the open bay door. Through the plastic strip curtain emerged the ass-end of a forklift. We gathered like fat kids eyeing an incoming ice cream truck. As two employees guided the forklift, my hopes lifted. I stood close to where they would drop the pallet. As it turned, I laughed seeing it was just a pallet of wooden fence pickets.

After the pallet dropped, the two men cut the plastic straps with their box cutters and bolted out of the way. The mob flew around me. I chuckled as they brushed against me, consuming the pickets. I was too tired to fight, too tired to get out of their way. I was ready to go home with what little I had.

As I dragged myself to the register, Chippy caught up, pushing a cart with twelve pickets. I laughed and asked him what he needed those for. He said he got them for me. I didn't cry, but I was speechless. I wasn't sure what I was going to do with them, but I took them.

Chippy said he wasn't going to bother with the television. It was overrated and he needed to get to his new job. He said he was a new hire, a desk job with the power company. "They're making us stay with them during the storm."

I was relieved. "If anyone keeps power during the storm, it's the power company, Chippy."

He gave me a hug and went on his way. He was the best thirty-minute friend I ever had.

An hour later, I was in my backyard. My wife came up behind me, watching. I was trying to use the scraps of picket fence, my interlocking 12 x 12-inch Rubber Tile Multipurpose Flooring, my Rustic 5.5-inch x 4 feet Weathered Brown Pine Wood Wall

Planks, 42-gallon garbage bags, duct tape, and 4 x 4 x 8 severe weather pressured treated posts to secure the three windows on the end of my L-shaped house. That was going to give us two small safe rooms for my parents, my wife, and our two chihuahuas when Irma finally showed. The rest of the house was in God's hands, testing the quality of a track builder and under-the-table subcontractors.

"Impressive," she said. I took a step back. My three windows looked more like abstract pieces of art you would see at the Dali Museum in St. Petersburg.

"Spent twice the cost of damn shutters."

She wiped the sweat from my forehead with her shirtsleeve and gave me a kiss. The neighborhood was silent. The banging hammers, thumping sledgehammers, grinding table saws, bursting chainsaws, buzzing drills, and rumbling generators were still. I felt like I was waiting for the Florida Passover. I only needed some iguana blood on the front door to mark us a faithful Florida domicile.

The wind rustled the oak trees above with growing intensity. The sun was still out. Irma was not expected until two in the morning, but she wanted us to know she was coming. The spaghetti lines had converged on the map, over our very house, straight up Florida's ass. After a long week of media-induced hysteria, hunting for supplies, hearing everyone's opinions about what Irma was going to do to us, and fruitless worrying, it was time to get on with it.

"I saw our neighbor Denise," my wife said. "Everyone around seems to be staying."

I told her misery loves company. I had to get back to work. But it was the wrong thing to say to her. This is the same woman who left her family in New Mexico, where there are zero natural disasters, to make a new life with me in Florida. This was her first hurricane. I was frustrated. The silence of the neighborhood, the increasing gusts of wind, and the ragtag appearance of my covered windows weighed on me.

"I told them you were looking for plywood," she said.

"This will have to do." I stared up at the collage of pickets screwed in over one of the windows. One in the middle and one across were darker than the others. My wife didn't know if I was being a smartass or religious. When I stepped back and gazed at it, she realized it was not an intentional cross I made. She smiled at the coincidence.

"We'll be fine, babe, because of you," she said. "And God. Mostly God."

"See you in there," I said.

She took a picture of the cross and headed inside. I interrupted the neighborhood's peaceful state with a few final bangs of the hammer, wedging a 4x4 within the sill to hold in my creation.

I stared at my accidental masterpiece, made a sign of the cross, and gathered my tools.

My wife came running back, shouting, "Somebody left a sheet of plywood on our driveway!"

"You're kidding."

No, she confirmed again, convinced our neighbors pitched in what they could. I was overwhelmed with joy, the kind that makes you weep because you are tired and helpless. I witnessed something inspiring, restoring my faith in mankind. I never expected a piece of plywood to do this to me. It gave me chills deep inside, the satisfaction knowing that humanity was still kind, gracious, caring, and generous in one's time of need. It was at that moment, humanity was…

"We should get it before someone steals it," she said.

We sprinted to the driveway to grab our sheet of plywood. I used it to secure one more window. We took refuge in our home.

#Thoughts&Prayers, #FloridaNative, #Igotthis, #FuckIrma.

Always Working

At any given time, there were at least ten teenage boys working the store. We were acne-sprouting, only-recently-post-pubescent, revved-up dynamos of frustration. Leaving any of us alone too long, from the trash compactor to the walk-in refrigerators, the bakery to the produce section, the loading dock to the beer cage, the parking lot to the dank employee lounge, increased the chances of a needed cleanup.

Smiley's Supermarket, store twelve, was in prime territory. It was only a short drive or medium walk from the Deerfield public beach. Professional-grade Floridian sun worshippers showed in the morning to gather sandwiches and beer. Families followed, invading like circus troupes with children in tow. In the afternoons, came the ladies. Not all at once, but in rolling, shimmering waves.

Returning from a full day of religious tanning, working in sprayed highlights to their teased lion mains, the ladies arrived in pairs. Two by two, they entered to cool their salty bodies.

The automatic front doorway was the best place to stand. You could feel the store's cold air conditioning rushing against the swampy 90-degree air. Our manager, Mr. Barker, always yelled at us to stop dancing in the doorway like Michael Jackson, flapping our aprons. We were wasting the cool air and scaring the customers that didn't get the tribute to the gloved one.

The ladies slowly entered through the doorway. All took notice. I wished we could have used the intercom to announce them in the voice of a strip club DJ. "Gentlemen, making their way down the black, non-slip carpet, let's give it up for the very… sexy… Christina… and Samantha." The ladies would pose for pictures for their adoring paparazzi. The boys would align the entrance dancing, doing wheelies with the shopping carts. Some of us were expert tricksters on the carts to Mr. Barker's frustration. He watched me ride from one end of the parking lot to the other. I followed the slope and used my foot against the rear wheels to turn left, right, and control the speed. I was king of the lot. He chewed me out. But I know deep down inside, he was jealous. It had to be a record.

The ladies, the stars of the show, wore similar outfits, like it was decided in a national convention. A gavel dropped. The women decided the best way to a young man's fullest attention, was a pair of short jean shorts. They were to barely cover their bikini bottoms. Bikini tops were to feature the brightest fluorescent colors. This included neon green, pineapple yellow, firetruck red, and orange peel orange. These were the hottest colors offered that year at Ned's Surf Shop by the pier, where all the cool kids shopped. Such an outfit would cause a boy to walk into solid structures and become a hazard to all around.

Their minimalist ensemble came with bedazzled flip-flops to click and clank. They popped sexy rhythms across the store's sticky floor, the one we skipped cleaning when Mr. Barker wasn't watching. We spent most of our time trying to ride the industrialized high-speed floor burnisher. It only took a few violent tosses across the store to realize that spinning bull was impossible to ride.

Some ladies wore baseball caps. Their ponytails flowed out the back. Others kept their hair draped across their freckled shoulders. The shorter the shorts, the bigger the hair, the more fluorescent the top… the more dominant their mating signals were to the young males circling. The eyes of the hyenas followed the bouncing neon signals.

They grabbed their Snapples, Jolly Ranchers, lotions, and potions. My friend's older sister Kay always smelled like Aloe Vera. She worked hard to tan to the color of our eggplants in produce. I feared someday she would combust into flames. We would find only a singed bikini in an indentation to the coarse beige sand on the beach. Other ladies moderated their tanning ambitions, resembling mangos, crossing into shades of yellow, orange, and red.

In the next league up, were the college girls flowing in to restock on fruity wine coolers. Some had real ID's. Some did not. It didn't matter. It was Florida. As they entered, the boys went to full alert. They signaled each other, eyes bulging, like cheetahs stalking gazelles. The ladies were aware, giggling, smiling, flipping their hair. They posed in full view. They pretended they needed more time to make their selections, standing in their bikini tops by the cool air of the beer display.

My friend Gary once grabbed a can of Spanish peanuts and headed to the same aisle as two college girls. He pretended he had a very urgent price check. It was a smooth move until he walked into a structural column. His face made a loud ding into the metal wrapping for all to hear.

They asked him if he was okay, but he didn't stick around to respond. The ladies continued their walk with full reign of the store. Back and forth, they clicked and clanked to the undivided attention of the entire male staff of Smiley's store number whatever-we-were. But make no mistake, we were the prey.

Lured by beauty, we were victims to our still-developing, fumbling instincts.

When I wasn't the fifth best bag boy, as Mr. Barker once declared, I was also the gum scraper. That meant I got the privilege to wander the store carrying a broomstick with a razor blade on the end. My job was to find gum on the black and white marble-patterned floor. My ability to find it was a gift. It afforded me occasional freedom. It was a break from pretending to do the toilets, stocking the shelves, and taking some old lady's groceries to her car.

Gum scraper was a great gig. No matter where the ladies were, the gum scraper had that freedom to be nearby and look busy. The ladies knew. Some even walked a little sexier if that was possible. They clicked and clanked their flip flops as the zombie army of drooling boys circled.

Frankie Fitzgerald once walked straight into our huge 4th of July soda display. It was a solid wall of red Shasta, white Diet Coke, and Blue Pepsi cans made to look like an American flag. We lost three twelve-packs from that accident. My friend Chris and I did our patriotic duty and got the display back up within two hours. It could have been done in ten minutes, but it was hot out. It kept us inside, in the air conditioning.

Often, Mr. Barker would plop down from the back office, astonished to see abandoned registers. It was only customers and the old ladies at the register. None of his boys were to be found. He would waddle outside to scan the parking lot. Calling no joy, the order followed over the PA system.

"All bag personnel report to the front."

Few of us ever reported back until he called us by name. If Mr. Barker called your name three times without reporting in, you could get sent home. Unless I heard "Joshua to the front" at least twice, I ignored his beckoning. This was especially true if I had gum scraper duty.

It was Mr. Barker's way of saying "I know you clowns are up to no good and you better get your asses out front right now to bag groceries." When it happened, I reappeared like I was coming from the bathroom, ensuring the toilets were clean and the paper was stocked. Other times pretended to return from an incredibly productive round of gum scraping. If Mr. Barker was near the bathroom, I could drop out the back loading door, grab a couple of carts in the parking lot, and make an entrance at the front. It would look as if I had been out there all that time, dying in the swampy heat, in my stupid long sleeve shirt and tie, rounding up carts. But there were too many of us boys for Mr. Barker to manage.

Most of my shifts aligned with Mr. Barker. He was the best option. If you looked like you had a plan and were doing something, he'd move on. He focused on those sneaking in a smoke out back, taking tips, and stealing individual cans of beer. He was also on a mission to find those breaking items for the "write-off box."

The write-off box was where we tossed the damaged items. It didn't say or care who broke the items. If you broke a package of cookies or "some customer" broke a package of cookies, you placed them there. Within minutes, the contents would disappear. The boys quickly consumed them like starved rats. There was no sense in letting them go to waste.

"Minny" Michael was notorious for write-offs. He would break a six pack of soda, a bag of potato chips, a loaf of bread... whatever he felt like when he was hungry. This was until the famous ambush. Mr. Barker hid for over two hours, waiting like a Marine sniper. He jumped out of the beer cage just as Minny ripped the seal to a package of donuts. Minny was startled and almost choked to death on a chocolate glazed golden cake donut, that stealing bastard.

When they added the tilted mirrors along the store's back wall, Mr. Barker was able to gain a greater viewpoint. He could watch us all avoid work, circling like sharks, tracking scents of sunscreen, jasmine body sprays, bubble gum, and wine coolers. But he couldn't see everything. There was value to knowing the limits of the mirrored wall.

When the ladies finally approached a register, baggers miraculously reappeared. Mr. Barker stood in the front, holding the intercom receiver, watching his cattle return home.

"Where have you been?" he asked me.

"Gumming," I said leaning the stick against the wall and heading to the register.

"And where the hell have you been?" he asked Chris.

"Getting carts," Chris said, pointing at the row of carts in front he had nothing to do with. I was impressed with the ease at which Chris claimed the work, even after coming in from the opposite direction, nowhere near the carts. Mr. Barker looked confused and ran off to do an override at register two.

Baggers had to guess which register the ladies were going to pick. It required precise timing and intuition. It was a mix of mind-reading and human psychology that got you there right when it was their turn. You had to judge whether the customer in front of them needed a carry-out or would carry their own bags. Would they get behind the massive order being unloaded by a businessman, or would they line up behind the old lady with only a few items? It was difficult to know which one they would pick though I knew the one they should have picked.

The correct answer was the businessman, even with a $200 order. That old lady was likely lonely. She was looking for conversation and didn't get out much. She wanted something she forgot. She grabbed at least three items we failed to put a price tag on requiring a price check. She was going to pay by check. If you had my level of experience, you would have known all of this.

"Hellooo," Blue-Hair Mildred would shout from register four. "Big order. Somebody help me?"

No one liked bagging for Blue Milly. She smelled like cheese and criticized baggers in front of customers for putting the eggs and bread on the bottom, mixing the wet items with the boxed items, putting produce with cleaning products… or something. I didn't listen to her or care.

The meanest cashier, Angry Alice, called your name like a drill sergeant for all to hear. You could only pretend to not feel the heat of her stare. I once passed a massive two cart order at her register to bag a single pack of wine coolers for two college ladies at the express register. They wore the brightest matching neon orange tops, visible from space. I smiled. They smiled. A beam of sun went through the store's front window and shined a golden aura onto their magnificent…

"Joshua!" Angry Alice shouted across three registers. "Get your butt over here."

I pretended she was yelling at someone else. Joshua? Never heard of the guy. Like a smooth operator, I offered the bag and then pulled it away before they could grab it.

"It's heavy," I said. "I should take it out for you."

They giggled. "If you want," said the one twirling her butterscotch hair.

"Is that crazy cashier lady over there yelling at you?" asked the one with the bigger…

"Joshua!"

"She does that," I said. We passed the old lady pushing her full cart from Angry Alice's register. She had to balance her walker on top of her groceries. Other baggers could have helped her, but they were watching me. I was a young man of incredible focus, hand-carrying a single bag out for the glowing ladies.

Kenny Kilburn did something similar, but came back with, not one but, two phone numbers. Two numbers from the same order! That was the shit legends were made of. He wasn't much in the looks department either, proving confidence was key.

If there was a hall of fame to pay homage to the trailblazers before us, a tribute to working-class baggers, they would name it after him. The Kenny Kilburn Hall of Greatest Baggers. After high school, Kenny made assistant produce manager at Store 15. It was a bigger store, closer to Fort Lauderdale. Folks say Store 15 is no joke. He did well, bought a white '89 IROC with chrome rims and neon green underbody lighting effects. We looked up to him.

Kenny was calculating. Baggers not only had to time their turn at the register, but how long of a distance they had to work their charm. If it was a short trip to the car, I weighed asking for a number against being cool, laying the foundation for a future discussion. One of those, "hey, catch you next time," moments. It was an important judgment call.

I had a long, tenured, five-and-a-half-year career at the store. In that time, I met some real heartbreakers. After Kenny, of course, I was one of the top two baggers regardless of what Mr. Barker had to say. The other was Jason, my nemesis. Jason had a talent ignoring cashiers, even dropping an order in the middle of bagging it, to walk up to another register when a "looker" arrived. That was a level of commitment and audacity few could follow. His timing, confidence, charm, and lack of give-a-shit to the customer was unmatched.

One time, I was about to bag for Carrie, the captain of the girl's swim team. She was standing in line with her friend Teri. I only had to bag a gallon of milk for the old lady in front of her and stick around to finally meet Carrie. But Jason, that son of a bitch, had other plans.

Jason walked up behind me and asked the old lady if she wanted someone to carry her heavy gallon of milk to her car. She said that'd be lovely. Indeed. Jason then slapped me on the back and said, "This young, strong, gentleman will be glad to." She thanked him. I had no choice. Again, for those following at home, she thanked *him*, that no good son of a bitch, for what *I* was going to do.

It was so genius, I went. Jason somehow committed me, in front of the old lady, Mr. Barker, Angry Alice, all the baggers… the entire store. I carried the lady's bag, looking back over my shoulder. That son of a bitch then slid into my position to bag groceries for Carrie. I returned to the register from the parking lot and came up to him, not saying a word. He quietly waved a piece of paper in front of me, smiled, and placed it inside his shirt pocket.

"Game on, asshole," I said to him.

I wanted to smash a customer's grapefruit in his face right there at the register. I wanted to rub surfboard wax across the windshield to his crap blue Pontiac. I wanted to egg his car. I wanted to cover his car in popcorn so the seagulls could shit all over it. That was all standard level one Florida retribution stuff. But I didn't. I had to admit he won that round. I underestimated my enemy's capabilities.

I got him back two long weeks later. He was sweet-talking a looker in the parking lot. He leaned in through the open window, as the cute girl sat in the driver's seat with the car running. No one can confirm whether it was myself or someone else resembling me that left a shopping cart behind her car.

She backed into it, scratched her car, and had a total meltdown. Everyone in store twelve heard her yell at Mr. Barker. Not only did she blame Jason, but she also demanded the store pay the damage to her new Pontiac Firebird. Mr. Barker gave Jason a stern warning that day. More importantly, he and the girl never went out.

Jason never knew I was the perpetrator of this heinous crime. It bothered me. Two months later, I told him. Not because of guilt, but because I wanted him to know. I drew a line in the sand, telling him to his face, outside aisle three, while stocking the Veterans Day Baked Beans pirate ship display.

I had no idea what the pirate ship or baked beans had to do with our nation's veterans. None of Mr. Barker's displays ever made sense. He was responsible for the Halloween Hotdog sale, the Easter Bunny Burger Burn, the Memorial Day Candy Extravaganza, and the Christmas Cold Beer Bonanza. The only one that made any sense was the American Flag of Soda display for the 4th of July. I am positive he stole that from the great Kenny Kilburn at store fifteen. I also felt the bunny made of ground beef emotionally scarred some children, but it was not my concern. For Veterans Day, Jason and I had a mountain of canned beans to stock. Our job was to dump box after box of cans into the pathetic cardboard display painted to look like a pirate ship. We stared each other down like gunslingers as we did it.

"I could have lost my job, dickhead."

"Well, hope Carrie was worth it," I said.

He smiled. I threw the beans harder into the display, closer and closer to his side. He did the same. Any moment, we could have had an accidental misfire. Someone could have been beamed in the head with a can of maple or hickory smoked baked beans with pork. A total war would erupt on aisle three.

The store was getting too small for the two of us. Other baggers waited for it to go down. Pedro from Produce told me folks would check Mr. Barker's weekly schedule posted in the lounge. They were hoping the two of us would get scheduled on the same night.

In the interest of not getting fired, we decided to split prime days. He took Sunday. I took Saturday. Weekdays after school were slow and not worth fighting for. It was still a big store with enough room to avoid each other if it came to it. But our paths crossed from time to time. The holiday weekends were all hands-on-deck and often full working weekends for us.

One fateful day, we were both on shift, when Summer Parker walked in with her mom. Summer reigned as the most popular, prettiest cheerleader in my rival school. Like the rest of the boys in the store that day, I tracked her from the first step through the doorway. After years of experience, I knew bagging at register two, I could use the angled mirror on the back wall to track most of her way through the store.

I think some old lady asked me if I would mind carrying out a few bags. I remember smiling and moving her along. She eventually made it to the bus stop or some place. All I know is I remained focused on Summer's precise whereabouts. I was estimating her ETA to the register area. I had to calculate which register Mrs. Parker would choose.

Summer's jean shorts were low and loose at the hip. They showed the fluorescent green sides to the bright green bikini bottom pressing her hips. She proudly wore her white Poison tour t-shirt. It was cut at just the right length over her bright green bikini top. She clearly wanted to show the pale white scar across her tight tanned belly.

I already knew the scar was from a recent painful wrapping of a Portuguese Man O War last week. I too was hit, like everyone else in the ocean that day when the wind shifted in from the east. The massive offshore bed of sargassum seaweed and man o wars drifted to shore.

One by one, surfers, boogieboarders, and those wave-surfing were stung. Specs and full-length strings of the sticky purple menace made their way onto people's skin. One surfer was hit directly in the face, blue bubble and all, while duck diving a wave. His buddies had to pull him to shore and carry him to the lifeguard station by the pier. I heard the screams. They spent an hour extracting the sticky, gum-like purple matter off his face with a set of tweezers, bit by bit. I imagined it was like an alien tentacled lobster-meets-octopus creature swallowing his face. Horrifying.

My sting burned intensely wherever the purple tentacles stuck to the skin. The burn lasted over an hour. Many of us learned to keep a bag with Bactine and baking soda. Together, they made a cooling paste to apply to the wound. It helped but not enough.

Summer made her white scar look like an accessory and wore it with pride. Mine was around my arm, like a pale tribal arm tattoo. I had another on my leg but not as easy to show off.

Despite the aroma of the bakery fighting the vinegar spill we were ignoring on aisle eight, I picked up on Summer's strawberry bubble yum. I smiled, watching her grace the store, aisle to aisle with her mom. I knew from the latest intel that Summer broke up with her boyfriend from the local surfing gang, the Yolo Dregs. South Florida is not exactly known for its surf. This might explain why the Yolo Dregs were always pissed. Instead of surfing, they had to spend their time fighting other gangs of bored preppy kids at the mall. Either way, it was soon "go time."

"Romeo." Angry Alice snapped her fingers at me as I continued bagging someone's soup cans on top of the bread.

Summer followed her mom, closer and closer to the registers. The line at seven was too long. Register eight was my bet.

"Son of a bitch." I watched Jason slide toward the register. I didn't even see him walk in. He took his position at the register. "You're kidding me," I said to myself.

"Hey," Angry Alice repeated three times like a barking dog until I looked her in the eye. The man at the register tried not to laugh at Angry Alice's drill sergeant routine. He was unaware I might have thrown his drain cleaner in the same bag as his pork chops.

Angry Alice saw the surrendered look on my face. I already calculated that the current customer at register eight was not going to need help to the car. Summer was next with her mom.

It was a large order and Jason, that son of a bitch, was going to get to take them out to their car.

I approached Angry Alice, defeated. She snapped her fingers at me. "You bag exclusively for me the next two weeks and I fix this."

"What?" I asked, staring off toward register eight.

"Look at me," she commanded. The customer shook his head laughing as he continued writing out his check.

"I fix this, you bag for me. If I get a big order, your sorry butt is here helping me." She leaned over me and took the milk out of my hand. She placed it in a separate bag, preventing me from throwing it on top of the man's red grapes. "And you are going to bag correctly," Angry Alice said. "Deal?"

"Fine."

"Have a nice day," Angry Alice said to the gentlemen. He took the cart from me, knowing not to even ask if I'd help him to his car. Angry Alice asked again, "Deal?"

I agreed. The customer in front of Summer's mom finished paying. Jason pushed the cart to her with zero offer to help and immediately jockeyed for the first items to Summer's order. Summer was not paying attention, placing items onto the conveyor for her mom. He waited to launch his charm offensive. I was soon to be the loser on register six with Angry Alice.

Angry Alice gave a nod to Sassy Sherry at register eight. She reached for the cookies on her conveyor belt from the next customer. Without scanning it, Angry Alice lifted the package into the air for all to see.

"Jason," she shouted two registers down. Sassy Sherry made Jason look back at Angry Alice. He did not want to, but she gave him no choice.

"I need a price check! Now, Jason," Angry Alice shouted.

I stood there useless, confused, unsure what to do. Jason looked at me, wondering why I was not doing the price check. Without further explanation, Angry Alice shouted louder for all to hear, "I need him to bag. Jason, price check… right now, young man!"

The entire store watched Jason. He stood motionless behind his bagging station. Sassy Sherry told him, "You better help Alice, Hun." She laughed, "Don't make her tell you another time."

Summer continued listening to her headphones, placing the final items from the cart onto the conveyor belt. Jason slowly stepped away from register eight and made his walk of shame toward me.

"Go, kid," Alice said to me.

I headed to register eight to replace him.

"What the hell?" Jason said to me.

"Tough break, Fuckstick," I said in passing with a smile.

I made my way to the register and greeted Summer's mom. I asked her if she preferred plastic. "Sure," she said. As the bouquet of fresh cut flowers passed the scanner, I asked her if she would like to hold the flowers.

"Ah, hand them to my daughter," she said fiddling through her purse.

Summer lifted her head. She pulled off her headphones and placed them around her neck. I never forgot her first giggle toward me. She gracefully squeezed by her mom to get to where I was making all the magic happen, bagging her mom's groceries.

I handed her the flowers as if I purchased them myself.

"I hope he wasn't bothering you," I said.

"Who?"

"Exactly." I placed the peppers with the cucumbers, papayas, and lemons neatly in the same bag. Jason sadly drifted by carrying the package of cookies while Summer and I continued our flirtatious dance.

"Move it, Jason," I heard Angry Alice yelling in the distance.

Summer asked me if I was from her school. I played it cool and asked her where she went. She said Boca. I said Deerfield. She smiled like I was now something even more exotic, something not from the usual menu. She flung her perfectly straight sun tea hair as she wet her lips in slow motion… at least that's how I remember it. And yes, she was an intoxicating breeze of coconut body lotion and strawberry bubble yum, exactly as I had guessed.

Unlike all other orders in my legendary bagboy career, I ensured the eggs were on top. I kept the cold stuff somewhat together and the dry boxy items separate. It was like they showed in the boring training video. I even packed the bread separately and put most of the cans on the bottom of the cart. I wanted her mom to appreciate this level of effort, something you rarely see from any of the bagboys.

Her mom finished paying Sassy Sherry and quickly offered to take the cart, appearing to be in a hurry. She grabbed the cart. I glared down at her hand. I refused to let go. There was no way I was letting this one get away. I took a deep breath, looked up, and smiled. "It will be quicker if I help you, Ma'am." I told her it was my job. "Besides, my boss is watching," I joked, pointing at Mr. Barker telling Jason to stop moping around.

Summer's mom agreed and led the way, walking briskly, trying to find the keys in her purse. She was a non-stop multi-tasker.

"You hang out down at South Breaks Beach?" I asked.

"Sometimes." She flung her hair over her shoulder. She somehow knew it would drive me crazy.

"So, were you also part of the man o war drama last Thursday?" I said knowing very well she was. I played it off like I never noticed the cool white scar across her stomach with the pierced bellybutton featuring a small fake emerald. I knew it was her birthstone.

She ran her fingers along her stomach to show the scar… like a model running her hand down the lines of a hot red racecar. "Not bad," I said.

I pulled up my sleeve, proudly displaying my own battle scar.

"I heard you got hit twice." She paused. She not only knew of me, but she cared I was hit twice.

I played it cool, like I didn't notice. "Yeah, the leg too."

We walked side by side, slowly pushing the cart. We enjoyed small talk while her mother continued racing ahead for the car. Her mom already opened the trunk and fired up the car to get the air conditioning running. A gust of the wet, salty ocean breeze carried Summer's scent across the freshly tarred parking lot. Hot tar and coconut are intoxicating when combined, if you didn't know.

It was a quick walk, but we nailed the main topics. This included which hair bands we were into, what we knew about a 1972 Camaro jumping the drawbridge last Friday night, a cocaine bust from a cigarette boat stopped at Hillsboro Inlet, and the rumor of a keg party at some rich kid's house on the A1A Hillsboro Mile. My answers were Def Leppard and Warrant, it was really a Chevelle that jumped the bridge, it took a helicopter to catch the badass cigarette boat, and I knew a guy that knew about the party.

I then worked up the courage to give her my beeper number. It was also to show off that I, a sixteen-year-old, reached the pinnacle of my life to warrant a beeper. At the time, only important people, doctors, and drug dealers with badass cigarette boats carried beepers.

I tossed the final bag with the eggs somewhere in the trunk. I wasn't paying attention. It didn't matter. My focus was on her. "Well, beep me."

Summer snatched my hand and wrote her home number on my palm. "No, you call me." Her hand grabbed mine. She smiled holding it out, writing her number, all in slow motion. It was a heavenly moment before her mother shouted at her to "get in the car before the ice cream melts."

I backed away with the cart and watched my love drive away. The sun began to set over the purple metal roof of Meryl's Merry Liquor Store. I didn't even worry over the fact that I couldn't remember bagging ice cream for them.

I returned like a triumphant warrior, marching through his village after a glorious victory. I skipped every cart in the parking lot Mr. Barker likely expected me to bring in. I passed Jason at the front doorway and threw my palm in his face, fast enough to make him flinch. He saw the number.

"So nice," I said walking away.

Jason stood in unrecoverable, eternal, ass-kicking defeat. I then raced to Alice to borrow a throw away receipt to copy the number before my sweaty palms smeared the digits.

"Happy?" Alice asked.

I thanked Alice and kept my word. I bagged exclusively for her (and Sherry) that week and the weeks that followed. I did so beyond my two-week contractual obligation. As Summer and I continued dating, I found myself bagging for Alice on a regular basis. I was in love and my days of wandering the store with the other hyenas was less than before. In time, I got to know Alice and she became a "store mom" to me.

Alice told my mom she knew Summer's mom from church. She remembers Summer when she was only a baby, her mom holding her in morning mass every Sunday.

Alice confessed that once she recognized Summer was the star of the show, she wanted to step in for the assist. She said she thought Summer, being from a good, God-fearing family, would be a better match for me over any of the "neon-booby beach bimbos" we bagboys tripped over. She didn't think Jaimie would straighten me out. But she also wouldn't corrupt me.

To her credit, Alice was right. Summer and I corrupted each other equally. Alice also confirmed that she enjoyed destroying Jason's spirit. She called him an "arrogant shit." She believed each day Summer came into the store with her mom, blowing me a sweet kiss, "humbled that little asshole." Jason was like a defeated enemy, forced to bow in shame before his conqueror each day.

I dated her for a long time, almost six months. Summer, along with Jamie, Amie, Cindy, Katie, Jenny, Sandy, Brandie, and others ending in *ie* and *y*, were lovely acquaintances from my tenure at store twelve. It was a more personable time. Now, I guess kids use apps, websites, games, or other weird nonsense on their smartphones to find a date, like ordering a pizza. There is no chase, no commitment.

Boys today will never know the thrill of finding a beautiful woman, following her every move, planning how you are going to cut off all the other hyenas and win her heart. Today, some would consider it stalking, toxic manliness, or whatever they choose to complain about these days.

Back then, I would have preferred meeting these ladies at the beach, a club, or a party at some rich kid's house on the beach that we could trash, run, and not feel bad about. But I was a working-class man. Always working.

Angels in the Marina

"The two best days owning a boat are the day you buy it and the day you sell it," Samuel said. Pops watched the storm from the cushioned seat in front of the center console. Samuel wasn't sure if Pops heard him over the incoming gust and the rocking of the boat. Pops waved his right crinkled hand across the sky in front of him. It followed the distant dark purple and gray swirling wall. His arm had quarter-sized spots of matching purple, showing how easy his skin now bruised. Thunder trundled the horizon, a warning from a hurricane a day away.

Samuel reeled in the two lines and placed the hooks into the cork rod handles. He positioned the poles into the holders at the stern, one on each side. Sweat rolled down his forehead and dripped off his nose. What he didn't wipe with his bandana disappeared into his thick black, expertly trimmed beard.

Samuel couldn't tell how soon the storm was coming. He just wanted to know why the 115-horsepower outboard to his boat failed to turn. Messing with the rods allowed his mind to reset.

"Let's get her going," Pops said.

"I'm working on it."

Samuel thought back to when he first got her, not long ago. It was supposed to be a father and son project, an opportunity for Pops to pass on what he knew. Pops was the sailor, a Merchant Marine, a man that knew the sea. He sailed the big ships, usually moving fruit of all sorts, from papaya to bananas. The usual stops were Guatemala, Cuba, and New York in the 1950's. In his fifteen years at sea, well before Samuel was born, Pops grew familiar with many of the ports this side of the world.

That morning, Pops had three key points to settle with his son. As soon as his old beige Crocs touched the deck, Pops was ready. One, it was necessary to name her. Two, it had to be a woman's name for luck. And three, he couldn't believe his son hadn't gotten around to it.

"Name her already," Pops said. He smiled, appreciating the 18-foot length of the boat. It was a sturdy, humble boat, perfect for his son's first time at the helm. Forty-six years to finally become a captain was better than never. There was something satisfying about pushing away from a mainland hell bent on destroying itself. All Samuel read on his smartphone these days disturbed his soul. The boat was a refuge from the noise.

People were wearing masks and not wearing masks, getting shots and not getting shots. Everyone snarled for the blue team or the red team. People were offended if you weren't offended when they were offended. The world made less sense each day. "Fuck them," Samuel would say with a smile each time he took the boat out of the marina. He felt a disconnecting from the wired world, like a plug being pulled from a socket, each time he made his way out the Hillsboro Inlet. Out the rock jetty and into the Atlantic, he enjoyed seeing the mainland behind him get a little smaller. But he was never sure enough to watch it disappear. Although the ocean separated him from a mad world, Samuel was entering another he didn't know. He was still hesitant and only had hours truly getting to know the sea.

"It's bad luck, no name," Pops said.

"Kind of busy," Samuel said looking into the well on the starboard side, underneath the cushion seat at the stern. He kept staring at the little red dial. He wasn't busy. He was hoping his angry eyes would make a difference as he flipped the "switchy thing" from battery one to battery two. He checked the cables and kept switching the dial. It became harder to ignore the high wall of clouds moving west toward them. He turned the switch off in case it was to reset itself. He was sure it didn't work like that. But he did it anyway.

The incoming storm was not Hurricane Whitney. It was a little hint to the madness to come. She wanted to sit and spin in the Atlantic, south of the Bahamas. It gave her more time to stir into a bigger mess. He equated it to his wife sitting on the couch, arms folded, not saying a thing, getting ready to do some damage.

Samuel thought all hurricanes should be named after a woman. When they found the most threatening hurricane, Samuel wanted it named after his ex-wife. Hurricane Traci… *with an i, not a y or ie,* but only an *i* on the end not followed by anything else, which all the world had to know to accommodate her constant need to feel special, above all the other ladies at the Sapphire Cabaret off of Federal Highway which, according to her, was classier than the other strip joints until she left and married Samuel's sorry ass. Her words.

"Hurricane Traci" sounded like the perfect angry, unforgiving, unrelenting, cheating, self-revolving, trailer park-destroying homewrecker. Samuel didn't know how a hurricane could cheat, but he had to press on.

"Doesn't work like that, son." Pops said. He explained that NOAA had a predetermined, alphabetical list of names.

"I know, Pops."

"Traci… with an *i,*" he laughed. "She had your number."

Samuel turned the battery switch, jumped to the console, and rotated the key. The motor cranked and cranked. It would not turn. He wanted to hear anything besides Pops reminiscing over Samuel's ass-handing divorce. He tried to drown out Pop's rambling with more attempts to start the motor. Samuel ran back to the stern, slapped up the cushion, and turned the battery switch off. On his hands and knees, he stared at the cables.

"Ever use that radio?"

Yes, he said, thrilled to switch to Pops laughing about his splurging on a nice radio.

"You spent too much on that thing if you ask me," he said. "Need to be quiet to fish."

"Told you I don't use it when I fish," Samuel said. He touched each of the cables, but there was nothing wrong with them.

Lightning flashed the horizon bright white. Another long roll of thunder sounded over the choppy water. Sweat rolled down Samuel's neck, down his broad tattooed back. It made its way through his shorts, down his muscular gym legs to his flip flops.

"Doesn't look good," Pops said in between sips of his beer. He smiled at the lightning show like he was cheering for the storm.

After Samuel's mom, Gloria, passed last year, Pops claimed to have a clearer view of life. He said growing old was "like watching movers waltz in to take your shit out of the trailer you called home." Loved ones are taken and you sit alone, waiting to be evicted. All you can do is watch everything get thrown away or given away. They occasionally ask you what something is or if it is still good. But you don't care. You can't take it with you, wherever you are going. The last thing to go is you. Pops said at some point, you stop being mad. You grow numb. Your ride comes to a slow end as the roller coaster returns to the start for someone else.

Samuel wanted the day to be a good one, a quick run of the boat to ensure everything was in good order. They would then secure it a final time at the marina. The forklift would put it up safely in the rack. Samuel would walk away knowing it was as ready as it was going to be for the hurricane.

Boaters crowded the water. Jet-skiers, families, and fishermen were out to enjoy a final day while they could. They didn't have to share the waterways with the clueless tourists in their rentals. Ivan's Watersports & Rentals was already closed and buttoned up. His armada of old pontoon boats sat secured on the gravel lot beside the boat ramps.

As the boat traffic returned into the inlet, Samuel grew weary of being the last in. He tried to keep his head up, staring out at the horizon as his stomach twisted and his heart raced. He wanted to vomit, staring into the rocking boat too long. His skin was turning red, feeling warm and flush.

"What wrong with you?"

"Nothing," Samuel said, his knees on the deck. He popped his head over the side of the boat and started to spit into the water.

"Have a beer," Pops said. "It'll settle your stomach. You got them damn land legs."

"I'm fine."

Pops took another swig of his beer. "Traci with an *i* had better sea legs than you."

"Yeah, well she wrapped them around anything."

"They're why you married her, son."

Samuel felt his stomach churning.

"Fancy beer," Pops said. "What do you call it?"

Samuel looked again at the battery switch.

"Craft beer," he said taking a deep breath, pushing the air down into his stomach.

"Never heard of it."

Samuel's lunch tried to resurface, like a submarine performing an emergency blow. He turned the battery switch OFF then ON. He hoped something would catch, turn, click, anything. He saw power going to the console and decided to hit the radio ON button. Pit Bull blared out from the speakers for all the east coast to hear.

"Loud enough for you?" Pops said, covering his ears, grinning. Samuel quickly tried to turn it down while staring at the power going to the rest of the console. The Latin beat, horns, and rapping initially shook the boat. Samuel played it off like it was not from his phone's playlist of favorites. It was and he just wanted to get the engine started.

"Fish don't like whatever that is."

"I said I don't use the radio when I fish, Pops."

"What was the last big catch you had?"

"A thirty-inch Kingfish," Samuel said. "Three weeks ago."

"No grouper or snapper?"

"No, Pops."

Pops finished his beer and crushed the can. "Well, you got to go out further from shore for the good stuff."

Samuel said nothing.

Pops asked for another one of those fancy craft beers.

"Kind of busy, Pops," Samuel shouted staring over the outboard. "Give me a minute to think."

"No hurry." Pops slapped his knees and nodded his head to the faint sound of Pit Bull playing in the background. Samuel flapped his sweat soaked Bundo's Gym tank top with one hand while the other handed Pops a sweating beer. He jumped back to the console, ready to turn the key.

"Throw this away, please," Pops held up his can in the air.

"Dammit," Samuel mumbled, grabbing the empty. He threw it into the empty baitwell behind him. It made a loud clink. He slammed the lid shut and grabbed another beer from the cooler to roll across his big forehead.

"Won't start?"

"I don't know yet. Just give me a second." Samuel jumped back behind the console to stare at everything not going on.

"It either works or it doesn't," Pops laughed. "Turn it."

Samuel rested his butt on the cushioned seat, waiting for his aching back to adjust. He took a deep breath and turned the key. It kept cranking and churning without catching.

Samuel caught himself before launching into a tirade. This boat and Samuel were not meant to be. It was pretty. He took it home. He still didn't have a name, and he no longer cared.

Pops looked up to the incoming storm like he was ready to embrace it. He would forgive Samuel's failure as a captain. He was ready to ride the lightning to the next life. The winds gathered around the boat and the wind made more white cuts into the dark blue waters.

The boat shifted, rocking in the gusts. Hillsboro Beach moved from the port to starboard side as the boat tossed back and forth. "Is that Pompano Beach?"

"No, that's…" Samuel stopped rubbing his head and looked at up. "Which one are you asking about?"

He pointed to the beach south of the inlet.

"Yeah."

The thunder grew louder and more frequent. Samuel felt it in the boat, rattling from the deck to his knees. He heard music faintly from the radio.

"You have power," Pops said. "So that isn't it."

Pops cupped his hand to his right ear and leaned toward the starboard twelve-inch speaker. Samuel was not in the mood for more judgment of his tastes in music.

"Try again," Pops said before sipping his beer and making a face. The bitter taste of the IPA was still hard to get used to.

Samuel turned the radio off and saw the power still lighting up the different dials in the console. The fancy depth finder and chart plotter he purchased, but never got around to learning how to use, was fully lit. Lots of colors, numbers, and moving things he only generally understood. His unnamed boat continued to rock and drift toward the sandbar off Hillsboro Beach. It was not too far north of the red rock reef.

"Want to put down an anchor, son?"

Pops watched the nearing shoreline. A green and brown collage of pine, live oak, and cabbage palms stood anchored in the beige sand. "Trying to get us out of here, Pops. Just watch for that reef. I need to figure out why this fucking thing won't…"

The boat slid to a stop with a loud thump. Samuel froze, certain they had hit the reef.

"Reef's over there," Pops said, pointing at the Lighthouse two hundred yards south of the boat. "You said the lighthouse marks the north end of the reef. So, we're good."

Samuel popped his head over the side of the boat. He was relieved to see the beige sand below. Pops soon began talking about lighthouses and the time they beached a cargo ship during a storm. They were running from a hurricane, into the mouth of a port, head-on. They missed.

"Help me, Mom," Samuel whispered up to the clouded sky.

After Samuel's mom Gloria passed, Pops moved to a trailer in a friendly retirement community of similar boring white trailers. They had a small pond with huge black and white ducks that owned the streets. At the lake, there was a four-foot alligator named Caesar everyone left alone. They had a clubhouse to play cards and dominos. It included a community pool. Haitian landscapers mowed all the patches of grass. Everyone had a golf cart and often drove shitfaced.

Pops knew the divorce and the loss of Gloria was too much on Samuel. He declined Samuel's offer to one of the spare bedrooms. He was not going to burden his son.

Pops also knew he wasn't feeling the same anymore. Somewhere, some cells, some part, some organ, some... thing was not working like it should. He had no intention to figure it out with the doctors. He wasn't going to sit another day in a hospital gown with his bare wrinkly ass hanging out. He had no desire for the tubes and machines they would connect to him. He was sick of cold clinics, giving more stool, urine, and blood samples, sitting in scanners, and taking any more medicines. He enjoyed talking to certain nurses, especially the Spanish-speaking ones, but that was not enough.

Pops concluded that refusing care was not suicide. It was simply living and going out with your head up. Long, serious quality of life discussions with his always-preoccupied son had no value. One day, his ride would end and he hoped his son would finally get going to his own destination, wherever that may be.

The accident ending Samuel's career in the Army, the years spent in the gym rebuilding his core to support his busted back, the years building a new career selling homes in time for the greatest migration to Florida, the years becoming a dedicated husband to Traci with an *i*, the divorce to Traci with an *i*, and the loss of his mother was quite a journey. It had lots of movement to no destination.

Samuel was closer to Gloria. Pops couldn't blame him. She was special. Pops had trouble breathing just thinking about her, but more so given whatever was ailing him. He had unshakable faith she was waiting on the other side, sometimes calling him.

Last year, Pops said the right thing to get Samuel to buy a boat. He said, "Boating may not be your thing." A few weeks later, Samuel called Pops to tell him he "pulled the trigger on an 18-foot center console fishing boat."

"You'll remember the day, son," Pops said over the phone.

Samuel wanted to learn the intracoastal waterway and every little park's shore. He wanted to take in the sinfully huge waterfront mansions. Twelve of them were sold by his real estate team. From Fort Lauderdale to Pompano, Lighthouse to Hillsboro, Boca Raton to West Palm Beach, sat miles of waterfront castles. Sprinkled amongst them, stood the "holdouts." These were the original homes from the 1960 to 1980 eras. They were single story, lower elevation homes from a simpler time. Their owners were from the older generations, waiting on their own rides to end.

Samuel would learn each unique inlet; Port Everglades, the Hillsboro Inlet, and the Boca Inlet. Some were wide. Some were fast. All had the big black rocks on each side.

He heard the swift pass in Boynton Beach was a challenge. It was more a throughway between the intracoastal and the Atlantic Ocean than a traditional inlet. The narrow 130-foot-wide cut had a turn with a limited view that required "committing to your decision." Once in the path, there was no going back. Hopefully no one was coming from the opposite way, that same moment.

"Where we at? Anything?"

"No." Samuel continued to stare at the console. He turned the key again and again. "It's like the gas isn't hitting it. It's cranking."

Samuel exhaled to himself, "The two best days owning a boat are the day you buy it…"

"And the day you sell it," Pops said standing behind him. "That's bullshit, son."

Samuel folded his arms.

"Is the throttle in neutral?" Pops asked.

"Yeah." Samuel looked down at it again, relieved it was. If it were not, it would not start. That was just one of the rules.

The boat rocked further sideways, pressing into the sandbar. It was from the wake of a passing 40-foot speedboat, before making the turn into the mouth of the Hillsboro Inlet, around the large pilings of black rock. Pops waved as they passed.

Samuel extended his middle finger at the captain. They were in a bad position and still, that boat didn't offer to help and made it worse with their wake.

"Nice boat," Pops said squinting. "I like the lines on that V-hull. Must be pushing 400 horses."

"Well, get a ride with him and leave me here to wreck."

Pops laughed. "Let's go, son."

"Would if we could."

Pops scanned over the center console, up and down, left to right. Samuel waited for him to find something to blame him for. He prayed the boat was busted. Samuel would have been happier to die stranded in the ocean than watch Pops conclude his son didn't know what the hell he was doing as a captain. Samuel smiled imagining the hurricane shooting a lightning strike to his fuel tank. The explosion would lift his 230-pound carcass and unnamed boat into a glorious green and red fireball for all to see. The mushroom cloud would rise above the 137-foot Hillsboro Inlet Lighthouse.

Pops tapped the throttle and saw the glow of the electronics across the console. He never touched the ignition.

Samuel watched his eyes drift down to where the red curly safety lanyard dangled the unconnected kill switch. Pops smiled and headed back to his seat up front.

Samuel slowly approached the console shaking his head. He connected the kill switch, closing the circuit that allows the connection to generate the sparks that ignite the fuel in the engine. The outboard motor immediately woke from its stubborn churning as Samuel turned the key.

Samuel left the motor running in neutral and quickly jumped in the water. He used every bit of his expensively tattooed gym muscle to push from the sandbar and free the unnamed boat. It was a valiant five-minute effort, as Pops directed from above on the boat. Samuel wasn't listening and continued to push the boat into the waves away from the sandbar. He then climbed aboard from the ladder on the stern, exhausted, defeated, but not done.

Before Samuel could push the throttle, Pops shouted in the wind, "Let's go, son."

"Don't jinx me, Pop!"

"Have a little faith, son. Let's go."

Samuel pushed the throttle. The boat rose from the plane, lifting from the water's surface.

The engine kill switch. Son of a bitch, Samuel said to himself. Like it was designed to do. If the captain were to fall over, attached to the lanyard, the u-shaped plastic kill switch would pull off. It would then disable the engine. This would keep you from watching your boat leave in an endless straight line. It would also keep it from coming around in a circle to run you over.

Samuel was angry seeing they could have been home an hour sooner. He had to focus on the weather at hand and the time left to get in. He threw the throttle down to the boat's max speed of 28 knots. Samuel was certain that was around 32 miles per hour.

Pops held his Army hat as the breeze swept by him from the bow. As a Merchant Marine, he enjoyed wearing Army hats, proud Samuel followed his own path, a different rollercoaster.

The boat made its graceful curve to the right, then left, following the rocky sides into the inlet. Samuel slowed as the boat began to overtake a wave in front of them, rolling into the inlet. He had to wait for his boat to make its way over the wave, balancing its bow and stern just right. Frustrated he had to deal with the wave, he eventually hit the throttle. He landed in front of the wave, ensuring the bow remained above the water.

"Nicely done," Pops said.

They passed Pompano Beach, its shoreline to their left, the port side. Samuel and his friends used to jump in from the docks there and illegally snorkel in the inlet to spear fish and look for lobsters in the rocks. Across the way, was Hillsboro Beach to the starboard side. Long ago, Samuel and his friend misread the changing tide when they tried to cross the inlet. Luckily, a crew from the Coast Guard station nearby threw them a line and pulled them out. He smiled thinking about the stupid personal history that made this inlet feel like home.

Channel markers passed, green to the left, "red right on return" as Pops always liked to say. Several of the marker posts were permanent nests for the white and dark brown ospreys. A public park along the intracoastal was full of customized 4x4 SUVs. They were there to pull their jet ski trailers in and out of the water. More than fifty jet skis spent their day stirring their usual havoc around the park. They raced the stretches of the intracoastal not decorated with "No Wake" signs.

They enjoyed the day like the rest, before crazy Whitney was going to have her tantrum. Pompano, Hillsboro, Deerfield, and Boca Raton beaches were full of families earlier in the day. Earlier, blue, green, red, and turquoise umbrellas spotted the beige shorelines in front of new sinful mansions and old family condos.

The storm's wall smothered the sun. Samuel slowed the boat to a minimum wake under the bridge, just as the sign said. A row of indifferent pelicans watched, perched on the wood funnel structure. He then made a sharp right turn into the channel, to the marina. Pops smiled and regained a hold onto his hat. The white poles jotted by full speed, right, then left, right, then left, all the way in. Pops pointed to a pod of dolphins thirty feet out, stirring the waters, chasing easy kills around a spoil island.

Samuel idled into the marina.

"Just in time," Pops said. He got up to see if Samuel needed help docking the boat.

"Just stay seated, Pops and let me focus."

"Sure thing," Pops said.

The wind picked up from the West. The outgoing tide, the position of his boat, the boat already at the dock leaving less space to pull in, the incoming clouds, the music from the nearby restaurant on the water, the people from the restaurant watching, the people at the marina watching, the day of the week… everything weighed on Samuel as he steered toward the dock.

He needed everything to be still for just one damn minute. He needed to dock without ramming the other boat already there. He didn't want to miss the dock and get caught in the wind or current, slamming into the seawall. He didn't want to accidentally thrust his boat full speed into the dock. He didn't want to sink his unnamed boat right there. He didn't want to hold up the nonexistent line of boats behind him from getting pulled out before a monster hurricane arrived. Samuel was certain he was a horrible captain and the death of everyone.

"It's gonna be tricky," Pops said sitting comfortably up front.

Samuel tapped the throttle forward, then back while turning the wheel, forward while turning the wheel the other way, back, more back, forward, and back. The boat made its slow and easy turn toward the dock, into the wind, and slid into the spot.

"Nicely done," Pops said.

Samuel tied up to the dock and jumped out.

"That kill switch sure was…"

"I made a damn mistake," Samuel shouted.

"What's wrong, son?"

"Everything! Nothing." Samuel briskly helped Pops step out of the boat and handed him his cane. "We could have been back a while ago. I screwed up. I forgot the kill switch. That's that."

"You're making a bigger deal of it…"

"Am I?" Samuel said. He took a deep breath. "Please just head to the truck and let me get the boat squared away."

Pops shrugged and began his labored walk to the parking lot.

A massive red forklift rested at the water's edge, over the seawall. Its front tires pressed firmly against the metal stop rail. Its extensions hovered over Samuel's boat tied to the dock. An old man sat in the forklift smoking his cigarette. He appeared in no hurry to retrieve the boat and put it on the three-story stack behind him with the others.

"We're all done, if you can put it away."

"Sure," he laughed. The white smoke from his nose sunk into his long chalky beard. His dirty red knit hat matched the forklift. "You're going to want to tie down the bimini. Stow the rods. Center your motor. Get all your shit off that boat and into one of them wagons. Anything that's gonna fly. Toss the cushions in the hatch and turn off all your batteries. And don't forget your key. It's going straight to the rack. It will get washed in the hurricane."

Samuel jumped onto the boat, doing all the man instructed. He paused to see Pops was still a long way from the truck.

The man turned off the forklift. The palms rustled in the breeze. "You got time to make things right," he said. He put his bare feet on the console and looked out at the water, taking a deep drag. Samuel continued doing as told, prepping his boat for its best chance against the predicted 120 mph gusts.

Samuel threw everything in the plastic black wagon and gave a thumbs up. The old man focused on inhaling his cigarette, making it disappear like magic. Samuel stood, waiting for him to exhale, die, or say something in a cloud. After the smoke finished staining his lungs, taking the full tour of his old, plump body, he sat back up. Samuel never saw smoke come out.

He leaned toward Samuel, pointing at him with the butt to his cigarette, waiting for Samuel to come to him. Samuel let out a noticeable sigh, dropped the wagon's handle and approached the forklift.

"What?"

He made Samuel wait as he pulled another cigarette out from behind his ear, underneath his long, white, straggly hair. Samuel looked at him like a magical cigarette PEZ dispenser.

"Got a cigar back there?" Samuel joked.

"No."

He lit the cigarette with the cherry of the outgoing cigarette. He took another deep drag, making Samuel wait. In the corner of his eye, he saw three more late boats idle into the queue. Samuel pointed them out. The forklift operator didn't look.

"Smoking's bad for you," Samuel said.

His eyebrows lifted above his sunglasses. "The hell you say." He twisted off the lit cherry. It dropped to the steel of the forklift where he squished with his flip flop. Samuel stared at his nasty yellow toenails pointing for the heavens. His feet showed deep hardened wrinkles, matching the ones on his cheeks and purple nose. "You still have time to make thigs right," he said to Samuel.

Samuel looked back down at the boat, hands on his hips. "It's good to go. Take it," Samuel exhaled.

"Not the boat." The old man nodded, looking back at Pops slowly making his way to the truck.

"What? You're a fucking counselor?"

He chuckled at Samuel, staring. "You're rattled, kid."

"Bad fucking day, man," Samuel said. "That's all."

"What?"

"Really? Ok, the storm, the boat, Pops, just about everything today," Samuel said. "Besides, what business is it of yours?"

The man leaned back in his worn leather seat, making a noticeable fart sound. "I've pissed more salt water than you've sailed, son."

"Awesome," Samuel said wiping the sweat from his forehead. "You should see somebody about that."

"Well, if you listen, I'll tell you the secret."

"THE secret?" Samuel said. "Well, I gotta hear this. What's the secret, Forklift Man?"

He paused, waiting until Samuel appeared willing to listen.

"You're not a captain until you run out of gas and run aground."

"Well, thank god because I ran aground today," Samuel said.

"Excellent. You're still not shit," the old man laughed. "But you *are* halfway there."

Samuel watched his boat rock in the wake of a passing boat. The storm was still making its trek west toward the mainland.

"It's great what you got," the old man said staring at Samuel.

"What's that?"

He turned in his seat. Pops was still only fifty feet away, slowly making his way. One foot in front of the other, he tried to walk upright and distinguished, cane in hand, to the marina parking lot. A gust of stale fishy air made its way across the water. He closed his eyes and inhaled the breeze with a smile.

"I'd give anything in the world to fight my old man one more day," he said to Samuel.

Samuel watched a tear escape the old man's sunglasses, retreating into his nasty yellow and white beard. Thunder cracked all around them, startling only Samuel.

The operator fired up the loud forklift. Samuel jumped back and ran down the steps to the dock to guide the boat into the lowered forklift arms. The forklift lifted the boat and pulled it over the pavement. Samuel quickly remembered to unscrew the drainage plug. He stood and watched the water flow out.

"You're going to be fine, son," the man shouted over the forklift's rumble.

Samuel backed away and watched the old man reverse with his boat. The forklift turned and ran full speed to the racks like he was being timed. He placed Samuel's boat perfectly in the second row before quickly backing out and racing back.

Samuel started pulling his wagon, watching the forklift. The operator slowed it down as he passed by.

"Take care of Pops," he shouted, staring forward. The man wiped his cheek before speeding off to the dock to retrieve the line of idled boats waiting.

Samuel waved. The man did not wave back.

Pops continued toward the truck. Samuel caught up and placed his arm around his shoulder to guide him to the right truck. "They all look the same," Pops said.

"Yes, they do," Samuel said, using his other hand to pull the wagon with their things.

On the drive home, Samuel asked Pops if he ever had any bad days on the water.

"God yes," Pops laughed. "But they were still *good* days."

Samuel never saw the forklift operator again. When he asked, the marina didn't know who Samuel was talking about. The marina's owner said they were short-handed that day and his manager likely borrowed help to prepare before the hurricane.

Today, Samuel rides out the Hillsboro Inlet into the Atlantic Ocean aboard "Faith" alone. The radio is off. He listens for Pops. He imagines him still riding up front, doing what fathers do. He is staying out of the way, having a beer, giving an impatient son a chance to fight every damn thing, to come around to embrace challenges, or to tire out and eventually figure it out.

"I'd give anything in the world to fight my old man one more day," Samuel says as he heads out to sea, farther than yesterday.

(For my father Jim, 1930-2022).

The Great Wall

"Julio, we need you in right away," he said. I wondered what emergency needed me at a supermarket at four in the morning. My shift was not until noon. "I'll brief you when you get here," Mr. Adams said. He used his military tone, like I was one of his former Marines ready to jump in for a secret and dangerous mission. He said it was bad. I said "OK" and hung up. I was unsure if I had anything to do with it or what happened to our town last night.

I rocked back and forth, trying to roll my limp body out of bed. My jeans were damp. I felt the coarse beach sand on my bare feet as I rubbed them together. I tried to remember the name of the girl I gave my favorite flannel shirt to. We made our joined imprint in the sand until the sirens. Like the other teenagers, we scattered in different directions. Some ran to the abandoned barn on the old McDuffie Farm. A few of my friends broke into the closed down Tiki bar. Others were in the pines, behind the Best Western, and in the backs of cars and pickup trucks.

I purchased that shirt two weeks ago at Brandon's Outdoor Outlet and Bait Shop, a shop we all called BOOBS for short. Brandon Myers named it that when he was a young entrepreneur. It caught on and he was forever stuck with the joke.

I had never seen this girl before. She had huge brown eyes, a slender body, and the straightest long black hair I had ever seen in this humidity. When she grabbed my hand after the game, I was done for. She wrote her number on the back of a neon flier for her friend's terrible folk rock and techno fusion band. They called themselves Mud Heathens in Monochrome. I had it in my back pocket. Two of the digits smeared. Only guesses were going to lead me to her and my shirt ever again.

I put on the pink polo with the Smiley's logo on it. It was dirty from yesterday, but it didn't sound like it was going to make a difference. I hoped the smell would overpower last night's lingering stench. I made several attempts to pull the shirt over my head before falling to the floor.

Dad was downstairs, leaning on the countertop, sipping his black coffee. He was half asleep, tired from his night shift only hours ago, pouring concrete to what would be another dorm. He insisted on driving me. He was not going to let me ride my bike in the dark. Dad gazed out the window over the kitchen sink. The glow of flashing red and blue lights painted the cypress trees in the dark wet distance. "People lost them damn minds," he said.

Dad tossed my bike in his truck to ride back. He smiled as I slid into the truck and closed my eyes. "They gonna love you today," he laughed. The smell of smoke and many alcohols seeped out my sixteen-year-old pores. He didn't lecture me. I was being punished enough, called to work only minutes after sneaking in from a long night out.

For most of its history, our town of Reynolds was a three-gas station town. It had two supermarkets and one to two car dealerships depending on the economy. The tractor dealership was larger than any of the car dealerships. My mom worked at the only elementary school, next to the only high school. The mall was always on the edge of closing, remodeling, or expanding.

Reynolds was far from any beach or desirable body of water. This made it affordable for immigrants and an eroding, retreating, blue-collar population. Eventually, it was no longer just poor white farmers, my family, field laborers, and those who didn't want to be found.

Anything in proximity to water was conquered by massive waves of Northerners. They were fleeing their own mess. New Yorkers had no idea declaring New York a sanctuary to welcome immigrants meant welcoming immigrants. They even tried to declare New York was "full." Many immigrated to Florida. Those who loathed Florida and scoffed at it with their noses in the air, were first to move here. They soon enjoyed the low taxes and freedom to move about. Other states were still wordsmithing their draconian policies in case of future lockdowns.

Desired homes along the outer edges of the state, touching the Atlantic or the Gulf, rocketed in price. Only the rich could afford the increased prices, taxes, and insurance. Inflation was another kick to the balls on the middle class. It took its toll on the value of a hard day's pay and whatever social security the retirees had to survive. It didn't take long for the state's center territory to attract more Floridians. It was the only affordable way to own more than a few feet of dirt between them and their neighbors.

Whether retreating east from the Sun Coast and Culture Coast, or west from the Space Coast, Treasure Coast, and Gold Coast, our town awaited. Reynolds and the other little central towns no one cared to know, saw more inbound moving trucks.

Reynolds was always fifteen miles further than anyone would want to live. There was grass, dirt, trailers, farms, some agriculture, and swamp. Single lane paved roads were shaded beneath live oaks dripping in Spanish moss. Dirt road offshoots lined with irrigation ditches. Muddy tributaries flowed from distant freshwater springs. Most of the land not used for farming was a deep green, full of pine. Farmland produced strawberries, okra, and watermelon. A family farm, owned by one of the original families that settled here, grew colorful orchids. They also produced shrubs and palms that made their way across the state to landscape the more expensive residential areas.

Most were religious on Sunday. Five dollars in the weekly offering basket at Saint Anthony's Catholic Church was from the rich folk. The majority gave thanks to God in singles. Father Alejandro welcomed all after mass for a free pancake breakfast. It was often the best meal of the week for many, to include my family. Dad worked hard and reminded me my afterschool job at Smiley's was a privilege.

One day, a new settler discovered Reynolds. After making his fortune with the protected offspring of a few politicians, he wanted to preserve his legacy. His ego was as huge as his wallet and the land was cheap. He offered the commercial growers and family farms far more money than the land could ever produce. Generations of farming, of struggling and surviving off God's land, swiftly came to a close. Someone else would tend America's fields somewhere else.

Reynolds shook as bulldozers, cranes, and cement trucks entered the town. Somewhere behind the dust, a new university would emerge. Select pines and small lakes stayed intact. They were to be part of the campus scenery. Modern buildings were set to sprout between the natural features. Cement and rebar settled over the fertile farmland. Plant City would remain Florida's strawberry capital. No one would miss the few that tried to come from Reynolds. The family that grew the orchids, pioneers of Reynolds, retired to the white sandy shores of Naples.

Florida offered over 150 four-year universities and colleges. Thomas Haney Younger III felt another one bearing his name was badly needed to educate America. Younger University's birth was quickly cemented in with a brick academic building, a matching dorm, and a deluxe state-of-the-art gym. Priorities.

The next phase included a gourmet coffee shop, a swimming pool addition to the gym, and a 31,000-capacity football stadium for the Fighting Sharks. Several universities had sharks for mascots, but none had "Fighting Sharks," which I thought was redundant. It was also odd considering the school was the farthest location in Florida from an actual shark.

Before the first season even began, a freshman visiting New Smyrna Beach was bit by a small bull shark. She got away with only a small chunk of her left lower buttocks missing and a few stiches. Less than a day later, her fellow students protested, insisting sharks were offensive, even if smiling and cartoonish on the helmet.

The school immediately caved and changed its mascot to the Fighting Lionfish. It was to bring awareness to the non-native fish overpopulating Florida's reefs. It was an invasive species with no natural predators, wreaking havoc on the balance of reef life. Again, the mascot's habitat was still nowhere near the school. But the mascot change lasted only three months when someone pointed out the obvious. They chose a pest even the tree huggers said needed to be exterminated. Glorifying it on a red, white, and black football helmet was offensive.

They eventually settled on the Alligator Snapping Turtles, even though most of them were in the Big Bend area of Florida, well north of us.

They should have picked a mascot from all the local wildlife. There was a wide variety fleeing daily from their natural Old Florida habitat to make way for Younger University's bulldozers. Sandhill cranes, foxes, black bears, bobcats, and two Florida panthers scattered. Some with their offspring in mouth. If there was any truth, they would have named themselves after the ever-present mosquito population. It had zero intention to relocate.

The university eventually added more academic buildings. But first, the football team needed its world-renowned weight room. It needed a practice field and of course, the 31,000 new hunter green and tan plastic stadium seats. They replaced the dark red seats, from when they were Fighting Lionfish. Those seats replaced the midnight blue seats when they were Fighting Sharks.

The stadium could host more butts than the number of people in the ten nearest towns combined. Whether named after sharks, fish, or turtles, the football team sucked. Losing quickly became a time-honored tradition for the Younger University Alligator Snapping Turtles.

"Idiots," my dad said as we drove by a flipped pickup truck lying next to a downed powerline pole. The police waved us by with their flashlights. I sat in the passenger side with my head against the window. The power company trucks surrounded the scene with their flashing orange lights. Men in neon yellow road guard vests were assessing the damage.

"Hope to God you weren't part of that," Dad said.

"No, Dad."

"Momma's gonna ground your butt for some time. Hope it was worth it," he said. We stared at the kids being questioned by the police outside **BOOBS**. They were sitting against the wall with the mural of a smiling bass, their hands cuffed behind them.

"Friends of yours?"

"No," I said. "Stupid college kids."

"If you go, I'm not sending you to do stupid shit," he said.

"I know, Dad."

We passed a burning dumpster along the highway. Its flames were several feet high and continued unabated. Three volunteer firefighters watched it, saving their water. In the distance, police lights sparkled the bridge. A few campers remained in the stadium parking lot, with people still partying from last night's game.

Dad pulled into the supermarket parking lot. He shook my shoulder until my eyes opened.

"You sober?"

I sat expressionless. What happened last night was not my fault, but for some reason I still felt guilty. At the same time, I kept thinking about her. Worth it. It made me crack a smile.

"Good enough," he said. We saw Mr. Randolph's amorphous silhouette in front of the pale white emergency light. The glass to the entrance door was smashed and broken. Mr. Randolph stood with a few of the other bagboys and stockboys.

"Aye," my father said shaking his head. "When the police finish questioning everyone, you'll have to tell me what the hell happened."

"I don't know, Dad."

"Stick to that for now," he laughed. He leaned over me to push open my door. "Out you go, young man."

My dad waved at Mr. Randolph. I flung my bike out of the back of the truck and used it to help me walk up to the store. Dad drove off and Mr. Adams' flat top emerged from the shadows.

"Full circle, son," Mr. Randolph said to me.

The other boys laughed. Mr. Randolph told Mr. Adams to proceed inside.

"You heading to the hospital?" Mr. Adams asked.

"No. I'll be okay," Mr. Randolph said.

"We got it from here, sir," Mr. Adams said.

Mr. Randolph placed his hand on my shoulder. He knew I wasn't sober, had no sleep, and reeked of alcohol. He gently smiled. "It's one of them moments, son," he said. "You'll be fine. Town too."

"What happened?" I asked staring at the broken glass doors behind him. He shrugged his shoulders and limped to his car. He held his hand on his hip and made a grunt with each step.

Amari and Kendal laughed, pointing at me.

"Don't put this on me," I shouted at them.

I could hear the crackle of the burning dumpster in the distance. Mr. Adams told us to get ready.

He grabbed the 4x8 sheet of plywood in front of the smashed front door. He moved it to the side for us to step in. I carried my bike over the broken glass. Each step made a special crinkle, snap, and pop. I leaned my bike against the American flag soda display in the front. Mr. Adams placed the plywood sheet back against the doorway. The frame was still locked. The glass was shattered, some hanging in the frame, the rest across the floor like pebbles.

We walked single file behind Mr. Adams into the unlit store. The emergency flood light pushed its white haze from the rear wall. It looked like a pale moon fighting the darkness. My friends Aidan and Manny walked in with me, like brothers do.

"Police didn't get you?" I asked. They grinned and nodded no.

Mr. Adams put his closed fist in the air, like a squad leader in the jungle. He was signaling his men to hold by the door leading to the back of the store. We waited in the dark, listening to the hum of the flood lights.

Mr. Adams tossed a box of black garbage bags at our feet. He said they were for our shoes and pants, though probably not worth the effort. Aidan worried about his new red basketball shoes. He spent several minutes taping the bags around his legs.

"You can try but they're getting soaked," Mr. Adams laughed. Aidan continued wrapping the duct tape around his ankles. "Bullshit they are."

I immediately sobered up.

I skipped covering my shoes and threw my garbage bags to the ground. I ran to Mr. Adams. "Tell me it happened."

I couldn't contain my excitement. "It did, didn't?"

He rolled his eyes. "Let's go."

Mr. Adams pushed open the door.

"IT HAPPENED!"

I shouted over and over again with joy into the vast open darkness of the back of the store. My excitement echoed between the tall pallets of boxes, over the dark river.

"Oh my God, it happened!"

"Happy?" Mr. Adams asked as the boys laughed.

"Of course not," I said. "But, no shit, it happened!"

"Get it out of your system, Julio." Mr. Adams handed me a flashlight.

He looked over his shoulder to the team. "Let's move out!"

I pushed Aidan and Manny aside to enter first, jumping down the sloped ramp into the black river. A single white floodlight high up reflected on the water. I started to dance in the ankle-deep waters. I laughed as Mr. Adams' flashlight showed how long the river went. "Some parts get much deeper, so be…"

"Awesome!"

"Okay," Mr. Adams said. "Try to be careful."

The waters went all the way down the corridor. It went past the walk-in refrigerator for the eggs, around the beer cage, and around the corner. The river continued down the corridor to the back of the Produce Department and behind the Meat Department. The departments were not flooded because of the slope and lower elevation of the back.

Aidan and Manny looked puzzled, watching me.

I waded into the waters, splashing like a kid in a water park. "It was the…"

"Yes," Mr. Adams said. He jumped in and signaled for the others to follow. "It's a little cold."

Before expressing any more joy, I felt required to ask the obligatory question. "No one died, right?"

No, Mr. Adams said. "Drains clogged with trash and boxes."

I found myself awake, alive, invigorated, revitalized, energized, excited, eager, impatient, fervent, thrilled, fixated, focused, jumpy, still nowhere near sober, but insanely anxious to get to the rear door, past the compactor, where the lift dropped to the truck loading dock. A massive rush of adrenaline overcame me.

Mr. Adams told us to keep pressing forward. We had to get to Mr. Gerard. I asked what our head manager was doing there in the middle of the night. He said when the wannabe riot started, some kids broke into the store. It triggered the alarm while Mr. Randolph and Mr. Gerard were doing the monthly inventory.

"When was this?"

"After midnight" he said.

"Who works that hour?"

"Managers taking their jobs seriously. Julio, there's always more to do."

Mr. Adams pushed ahead to lead the wading line. "Some moron crashed his truck into a pole outside," Mr. Adams said. "Pole came down and with it, the power lines. I guess that's when the alarms, lights, everything in town finally went out."

I halted in my tracks. I just wanted to hear it finally said.

"So, when the alarm went," I said, "someone…"

"Mr. Randolph," he said, "accidentally bumped into the wall." He looked to the team. "Into Julio's Great Wall of Soda."

My inner mafia boss voice was shouting, "Yes! There you go. That wall came down like a motherfucker. Said it would too. But what did you say? Huh? You said… it wouldn't. I was full of it. Hmm. Keep wading in all that soda. Feel it deep in your socks, in your pants. Maybe listen to me, next time, fuckers."

As my violent inner voice finished its tirade, I simply said, "Hmm, that's too bad."

In Mr. Gerard's infinite wisdom, he acquired all the soda products he needed for the rest of the year at a reduced price per unit. The problem was he wasn't sure where to put it. Truck after truck, soda came in and we did what we could.

We made a massive American flag with the different brand colors of twelve packs. The white packs of diet soda made stars and stripes with the red and blue brands. It was two weeks after the Fourth of July, but patriotism is appreciated year-round in these parts. When more white twelve packs of diet soda arrived, we added a Florida state flag to the front of aisle seven.

We then tried to replicate the Castillo de San Marcos of Saint Augustine. We used an intricate set up of plastic crates and 2-liter bottles. When we saw we still had half a truck remaining, we extended its walls where we could. The best space was between the Bakery and Meat Department. It was five feet high and grew until Mr. Gerard told us to stop. The bakery crew called it the "Trump Wall" and threatened to call HR.

In the seasonal promotion area, near aisle twelve, we made a large sandbox. We used crates lined with garbage bags. We filled the square full of sand and surrounded the exterior with a two-foot-high wall of twelve packs. We made a back wall of shelves with assorted two liters. The blue bottles were on the bottom to look like the ocean. The red bottles made a straight-line sunset horizon. The orange drinks made the sun. The white diet bottles made clouds. It was a genius work of art.

We placed two Adirondack chairs ($89.99) in the sand, an umbrella ($17.99), assorted coolers ($10.99 to $39.99) and moved on. Mr. Gerard had us surround the display with the overstock of sunscreen ($10.99 to $18.95) he also purchased. We took pride in our creativity. More importantly, we used up an ass-load of soda.

After all our clever constructions, three more trucks of soda were at the loading dock. Mr. Gerard called an emergency meeting with his assistant managers. When the meeting room door opened, Mr. Randolph came out first. Like a good field commander, he shouted to his mini army of wayward stockboys and bagboys waiting in the back. "STACK 'EM!"

Several of the minions behind me cheered, but I doubted they knew what it meant. In the corner of my eye, I saw Mr. Gerard, sitting in his cracked leather chair, his forehead resting in his hands, staring into the unpolished floor. He saw me as he picked up his head. He sprung up with a half-hearted smile. "Let's do this! And be careful!"

The bottles stayed in their crates. The crates were stacked as high as necessary, all along the entire length of the two corridor walls. We started at five feet. After the next truck, it was ten. It settled at fifteen feet high by two feet wide on each side, hidden in back from the public.

After a hundred or so crates, I admired the relentless vision to the project. Joking to the others, I named it the "Great Wall of Soda" much to the displeasure of management. The nickname caught on. Rumors made it to the other stores. The Great Wall of Soda became a legend. You only got the privilege to confirm its existence if you worked for the store. It made you not want to buy soda to see how long it could survive.

Management tried to dispel rumors of its existence. They hoped word never reached corporate. Even if every bottle sold before their expiration, or even in our lifetime, it didn't matter. The Great Wall of Soda was forever etched into the annals of Smiley Supermarket history. I imagined a bronze statue in front of our store of Mr. Gerard, like our own Florida Sun Tzu, would one day immortalize this historical moment.

Entrenched in the moment, I continued to dance in the waters. Soda was up to my crotch. "This is so awesome," I whispered.

"Mr. Randolph's lucky he didn't get killed," said Mr. Adams.

"Well, yeah," I said to cover my joy. I had to appear a responsible, concerned employee not imagining a fat man running for his life from a collapsing wall of soda, its fizzy contents rupturing as bottles shot into the air like rockets and missiles, exploding against the once-white walls, splattering the rest of the store's inventory, against the beer cage, and pounding into the solid metal walls of the dairy cooler. Several kegs were set off. The pyramid of 5-gallon waters was no more. Cardboard box towers of smaller cardboard boxes of product soaked and collapsed. It had to have been the most glorious domino effect, crate after crate, stack after stack, several minutes long, a barrage of internal, earth-shaking destruction for Smiley Store number 22.

"Gerard and Randolph were trapped," Mr. Adams said. He continued his story, wading the river. "Some trespassers got inside and made themselves at home. Don't know if they stole anything. At this point, it doesn't matter." Mr. Adams said Mr. Randolph eventually broke free and made it to the front office to see the safe was fine and call us for help. 911 was busy. When the power briefly came back, the alarm and lights scared off the trespassers. Mr. Randolph later turned the power back off wanting to further assess the damage and get Mr. Gerard out.

"I know he's still out there," Mr. Adams said softly looking out into the darkness. "He's out there."

Manny and Aidan were quiet, their mops in hand like rifles.

An older stock boy in the rear startled us, making chimpanzee noises. We joined in, laughing until Adams told everyone to "shut it."

"Get your game faces on, men," Mr. Adams said. The stale syrup smell grew stronger. My legs became heavier with each step as I went in deeper. Mr. Adams led the way, but I kept passing him. He repeatedly told me to slow up, staring out like a platoon leader waiting to get ambushed. "Yeah, he's out there alright."

"Well, yeah. I'm sure he is," I said, moving on.

Fifty-two years of ammonium cleaning residue stirred in with the massive flow of high fructose corn syrup, phosphoric acid, potassium sulfate, disodium phosphate, sodium citrate, and sucrose as the carbon dioxide bubbled. Two full racks of five-gallon water bottles emptied into the mix, a second order effect of the collapse. Emptied bottles floated like a plastic armada, drifting between the islands of broken crates and shelves. They flowed in a slow tidal shift to the rear loading dock.

I watched a bouncing box of animal crackers, imagining it like a miniature Noah's ark. I couldn't contain myself. I continued to shout how awesome it was. Each splash pushed a little wave further into the store itself for the rest of the morning shift to clean. Screw them. This was a momentous occasion.

"He should be around the corner," Mr. Adams warned.

Mr. Adams shouted "hello" around the corner.

"I'm here, boys!" shouted Mr. Gerard. Three flashes appeared on the ceiling above from his flashlight. He was behind a large wall of boxes, collapsed shelves, and soda crates. Mixed in the carnage were boxes of cookies, condiments, chips, salsa, tampons, and cereal. Aidan smiled aiming his flashlight at the boxes of tampons bobbing in the soda. "Should help soak it up, I guess."

"We'll get some daylight first so we can find a path to get you out," Mr. Adams shouted over the collapsed piling. "I'm underneath a lot of stuff, fellas, but I'm good," Mr. Randolph tried to laugh.

"Found it," Manny shouted, standing by the garage door to the truck loading station. Aidan and I tried to clear the debris against the door in the dark.

"Ok, boys, pull the chains and let's get it up."

We lifted the door. Aidan grabbed its bottom from under the waters. There was a pop and a suction sound as the seal broke and the door lifted. The river flowed like the Big Shoal rapids.

Mr. Adams told us to hang on to something as the black waters rushed by our legs. Debris drifted by. Manny punched open another back door. We celebrated as the early morning's bright orange light drifted in and more of the waters exited.

Everyone grabbed their wide brooms and mops to help the flow out the door. Objects continued to block and gather. "Don't let up, boys. If it's in the way, toss it outside and keep it moving!" Mr. Adams shouted like he's returning fire to an unrelenting enemy. Amari, Kendal, and Aidan tossed the boxes, five-gallon water bottles, and even three exploded kegs out the doors. We worked diligently to find a path and safely extract Mr. Gerard.

Mr. Gerard was on the ground, soaked in everything, under a cavern of shelves and empty milk and soda crates. His perfect tie and long sleeve shirt showed a festive pattern of orange, black, brown, red, and yellow liquids. He was tired, hurt, but smiling. Upon seeing us, he rested his head against the metal wall. "My rescuers," he giggled. "My butt's numb, so I'm not sure I can get up."

We carefully cleared the debris around him and helped him get up, supporting him until he found strength in his legs. Mr. Adams asked him how he's doing.

"Very wet, moderately bruised," he said. Mr. Gerard turned to us as he gained footing on the hill of debris. "But never defeated, boys!" We cheered and continued to clear a path for him to get through.

I overheard him whisper, "it is what it is," to Mr. Adams.

Something that day changed him. An always stern man, often frustrated at his house of wayward boys, was replaced by an even better man. It was possible I simply realized that day he was *always* a good man. I felt horrible hearing him ask so many times if Mr. Randolph was okay. Mr. Adams assured him each time he was.

The morning light made its way to the back, through the fire doors and the opened loading dock. Mr. Gerard and Mr. Adams approached while I tossed whatever I could into the compactor. Everyone around me stopped to watch.

"I'm giving you this one time, son," Mr. Gerard said aloud for all to hear. He smiled at me, his hand on my shoulder. "Go on now. Say it."

"Say what, sir?"

"Repeat after me," Mr. Gerard said, "I… told… you… so."

"I told you, sir."

"Feel good?" he laughed.

"No, sir," I said.

Mr. Gerard patted me on the back. "But you called it, son. I'm just glad none of you were hurt by my mistake." He took a deep breath and looked out at everyone.

Mr. Gerard then pulled me beyond the ears trying to listen over the gurgling drains. "As for this other mess," he said quietly, "you don't let anyone put that on you." Mr. Gerard looked at me again, nodding his head. "You got that, son? That nonsense outside… whatever this town does, that's on them."

"Yes, sir."

"We're all adults, right?"

I thought about what he said, what he could have said, and what he didn't say. I thought about the money he lost, the embarrassing mistake he made, and his owning up to it.

"We are," I said.

He looked at his watch and handed me his sacred keychain of store keys. "It's almost time." Mr. Gerard instructed me to make my way to the front, open both front doors, and let the cashiers in. I was to get registers one and five up and tell the four stockboys to the 7am shift to clean. They were to start around the doors to the Bakery, then Produce, and then the Meat Department.

At 7AM sharp, he wanted me to greet the customers and welcome them in… to excuse our mess. He was going to flip the circuit breakers once he felt it was safe and everything checked out. As I made my way to the front, I grew ever so thankful. I never imagined my joke would make this town act the way it did.

It was a joke I made a little more than a year ago. I was a high school freshman. First, I was a kid who had a wise-ass comment. Soon, I was a visionary. Later, a villain. I then tried to formally renounce my comment but, it was too late. My regrettable comment had spread like a wildfire. It became a town curse.

Some said it was offensive while Father Alejandro defended me during a Sunday sermon. He said there was nothing wrong with self-discipline, moral restraint, and abstinence.

All I said was no girl should date a Younger University football player until they won a game. I never directly used the word "sex." I never publicly called for a unified, town-wide sex-strike.

I never suggested a courageous show of solidarity, foregoing parties and urges until this pathetic, sorry-ass team won a damn game. I had no idea they would have a two-season losing streak.

Against my wishes, the idea had a life of its own. It won overwhelming support by the non-football playing frat boys in the university, of course. They originally thought "more for them."

As for the ladies, one can assume they were tired of dating losers. The ban was only on the players. But the news caught wind. Citizens of Reynolds soon claimed they, themselves, were abstaining from sex in solidarity. I never asked for that.

Even Mayor Roberto Ronaldo, a popular eligible bachelor, claimed he was playing along. It had spread like a dare. It morphed into a cute show of support before twisting into a cruel moral code. It eventually finished just short of law.

I was certain everyone was lying. There was no way everyone became a monk because I said so. I can't even get my blue heeler, Lobo, to stop licking himself. But whether true or not, I became everyone's poster child for their lack of sex. Thanks to me, Reynolds became the most sexually frustrated town in Florida, if not the United States, and possibly the world.

The opposing team chosen for the homecoming game was the next worse team in Florida. They hailed from an even newer university still building its stadium. More than half of its first string was out with injuries. They were down to their third string quarterback, who was also their shitty kicker. The local country radio DJ, Rob "The Rooster" said live on air, "If there's a game that's gonna get us all laid, this is it, folks. I'll be under the bleachers. Cheers." He then proceeded to drink live on air the rest of the day, playing old school R&B music to get everyone in the mood. Again, it was a country station.

No one called the station to complain. Instead, people got their tickets. It was the highest attendance in the team's miserable history. A redneck Mardi-Gras atmosphere began to build.

Aidan, Manny, and I started the pre-game activities in the parking lot. We did shots with the rest of our crowd from high school and work. The older kids had kegs in the back of their pickups. Most of the town was hammered before kickoff. The festivities continued in the stadium, whether carried-in or purchased at a stand. The game happening in the background was only a detail.

I missed most of the game. I heard the opposing team's third string quarterback threw an interception. This led to our kicker finishing with a 20-yard field goal. That's right. The kicker, of all people, was the hero. His night was sure to be unlike no other. The crowd roared and we sprung up to see the final score.

Younger University Alligator Snapping Turtles: 3. Springhill Polytechnic Fighting Sandhill Cranes: 0.

A cannon shot out and scared the locals. To date, no one realized we had a victory cannon.

It was official. Our 0 and 12 team WON. As I continued my way to the front of the store, I thought about her. She drank with me in the parking lot and then in the stands during the game. We drank too much and spent much of the game sitting together, her head on my shoulder. I closed my eyes to keep from spinning off my seat. I was happy.

The cannon startled me. I held my arm around her as the crowd sprinted by. They spilled down the rows, over the green and tan seats, over the rails, and onto the field. Frat boys were humping the goalposts on both ends of the field. They eventually fell onto the crowd, injuring a few below. Faculty, staff, security, parents, teachers, and teenagers alike turned their town upside down. No one was sober. Everyone had something on their mind. Some couldn't, and didn't, wait to get home.

Sheriff Bud Bradley told his deputies to "safely manage the damn chaos and make sure no one dies."

After the crowd rushed by us, we continued to sit and hold each other. My head was spinning from too much alcohol. She rose from the bleachers, grabbed my hand, and pulled me up. She whispered in my ear that she wanted to celebrate with me. She could have asked me anything and I would have said yes.

Holding hands, we squeezed through the bouncing crowd. We found our way around the kids dancing in the streets, around the burning car, an exploding fire hydrant, and a flaming dumpster. We navigated through the street parties, eventually finding refuge inside, away from the madness.

I faintly remember a beach. I placed my flannel shirt on the sand. We laid there laughing, holding each other while screams, cheers, fireworks, explosions, and banging noises echoed in the distance. We gazed at the pale light pushing against the darkness.

The chaos then caught up. We heard alarms again and fled. She scribbled her number and handed it to me with a long kiss. I watched her run down her street. I stumbled down mine a few blocks away. It was coming back to me, though most of my memory focused on her. Would I ever see her again?

I exited the back of the store, walked around, and reentered the front door to the, otherwise, dry store. I could see only some of the waters made it past the doors at the Produce, Meat, Deli, and Bakery departments. Some of the first shift were already inside, scrambling to clean the mess. They nodded as I walked by. They saw my pants, shoes, socks, and shirt soaked and stained. The power came back on with loud cheers from the back. Mr. Gerard must have felt it was safe again the pull certain breakers.

I proudly walked with his keys, to do the manager thing on his behalf. I explained what happened to the three up front as they prepared their registers. Ms. Connie Jo distributed the money trays. She was relieved the safe was untouched.

The first crew moved the plywood against the wall to enter. Seeing the broken glass at the entrance, it came back to me, the image of several kids fleeing the store as the alarm went off. I remembered running from an explosion, from a collapsed transformer, a burning car, and cheering students. I remember finding a place to sit in the cool sand after the town went dark and the alarms came to a stop. I remembered red and blue lights speeding by to the chaos by the bridge, near BOOBS.

I walked past the soda beach display and grabbed my flannel shirt lying in the sand. The imprints of two teenagers remained. I tossed it onto my bike and put on my managerial game face.

I approached the broken entrance and swept the glass to the side with my shoe. "Please excuse our mess, folks. Welcome and good morning!" I unlocked the broken glass door lying against the wall to make it official. The handful of waiting customers smiled, said good morning, and walked in like nothing happened.

She was standing at the entrance.

"Can I help you, Miss?" I said in my manager's voice.

She giggled at my wet, colorful appearance.

"I left some cute boy's shirt inside."

Cuda Killer

My design, my time, my hard labor, and my determined heart brought to life the most massive, secret, time-consuming, unapproved, unregulated, undisclosed, unsanctioned, non-unionized, non-profit, non-permitted underwater construction project ever executed by a ten-year old off the East Coast of Florida. It was my Area 51, my Atlantis, my Mona Lisa, my reef.

Each calm day consumed me. The breeze carried the salt air over a still and clear turquoise sea. A dedicated worker, I grabbed my mask and snorkel, ready to begin the day's labor. I ran across A1A from the apartment complex to the beach, diving into the ocean without stopping. I began my review, swimming ten to thirty feet parallel to the shoreline where the water met the coarse brown sand.

The voice of my hero, Jacques Cousteau, narrated my journey. His soft French accent played in my head like smooth jazz. I heard "And ze now I gently glide through pristine aqua, yearning to find ze marine life that awaits. It tis here, man and fish must coexist and ze learn from zeach oder."

My dad joined me many hours, snorkeling alongside me. Mom made me come in to put on some sunblock, guzzle some water, and woof down a hotdog she kept warm in tin foil. I then returned to my hard labor.

I gripped a small net while swimming for protection. Occasionally, I caught a few small fish along the way for my tank at home. Each new catch was another fish to look up in the Fish

Dictionary my dad got me. I learned what size they would grow to and what habitats they preferred. I learned about their enemies and their preferred prey. Each day after school, I ran home to see them and talk to them like friends.

I knew not to tap on the glass and not to overfeed them. I learned to replace the salt that built up on the outside of the glass as the water evaporated. The fish took shelter and congregated around the rock formations I made in the tank. It wasn't long before I found inspiration to build my own reef.

Swimming up and down the shoreline, I carried every rock of substance in vicinity to a single place. The spot aligned with the mast of an old Hobie Cat. It never sailed in my lifetime. There was nothing wrong with it. The old Canadian transplant that owned it was too sick, too tired to use it. I made it my marker, my constant west star. No matter how dizzy or tired I was carrying the rocks, I could pick up my head, see the top of the mast, and know where to go.

It was difficult as a four-foot kid to carry a large rock across an area five to eight feet deep. In time, and without drowning, I learned to bounce up for air while carrying a heavy rock. My head barely above the water, I gasped before dropping back down with the weight in my scratched, cut hands. I tried to run three to five steps before exploding upward with my feet, back up for air. I imagined I was training to be a Navy SEAL.

From the underwater thump of the first rock, I was being watched. I cleared my snorkel and floated still at the top. I tried to quiet my breathing. Nothing appeared and eventually, my nerves calmed. As I hovered over, I inspected the progress below. Additional trips down were made to perfect each rock's placement.

Holding my breath, I had seconds to decide how they stood. Were they better on their side or upright? For some odd-shaped rocks, what did upright look like? No two were alike. I had to calculate whether the rocks were better in a circle or on top of each other. I found myself designing my own Stonehenge with poor French narration in my head.

One day, my uninvited guest arrived.

"Out in ze distance, something lurked, curious to zis constructed thing. It tis but a shadow." I squinted harder into the emptiness in front of me. The sunlight's rays battled the clouds, presenting a puzzle of shades and light around me.

"I saw ze dart, a rapid torpedo jetting through ze shadows. Zis creature vanished, beyond vision, stalking me. Possibly, I was in harm's way." I remained still for minutes. My heart thumped, echoing in my water-lodged ear canals. A warm sensation took hold, like a bubble of fear, pressing in my chest. "I soon learned it was just ze gas from zis hotdog and I relieved the pressure, expelling from behind. Bubbles zepon bubbles."

I took heavy, concentrated flows of air in and out of my snorkel. I had to keep letting small amounts of water into my mask to swirl against the heavy fog and push it back out with the air.

My project was on a tight imaginary schedule. No one else knew or cared. Nonetheless, I told myself I had a deadline.

The first few rocks sat at the sandy bottom alone. A boring week of school, soccer, and television passed. All I could think about was the work awaiting me. I needed to get back to the water to see what happened.

Nothing happened. Rocks rested where I dropped them. It was a monument to my failure. I took measure of the moment, floating over the small, worthless, foolish structure.

Did I need to drop a long line of rocks leading to the rocks, like breadcrumbs? My eyes gazed into the sandy bottom. It stretched out into the fading blue wall beyond the thirty feet of clear water that surrounded me. It was an endless ocean bottom. My mask peeked out of the water, staring East. I saw the dark blue Atlantic reaching the far horizon. How, in all God's vast blue ocean, do I direct traffic to my twenty-foot piece of real estate?

I thought of the treasure hunters who searched endless miles of the ocean's floor. They did it with unwavering determination. It was easier to build than search, I thought. More rocks continued to drop from my hands. They fell like heavy feathers, bombing onto the sand and structure below. Each drop made a thump for all the fish in the Atlantic to hear. Something was happening here.

The next day, I returned with my next rock. As I was about to release it, I noticed three fish below. They were no more than one to three inches in length. They darted inside the pile of rock below. One, I recognized as a jackknife with its black stripes and curved dorsal fin. The other two were less attractive croakers but still welcome to my structure. As I placed rocks through the day, I was careful not to scare my first guests.

My construction project continued the weeks to follow. It grew easier to spot from a distance. My days began stepping out from the Hobie Cat on the shore, my west star. Depending on the tide, I knew I had to travel twenty or forty feet out to see the reef and what new fish made a home of it.

Different species and sizes started to appear. Some were visitors, stopping on the way to somewhere else. Others were regulars, new inhabitants of my creation. The more distinct ones I named. There was Jack the Jack-knifefish. Frenchy, the small

French Angelfish. Bo, the Beau Gregory Damsel. Then there were the croakers, the lane snappers, and a school of Blue Tangs... too many to name. Then came Skip the mudskipper, Robin the Sea Robin, Terry the Yellow Tang, Polly the Parrotfish, and Tommy the Triggerfish. For one day, I had a turtle I named Sebastian. He looked like a Sebastian. But he never stuck around. I missed Sebastian. I wanted him to stay forever. I would have built anything to his liking, but it was not his nature to stay.

I proudly showed my reef to my father and enlisted his help. Eventually, I brought a few neighborhood kids I trusted. Like a proud construction foreman, I explained how difficult it was to place the rocks. I detailed the strategic placement of each rock.

I had rules. Visitors were allowed, but they were not permitted to take any of the fish from the reef. The price of admission was one large rock. Two of the kids, Thorny and Samuel, contributed for a little while. But eventually, they felt it was too much work.

My attempts in underwater architecture came with lessons learned. A circular design maximized space to attract the fish. But the elevation of the structure needed to be tall enough to withstand the sand.

Sand was the enemy. I enjoyed surfing days. But they came with the risk of covering my reef. It would destroy my work and the inhabitants would disperse. Several times, I lost my reef to a storm. It was total devastation. Instead of continuing to build, I had to switch to salvage operations.

I stuck to my west star, the top of the Hobie Cat mast, to find my reef. My hands and flippers brushed their way through the accumulated sand. I poked a stick into the sand until I stumbled upon my treasure. For such recovery missions, the voice of Mel Fisher stood in for Jacques Cousteau. After sixteen years of heartache and persistence, he found the treasure of the Spanish galleon, the Nuestra Senora de Atocha. His persistence inspired me each time I had to excavate my reef. Instead of gold and silver coins, emeralds, and bars of silver, I dug for rocks. I did so with equal dedication.

Over two years, every moveable rock in a half mile radius made its way to my reef, aligned with the Hobie Cat, my west star. As I spent more time working on my reef, I felt I was becoming more popular. The shadows in the distance increased… or so I thought. None were so large to be a shark. But if one did appear, I was prepared.

I watched on TV an old man who swam with only cargo shorts and a mask, no snorkel. Tiger sharks, bull sharks, and even large great whites came at him, mouths open to chomp into his flesh. Each time, he calmly reached out, and tapped them on the nose, turning them away. One time, one came from behind. I was sure it was going to rip him in two. But he turned and slowly glided his hand into the nose like a kung fu master. I practiced as I watched the same episode over and over. If a shark ever appeared, I was ready to do some world-class nose tapping.

But the shadows were smaller and faster. The long shadow made me nervous. It became harder to concentrate on the job at hand. Off en ze distance, I knew… he was eh… watching. It was only a matter of time before we introduced ourselves.

One Saturday morning, I swam to my reef and he was there. The long, slender, silvery spear hovered above my reef, inspecting my work. He turned enough for his glassy black eye to stare at me. His mouth overflowed with pointy teeth. Sometimes he was three feet in length. Other times he seemed longer. I later concluded there were several, but the longest one was taking over my reef. I did not build this for him.

In the big picture, I had school and in time, I was nothing more than a visitor. When I appeared, all the fish should have bowed. I am not sure how a fish would bow, but some gesture, acknowledging my vision and hard work would have been nice. But when he showed, I feared I had lost control of my creation.

Each time I returned, he darted from his dominant position above the reef. From a distance, he watched me add more rocks. I felt like I was building his empire. He was king to my castle. I was now a serf, forced to continue building its walls and towers.

His presence made me nervous. I had to balance between not startling him and getting work done. Between being still and losing my breath. I wondered if I moved too fast to the surface for air, he would attack.

I read barracuda liked shiny objects. So, I never wore jewelry, a shiny watch, and I replaced my shiny metal hand-held net with one that had a wooden handle. I learned the barracuda was one of the fastest fish in the world at an estimated 36 mph. I imagined him spearing through my chest from behind like in an alien movie. Lifeless, I would float up with a gaping eight-inch torpedo hole, my heart missing.

At the age of eleven, I concluded barracudas were bullies and opportunistic assholes. At night, I wondered if I had lured all these fish to their deaths, to live in the shadow of the slender spear. Did I build a glorious killing ground for this asshole barracuda? Was this his territory... a candy aisle with a full variety to choose from to shred, maim, dismember, swallow, devour, scoff, gobble, gulp, and slaughter? I, alone, invited death to this beach, nothing more. It was a hard burden for an eleven-year-old to bear. My creation was beyond my control.

One horrible day, we found ourselves in another epic stare down. I only saw his eyes and teeth, his gills extending in and out. My heart was pounding. Neither of us were willing to budge. I stayed still at the top of the water, breathing hard through my snorkel only feet away. This moment was inevitable.

History is unable to say who threw down first. It seemed a mutual hatred. It was a moment in time where both gunslingers had enough. We could no longer walk around each other, avoiding a shootout. Face to face in the town center, all the fish watched. I was floated at the top. I clenched my fists in front of me, ready.

He shot at me like an arrow, a fired torpedo. I flung my arms under the water, punching outward. I twisted my body and kicked my flippers in front of me. I rolled into a ball. I spun and splashed in all directions. I looked for him, choking on the saltwater flooding my snorkel.

I didn't know it was going to come down to this. We established boundaries… a demilitarized zone of at least fifteen feet. I checked my chest for a gaping hole. I appeared unharmed but was still unsure. After regaining my composure and stance at the top, I cleared my snorkel. He was nowhere in immediate sight. But I knew, beyond the twenty feet of visibility, that big asshole full of teeth was regrouping.

Sprinting to shore, I grew angrier with each determined stroke. Thirty feet to shore flashed by me in rage. I crawled from the water, my hands and knees pounding the sand. I feared he was still chasing me. I tried to get every inch of my body completely out of the water.

My dad looked on from his beach chair. He thought I was clowning around, being a kid. I sat in the sand, checking myself, out of breath, saltwater dripping from my eyes. There was no bite or injury. Regardless, it was a day of infamy. Unprovoked, he committed an act of war. He crossed the line. He had to go.

History has shown the progress of society is often halted to enact war. This was going to be a very intricate plan that few eleven-year-olds could devise. After much deliberation and many drafts on construction paper, I finalized my plan. First, I was going to catch a bait fish. Second, I was going to use that fish on a fishing rod as bait. Third, I was going to catch the barracuda. Fourth, I was going to kill it. Again, a very complex, unheard-of, ingenious plan.

To kill it, I constructed a spear using a long stick and the end of a dart from the dartboard in the garage. This was state of the art shit. I knew to fish for him in the late afternoon when barracudas scrounged the shoreline… and before Dad got home. No one would be on the beach. It would only be boy versus fish.

I caught several pilchers from shore with the most focused throw yet of my dad's cast net. I selected the most alluring one. It was shiny, silver, and larger than the others. I placed the hook underneath his mouth, the point protruding out. At the strike of five in the afternoon, the fishing line went out.

The bait was flung into its sacrificial run over my reef. On the third, perfectly lobbed pass, the reel made its scream. I tried to set the hook, pulling the rod. My catch darted along the shoreline bending the rod as I tried to correct the drag. The line ran to the right, then the left, back and forth. I finally gained control, as I made my first cumbersome reels. Progress was undone with desperate sprints.

I wondered if it was him or a much bigger beast. Was it a shark? I knew this beach hosted lemons, bulls, nurses, hammerheads, and other sharks I had yet to punch in the nose. But as strong as it was, I knew it wasn't a shark. It was him. My nemesis was waiting to do this too. It was personal.

The rod bent in spectacular fashion. If only someone was there to see it! Part of me did not want anyone to see it, because I knew what was next. I was going to be the first fisherman to kill a fish. I knew this because I watched all the fishing shows. They always released their catch. They tagged the sharks and vented the goliath groupers. They released the tarpons before the sharks could tear into them. They admired the sail to the sailfish before releasing them. But this one was for keeps.

My arms were shaking and heavy. I managed to pull him near the shore's drop, where the waves met the beach. With the roll of the next wave, I yanked him onto the shore. His body shot out from the white caps and plopped hard onto the sand. I dragged him well beyond the water's grasp. The farther away I pulled him, the less hope he had to ever return alive to the ocean's sanctuary. He was on my territory now. He flipped with his last reserve of energy and spirit. The dry beige sand covered his body like flour.

I approached him, killing spear in hand. He jumped again, snapping, looking toward the sea. I slowed my approach, so he could watch me. Afterall, he loved watching me.

It had to dawn on him that I had all the time in the world. I could take my time, watch him gasp for air. I could poke him to death with my homemade spear. It was my choice.

"I didn't want this," I said. "It was you who crossed the line."

I looked over his sandy body, his gills flexing, his eyes staring at me. I had no idea where I was to stab him first. Again, I never wanted it to come to this.

A shadow appeared over me as I leaned over the barracuda.

"Whatcha doing there, eh?" an accented voice said to me. It sounded eerily like Jacques Cousteau. It was Hans Schauber, the man with the old Hobie Cat.

"You caught a nice cuda, son," he said. He leaned on his tall walking stick, shirtless with skin like his brown leather sandals.

"He's not nice," I said.

"Well, a nice catch. As big as you!"

"He tried to kill me," I said.

"Ju don't say?"

The barracuda started another round of flailing and flipping in the sand. His body tangled in the fishing line. It stopped again, exhausted, staring up at us.

"Eh, can't blame him," he said. "What ju gonna do?"

"Kill it," I said showing him my ready homemade spear.

"Ah, they're no good eating," he said.

"I know," I said. He looked over the spear in my hand.

"So, you going to poke him to death?" he said lighting a cigarette, cupping his hand against the ocean breeze.

"I guess," I said watching the fish flex his gills in and out.

"Ju have that power," he said. "His life in jour hands."

I gazed at its long teeth and nasty grin. Its black glassy eye still stared at me, covered in coarse sand. It was one of the two soulless eyes I remember coming at me. I recognized the scar on its tail. I had many days staring back at that scar. Out of the water, lying before me, he didn't look as big. Unless he blew a torpedo hole through my chest, a bite in the hand would not have killed me.

"Why you come at me, asshole?" I shouted at the cuda.

"Hey now," Mr. Schauber said looking around.

"Sorry, Mr. Schauber."

"He's neat though, eh?" he said exhaling a thick cloud.

"I guess."

Mr. Schauber looked inland, toward the west to see the sun begin its descent past the condominium. His Hobie Cat sat in the tall grass in front of a red sun and purple clouds.

"A good long life for him," he said. "Today, it ends. Over. Kaputt. His life in jour hands."

"I guess," I said, kneeling on the sand over my victim-to-be.

"Well, I leave you with him," he said. "Unless you need help."

I asked if he could help me get the hook out of his mouth. Mr. Schauber reached down and pulled it out with the pliers from my tackle box. I held down the cuda's head with a towel, but there was no fight left. Mr. Schauber started to walk away.

"I want to let him go."

Mr. Schauber stopped. "Ju do?"

"Yeah," I said. "Respect, right?"

"Jes, respect." Mr. Schauber nodded. He offered me a hand.

"I'll do it," I said dragging the cuda by his tail. I placed his body in the water. I pulled him back, then pushed him forward in the water to get water into his gills. They did it in all the fishing shows, like jump-starting a fish. It always worked.

Nothing happened. "Come on, butthead," I said. "Now you don't want to live?" His body was still.

I gave it a final push through the water. It glided like a lance. Its tail never moved as it sunk. Its body rolled clockwise, showing its shiny belly. It disappeared into the darker water, before a wave crashed into me and I lost sight of it.

"In God's hands now," Mr. Schauber said. He finished his cigarette and placed the filter in his swim trunk pocket. "It tis getting dark, son. I help you back," he said grabbing my bucket with the cast net. I gathered my rod, spear, and tacklebox and we walked back to the condos.

"I don't think he made it, Mr. Schauber."

"Hate to break it to you," he said leaning on his walking stick with one hand, my bucket in the other, "but fishermen occasionally kill fish."

"You sure?" I asked. "They always let them go on TV."

"TV's not real, my friend," he laughed handing over my bucket. I thanked him and ran off to my condo, next to his.

Mr. Schauber never judged me. He helped a child learn his first lesson in death and mercy, the crossing from something being in your control... until it is no longer. The cost was one barracuda.

He joined my dad from time to time. They sat in their folding chairs on the beach, in front of the Hobie Cat while I pressed on to maintain my reef. I never saw that cuda again. Other cudas came and went, but we all kept our distance. I did my thing. They did theirs. They must have heard the rumors.

I was the Cuda Killer.

But I was also the guy maintaining their reef. They watched me each calm day I could go.

Those days grew fewer as I got older, playing sports, working at the supermarket, and after I got my first car.

After Hurricane Andrew, the community reef was gone. I no longer had it in me to rebuild. I felt the cudas would live on, fine without me, elsewhere.

Just not here.

Here

It was heading elsewhere, there and not here. But here then became there. Everyone elsewhere, could rest their fear, saying it sucks to be there, now here. A week of honks and hollers, spending all their dollars, everyone was prepared but me. TV folk from there, and every elsewhere, screamed how bad it would be. Lines were shifting closer, Nature's Bulldozer, and "run like hell," they advised. All channels here and there, "honey, we're on everywhere," our destruction would be televised.

This was all on me. It was my idea you see, to move our life from there. Nothing wrong where we were at, a nice place to hang your hat, but I wanted to try elsewhere. I longed for the sea breeze, to see the palm trees, and never again shovel snow. A storm the size of the state, was about to seal our fate, and it was my fault, I know. I tried to be cool and strong, play it off like nothing's wrong, tell my wife it will be okay. I couldn't confess, I was kind of a big mess, thinking the end was on its way.

I tried to take measure, everything I thought I treasured, to pack it safely away. Most I couldn't find or understand in my mind, why I valued them in some way. Electronics are much cheaper. It's hard to find a keeper. I stuck to what I couldn't replace. Photos of when I was young, a toy that was once fun, and a painting of my mother's face. Found a letter from a friend, who sadly met his end, a young man way too soon. Then my dad's pocketknife, a guitar from my wife, and a record about some side of the moon. The rest was there, in a box somewhere, in the attic layered in dust. It was too hard to find, not seen for some time, and move on I said, "We must." If these things swept away, I'd be sad but okay, and try to pick up from there. I'd replace them with something, the same or anything, and store them the same somewhere.

I was ashamed to say, I didn't know the way, you're supposed to board up a house. Not in my résumé, for I'm in a cube all day, so I clicked on a mouse. Strangers on the screen, elsewhere all seem, to know what to do. Drill before screwing, be careful what you're doing, 5/8ths wood will do. Preparing to face this doom, I declared here our saferoom, to make the most glorious of final stands. The guest room would do, for one night to get through, this disaster and its many bands.

Men with empty carts wandered barren marts, for there was no wood in any store. Panic from East to West, certainly did its best, and everyone elsewhere had more. We all asked the same, hey whatever your name, are you sure it's not in the back of the store? Where's the next truck, does anyone here give a darn, that we need more and more? They had families too, and couldn't wait to be through, to salvage every minute they could. Days behind the rest, they all did their best, I couldn't ask them again for wood.

I stood there in defeat. I needed only a few feet to secure a single window. But there was no wood, I searched where I could, and soon we would begin the show. The power would go out, rain would flood the route, and the wind would do the rest. If the roof here didn't cave, we'd drink and be brave, and hope for the best.

I peeked out my gate, to see how great, everyone else was heeding the call. Some done already, others working steady, and some were not ready at all. I closed my picket fence, and began to commence, a search for any type of wood. Up the wooden steps I raced and crawled in the wooden crawl space, searching everywhere I could. Down again in defeat, there I took my seat, on my wood bench to have a beer. I stared at my worktable, only wishing I was able, to find anything useful near.

I laid in my lanai and watched time go by, looking at the cross on our wall. I said to the man, "I hope you have a plan," to help us here any way at all. I need some wood, like your cross if you could, so I may seal off that damn window. In six beers I found, inspiration all around, and the fence was the first to go.

Proud I figured it on my own, I considered the barrier a loan, from a fence that was never going to last. It was by no means pretty, in fact quite shitty, but beautiful for something made so fast. Thirty-one pickets, held by rope, screws, and wickets, would hold the winds and such. At the top I began to spray, a sign telling the storm to go away, I thought it was a nice touch.

The neighborhood grew quiet, no longer a loud riot, and the wind began to blow. The trees started to sway, the storm was on its way, and to the safe room we had to go. The power was down, to my phone I looked down, and the weatherman was still there. He was scaring the shit, out of all still watching it, saying it was coming here and not there. A reporter was at the beach, gripping a stop sign he could reach, the stores around him were all gone. In the dark I said to my wife, hey, I guess that's life, it looks like here the storm is still on.

Meeting Her

"Someday, you'll know when you found the right one," my father told me when I was younger. He repeated it after my divorce. I hadn't given it much thought until that day. My eyes caught a glance of what I wanted. Suddenly everything felt… not wrong. I had plenty of wrong these last few years to know.

The morning drive along A1A, from Boca Raton to Fort Lauderdale, was my needed break. It was a hypnotic passing of condos, palms, motels, hotels, mansions, and more condos. They passed to the left and right of my velocity blue Bronco. My spirits lifted seeing the Atlantic, crossing familiar drawbridges. I enjoyed the soothing hum of my 37-inch tires over the steel bascule leaves.

It was a Florida-frigid, 64-degree October morning, but I drove with the soft top back for the full effect of the beautiful drive. Summer's brutal humidity finally retreated. The air smelled of salt and fresh cut grass. The sun peeked through the clouds over the Atlantic, promising to warm the day.

Work kept me driving opposite to my past, where I once called home. Years passed since I had time to travel south along A1A. I felt I was passing a long line of friends I lost touch with.

The Emerald was a paler green than I remembered. It was a 15-story condo where two of my childhood friends lived. One still lived there, inheriting the unit from his parents. The other sold his for five times what his parents paid back in the seventies.

Three down was The La Fontaine, a white 10-story condo where I lived with my parents. Five condos from there, were the

Bachman Towers. Tall sabal palms surrounded the beige 12-story condos. Green flood lamps lit the palms at night. Many kids from my school lived there including my friend Thorny.

One day, a developer threw obscene money at the flip flops of all 48 townhome residents to the Royal Reef Club, sealing a real estate deal for the ages. The developer then grabbed the condo next to it. The Pelican Palace was fifteen stories of cracked concrete balconies, faded brown paint, and a decades' old hallway stench of what everyone was cooking. The few remaining residents faced an unsurmountable collective HOA expense to maintain the dated building. Each accepted their just-below-market offers like quick, merciful deaths to their dreams in exchange for avoiding prolonged excruciating financial torture.

The developer tried for the condo next door to that, but a handful of "holdouts" refused. No matter the amount, what they knew to be home would remain so the rest of their lives.

The 48 townhomes and tired condo awaited their firing squad until one day, in a synchronized bang, the bodies dropped. A short time later, five glass condo towers sprouted, each twenty stories high. Two stood on the intracoastal side of A1A, three on the ocean side. They called it The Tides Yacht Club. It featured a clubhouse overlooking the intracoastal. One million got you a bottom floor unit overlooking the parking lot. It made me think about how many millionaires relocated to Florida to warrant such demand.

As I drove by, I imagined us stupid kids sprinting barefoot across the hot tarred street. We dodged cars and ran across private properties to get to the beach. One time, my friend ran in front of a speeding convertible with his longboard. The car clipped Thorny's board. It cracked the fiberglass around the rear fin. One cried over a broken board while the other, a scratched quarter panel and busted headlight. An epic shouting match ensued until a cop came to resolve the nonsense. He was much kinder to us than to the driver. The cop's cool "no shit" composure, his thick mustache, and tight uniform of solid muscle apparently inspired my friend for life.

At night, we crossed the same road to find unlit spots on the beach. It was the place to drink, make out with our girlfriends, and smoke until the cops showed. If you lived in one of the condos, the cops ensured you got home safely. If you were not from there, they gave you a warning for trespassing. Cops poured the beer and confiscated the small joints. You only went to jail if you were fighting or doing anything to disrupt the turtle mating season. That was a serious offense in anyone's book.

Sadly, more condos along the way appeared empty, awaiting their final execution. The dust and rubble would settle. Fancier buildings for more millionaires would sprout.

Condos were originally for the middle class to collectively share a coveted piece of beach property. The property was equal in size to that used for most mansions. Five acres was standard for a CEO, a movie star, a ball player, or drug dealer. A condo used the same space for hundreds of families. The privileged strolled the same beach as their condo rift raft neighbors.

One time, an armada of barges came down the intracoastal to deliver fifty of the tallest palm trees I had ever seen. They were Mexican fan palms, each a hundred feet tall. A series of cranes were positioned along A1A. They lifted the palms from the barges, maneuvered them over A1A, and placed them in their tight row alongside a condo. The massive operation was so a ball player could keep his privacy, pretending there wasn't a five-story pink condo looking over his mansion.

The new wave of sprouting towers had no intention for the working class. Oceanfront was in high demand. Mansions were now meant for those the next level up. Individual condo units were twice as big as their predecessors. Only two to six units shared a floor. Each unit had full length, blue glass balconies. Their grand entrances rivaled those to four-star hotels. Some said it was a sign of progress. But it wasn't and it sacrificed more of our past than we cared to admit. I spent my drive wondering if our state's character was collapsing one condo at a time. Those who worked for a living were retreating inland so the world's richest assholes could play on the beach. Cocktail party elites who swore Florida was going underwater horded all the oceanfront property.

It all vacated my mind as I made my way to the five-day annual boat show in Fort Lauderdale. It was a time-honored tradition, the biggest party in South Florida for more than six decades. I went with my father every year as a kid.

My boat shoes touched the first dock and I felt at home. Everything troubling me fucked off to somewhere else. War, politics, my job, the economy, the loss of loved ones, my own mortality, my wrecked marriage, and everyone's bullshit failed to cross with me onto the dock. My only concern was not tripping over a baby stroller or bumping into people. The steel drum music quickly lowered my blood pressure. It was better than any medicine the VA prescribed.

The morning sun burned away any feeling of October by ten o'clock. The first bar I saw jumped out at me. It made me take a shot of whiskey. It was the start to what I knew would be a long weekend. The next several hours I flowed with the crowd. I toured the boats, avoiding any in-depth conversation with the salespeople. Traversing across seven marinas, I made my best effort to support each local bar tent and bar stand.

I had no intention to find her. I wasn't looking, expecting, wanting, trying, or ready. But I saw her.

"Where?" Thorny asked.

"I don't remember."

I remembered my soul, not my body, but my soul… gliding along the floating roll of the docks. I felt trapped in the shuffle of a sweaty, sea-sized crowd. I kept looking back until I could no more. She was gone.

"You were drunk."

"I don't think… dawned on myself… until I was, you know, like somewhere really elsewhere… somewhere."

"You're still drunk," Thorny laughed. "You needed this."

"What?"

"A break to pull that stick from your ass," Thorny said looking out across the marina. The sun was setting, shining its gold and red hue over the mansions to the west, onto the intracoastal waters in front of him. "What a day!"

Thorny was a boulder of tanned, tattooed muscle. He looked dumb, but he was far from it. He was listening, but not really listening. Thorny could only invest so much into my drunken explanation of events. He focused more on scooting his stool an inch to the right, then back, then to the left. He wanted to find the perfect view overlooking the boats from our high table under the bar tent.

"Did they call you to that scaffolding thing?"

"Yep." Thorny adjusted his seat, just in time to smile at the next round of passing young ladies. "Went down fast and hard," he said loud enough in his deep voice for the two women in bikini tops to hear. They smiled at him as he said "*hard.*"

We watched them walk away, their old husbands with their stupid golf hats and fat, almost-Cuban, cigars not far behind.

Thorny stopped counting the plastic cups accumulating on the table. They were full of pineapple rinds, orange peels, and cherry twigs.

"Lucky no one died," Thorny said. "I spent my day babysitting until they finally cleaned it up. Lots of news crews."

"Mom swore she saw you on the news," I said. "She kept talking about you in your tight little uniform."

"It's not like I have a choice after you add the vest."

"You showoffs would just wear utility belts and spandex if you could."

"So, Gloria noticed?" he laughed. "How *is* your mom?"

I nodded at the line to the bar.

"Speaking of spandex," Thorny whispered as two ladies walked by in their form fitting tan shorts and tight pink golf shirts. Thorny lowered his sunglasses, ensuring no doubt to any in vicinity he was checking them out. As they walked away, every man on dock nine saw the logo for "Haulover Excelsior Yachts" displayed on the backs of their shirts. "Well, I hope she wasn't at Haulover Excelsior Yachts. Way too rich for your blood."

With my thumb on my beer bottle, I flipped it to get the stubborn lime in. I put the bottle in his face and lifted my thumb.

"Why you do that?" he said wiping the mist from his face.

"I worry you don't even see it coming," I said. "Don't you cops have to have periperitary… whatever the hell vision?"

"Yeah," Thorny said. "So, we going to go look?"

"Thought you weren't listening."

"I was," Thorny said pounding the rest of his hurricane. "But even if you find her, you don't sound happy."

"I'm not." I stared out at the water, between passing bodies. The scent of fried grouper, hushpuppies, and roasted corn drifted in the wet breeze.

"Maybe I had other plans?" I finished my hurricane with a suppressed belch. I used the small circular table for balance as I tried to get up from the stool.

"Don't get ahead of yourself, bud. Besides, you never have plans," Thorny said. He tapped his empty cup to remind me I had the next round. That was only if I could make my way to the vendor along the dock without falling in. "I'm moving on," Thorny declared.

"From Ginger?" I started to pretend I was sober. "About fucking time."

"No, asshole. From hurricanes," he laughed. "Tequila, a little ice, and an orange slice, senor."

"Oh, ok."

"And what the fuck's wrong with Ginger, dude?"

"Nothing," I shouted heading for the bar. "She's great."

"Don't forget the orange slice."

I returned to the table and held onto it tight. "You wanted what again?" I said with my eyes closed.

"Water," Thorny said. "I said we should just stick to water."

"Shouldn't I go look?' I opened my eyes, taking a deep breath.

Thorny nodded west to the red horizon. "Day's done, bro." He lifted his sunglasses over the top of his salt and pepper hair. "Maybe tomorrow you get lucky. You recall enough?"

I sat back down and placed my head on the table. "One of the marinas."

"There's seven of them." He laughed. "Tomorrow is another day, bud. You've been going hard all day."

"*Hard…*" I said lifting my head, trying to sound like Thorny. People near us smiled before going back to their drinks.

After a long stumble from Bahia Mar, we stood at the Finbird Beach Resort entrance. "Night's still young," Thorny said. "You sober up enough, we could hit Sapphires on Oakland."

"Been sweating all day, man. I probably stink."

He leaned in and sniffed. "Fuck, you do. Like dead mullet."

"Besides, Traci is working there."

"She's stripping again?" he said. "I'll tell her you said hi."

The planet continued to spin. I stared into the shrubs. I saw a green and orange iguana eating away at the landscaping in the front entrance without a fear in the world. In the day they ran from the landscaping crews with the machetes. But at night, the bellhop is not going to go diving after them and they know it.

"I was kidding," Thorny said, his hands on my shoulders.

I opened my eyes.

"You ok finding your hotel?" Thorny asked, pointing to the front sliding door ten feet away.

"Yep," I said. "I got this."

"I'm late shift tomorrow, so good luck without me," he said playing with the app on his phone. "Text. I want to hear how it goes down."

"Yes, dear," I said as a car pulled up.

Thorny crammed into the back of a small white rideshare with three strangers, two in back and one up front with the driver.

I leaned in over the open passenger window. "How many clowns you fit in here, bro?" I asked. The driver flipped me the bird and pulled away. "Bye now," I said waving, laughing and pointing at Thorny sandwiched in the back. I gracefully turned and walked into the hotel glass door with a loud thump.

Tomorrow was only a few hours away. My mission was to jump back into the crowd of a hundred thousand people to search six miles of floating docks across seven marinas and a convention center to find her.

Unable to sleep, I brought a sixer of some local IPA to the pool deck. It had a smiling barracuda on the can, labeled Big Barracuda Bastard. It was a nice changeup after a long day of drinking hurricanes and margaritas, walking in the sun. I was working out a lot at the gym the last few months, since the divorce. I had finally finished a third round of tattoo work on my arms. It seemed like a nice day to show off the guns. When I returned to the hotel, it was too late to do anything other than acknowledge that my tan turned to a painful purple.

The pool bar was nice until the bartender kindly told me to "take that bullshit elsewhere," when I lit my cigar. I paid twelve bucks for that bad boy. No chance I was putting it out. It was a double maduro supposedly from Cuban seed, grown in the Dominican Republic, rolled by a Puerto Rican in a Greek-owned shop. I was new to this expensive hobby, but it lit fine and helped me relax. I plopped on the cool sand and leaned my back against a palm tree. I looked up to the stars and realized the difficulty seeing stars beneath the palm branches. Eventually, I slouched to see the ocean and the stars in the distance.

It occurred to me later how bad it was for a middle-aged back and big bony butt to sleep for hours against a palm. The waves crashed in a steady rhythm onto the shore, equidistant to the 80's music at the bar. It made a nice competition for my attention. But my mind was still focused on her.

"You a guest?" The security guy stood over me with his official flashlight. I showed him my official room key.

"Paid $450 for a room."

"How's the room?" he said.

"Lovely."

"Sir, it's two o'clock. Appreciate you going there."

I popped open another beer and told him I'd get right on it.

Hotel staff stopped caring after that. Real cops came earlier to escort drunk teenagers off the beach, back to their parents.

Day one was a hell of a party. I still had a day two in mind before going home to reality.

When I was a kid, we sometimes went to the boat show from the other side of the intracoastal waterway. We took a water taxi through the "Venice of America" to Pier 66. There, they had the super mega yachts. There were yachts and then there were personal cruise ships. They had helicopter pads and side doors that opened to deploy jet skis and full-sized boats.

As a kid, I dreamed of owning one of the little boats those rich assholes consider dinghies. Such a stupid name for a boat, but it was more than I had in my name, floating on the water.

The breeze kept the mosquitos off. I hated those bloodsucking bastards. Some were big too, as big as the lizard staring at me from the palm tree, flexing his red and yellow throat, like a mating call to other lizards. Either that or he was telling me off. His colors were like my tattoos. I tipped my hat to him and fell asleep again.

Sunrise was approaching and the stars were gone. I couldn't remember the last time I watched the sun rise over the Atlantic, taking it all in. It was probably back when my now ex-wife and I rented a place on Saint Augustine Beach. The row of tall three- and two-story homes looked over the white sand dunes and tall grass. We had a little white picket fence and a short boardwalk to the beach to sit and watch the sunrise. We got up a few of those mornings to go for a walk, back when we had things to talk about. That all went away. Her choice, not mine.

I gathered my empties. A man drove by on his all-terrain vehicle. It dragged a long rake behind it. He was clearing the beach of sargassum seaweed left behind from last night's high tide. He reminded me of the Turtle Man, cruising around with his big straw hat, flip flops, gloves, and bucket. I wanted to be him. He was the coolest guy on the beach. Lifeguards were dicks, but Turtle Man was king.

In the summer, myself and other kids in the neighborhood ran across A1A at sunrise. We scanned the beach for turtle tracks from the night before. Turtle Man would roll up, say good morning, and investigate. The turtles made the best dig they could with what energy and time they had. But eventually they had to plop their eggs and get back to the sea. Depending on the species, they laid between 50 and 200 eggs each time. Few would survive to adulthood and do the same.

The turtles tried to cover the eggs in their haste, but Turtle Man was always there in the morning to take over. The state authorized him to move the nests to a safe distance from the water and mark the nest.

Florida doesn't joke about its turtles and neither did Turtle man. Most of the time, we simply ran alongside his ATV and watched him do his work.

After he finished covering them, he tipped his straw hat and moved on. He had to keep going for several miles, salvaging the eggs before the tide got them or a fox or bird found them.

Later in the summer, we ran across to watch them hatch. At first light, their little heads popped out of the sand. Turtle Man was always there, waiting. He had his calendar and knew where to be. He was always on time, ready to protect the little creatures as they made their waddling sprints to the sea. They didn't wait for anyone, stepping on each other's heads, trudging toward the rising sun and the water. No one had to tell them. Centuries of DNA told them where they belonged.

But it was October, well-outside of turtle season. So, I guessed that was Beach Cleaner Dude… the other ATV dude with the less sexy, but necessary, job. I didn't want to be him. I then pondered over the chance he was the same dude and worked year-round. Regardless, that sound and the smell of exhaust from the ATV made me reminisce simpler times.

Yesterday, I covered all seven marinas. I remembered the fishing rods, knives, emergency beacons, and other vendor gadgets I played with at the convention center. I wasn't sure how many boat drawings I entered, but it was safe to bet everyone had my email to send me their spam. I remembered gawking at the mega yachts at Pier 66 and the beautiful sales ladies. One of them kindly reminded me they only take broker appointments to go aboard. They had to keep the rift raft like me off their magnificent ships. Like Thorny said, everything there was too rich for my blood. As drunk as I was, I knew that. She wasn't there.

I compared all the different builders, each with their own sections in the marinas. More young ladies stood in stretchy tan shorts and snug company polo shirts to lure boat buyers. Somewhere, she was there. I had the day to find her.

I remembered eating a lot. I remembered a buttery lobster roll, a grouper philly with a remoulade sauce, and a spicy ceviche. I skipped the carnival fare of fried foods, except for some amazing jalapeño hushpuppies. I could not recall how many drinks.

"Here we go," I said stepping off the water taxi, onto the dock at the famous Pier 66. Again, like a trance, I found myself spinning, enamored by row after row of towering mega yachts. It was easy to feel like everyone was a millionaire *but you…* if that was your only perspective. As I made my way along the marina, the boats decreased in size, bringing me closer to reality.

Most of the marinas were not tied to reality. Reality was across the water, downtown, where the homeless sought shade in the shadows of skyscrapers. When cold, they wandered like cats to the sun peeking on the sidewalks, between the glass and steel buildings. Daily, the local ministry offered breakfast burritos in exchange for a few words about Jesus. During the day, a few passing folks offered a few dollars. A soft grassy section in the park underneath a palm tree or a dry park bench made a place to sleep.

I was no closer to reality moving from the mega yachts to the forty-foot sailboats. No closer moving down to the thirty-foot cabin cruisers. I was blessed with a paying job, but knew I wasn't in my marina yet. The one closer to my economic status was still marinas away. It was my assumption; she was somewhere there.

My walk grew more purposeful, slower. I sensed I was getting closer to where she might be. Passing all the pretty women, all the pretty boats, and all the pretty women showing off the pretty boats, I kept trying to remember her. She was different.

It was coming back to me, seeing her at a sectioned off portion of dock with a large black tent. I kept imagining she was no longer there and I missed my only chance. Chances of finding her were, of course, zero if she wasn't even there.

I scanned the next marina for a large black tent. I saw dark blue ones, red ones, a few white ones, but not a black one until the next marina over. I moved faster toward the large black tent in the distance. I passed an impressive section of thirty-something foot long speedboats. They had two, three, and even four outboard motors.

Continuing my focused trek through the crowd, I passed a tall barrier of large red and yellow hibiscus. It separated the crowded dock of sweaty pedestrians from the park where others sat at picnic tables. They were taking a break with their plastic cups of margaritas and a variety of cuisine coming from the surrounding food trucks. The hibiscus reminded me of my garden, sitting in the backyard of the home I lost in my ass-kicking divorce.

I entered the tent, realizing it was for a personal watercraft and jet ski dealership. This was not it. I spotted a familiar red two-seater with yellow stripes. At a top speed of eight-six miles per hour, I imagined the colors would look like it was on fire zipping across the bay. A red and white flag faintly came to mind.

Another hour of walking back and forth, I spotted the red and white flag. It had bold black lettering, flying high over the black vendor tent on the wide dock. It was full of people.

Across the way was a bar tent. I grabbed a bucket of Coronas and sat at a little round table with a highchair. Potted palm trees swayed in the light breeze, their pots anchoring the tent.

A smiling crowd passed. Strangers occasionally joined me at my little table to catch some shade, swallow a hot dog, or slam a drink. The last guy told me how he sailed his 34-foot sailboat all the way from Long Island to Port Everglades. He had favorable weather along the way and made good time out on the Atlantic. Only a few days of difficult weather made him take the slower, protected, intracoastal waterway. He said he had been boating the last thirty-five years with plenty of close calls, but no bad days.

I laughed at his jokes and enjoyed his story more as my eyes confirmed she was there in the distance, in all her beauty. I watched the sun beam on her. I was relieved but my stomach turned, my heart began to race. Men walked up to her, one after another, staring at her. I swigged my beers, admiring her from afar, up and down, gracefully working the crowd.

Beer by beer, I worked up the courage. I was never so unsure of myself. It could have been the divorce kicking in. Maybe it was my long track record of mistakes. Some decisions were after serious wargaming, introspection, strategizing, and thoughtfulness. They still came out to shit. They ranged between disastrous to mildly failing.

Something this spontaneous was almost certain to yield improved or equal odds. Maybe that was the issue. Perhaps I thought too much. My mind drowned any good idea from the heart. Maybe it was time, five… six beers down, to go for it.

Like a cool action movie, I walked in slow motion through the busy crowd. I focused on her, straight ahead, as the bodies moved between us, in my way, then out of my way. I entered the tent with purpose, one step in front of the other.

The young blonde stood inside the tent, gorgeous, confident. Her soft green eyes and long lashes invited me in. She was out of place, like a Victoria's Secret supermodel in a central Florida gun show. The drool of surrounding men made the dock slippery. Her red and white polo with the company logo on the back was snug along her slender body. It stretched to the max around her orange-sized breasts. Her tight tan shorts were rolled up on the ends to make them even shorter.

She turned toward me as I approached. Her smile told me she knew exactly what she was doing. Her long blonde hair rested perfectly on her firm backside. I caught her eyes scanning me, from my flip flops to my sweat-stained Marlins cap. The other men watched her… watch me. Confidence was king.

"Hi. Can I help you?" She flung her hair around to her right shoulder. I moved closer toward her, squeezing between the crowd. I stepped in front of the drooling gaggle of men, the ultimate alpha move. My chest, which I had been working the shit out of at the gym, bulged toward her like bongos, dying to bounce a rhythm for her. My nipples pointed at her like compass needles. She put her hand up like she wanted to cruise it along my shaved chest. She caught herself, diverting her hand to run through her soft hair.

The breeze carried the scent of coconut from her tan skin, strawberry from her hair, lemon from her shirt. It mixed with the lime from the beer I chugged a minute earlier. I felt like I was in the sexiest fruit stand in Florida. My eyes caught the small beads of sweat running along her neck, stopping at her collar.

"Hi." I looked into her eyes, as green as the margaritas I slammed this morning. It was occurring to me that I possibly had a serious drinking problem to address later, but I continued into the moment.

"Hi." She giggled, realizing she already said hi.

The fourth finger to my left hand was cool, dry, no longer constrained with a golden noose. It was okay to move on and be happy. My ex-wife was on stage, only miles away, dancing to the delight of whatever hard-up dudes go to a strip bar at three in the afternoon. The sun peeking through the tent warmed my face, a simple reminder to keep living.

I could hear the Canadian-accented voice of Dr. Lorne Livingston in those self-help motivational videos I watched after my divorce. He was telling me, "Jump to it. Put what you want in front of you. Don't be sawry, eh. Find that courage. Go get it!"

I took a deep breath. It was time to speak from my heart.

"Excuse me," I said, stepping to the right of her and ten steps forward. I left her with the surrounding men, all watching me.

The sign said, "Please remove your shoes." I ignored it like a badass. I kept my flip flops on. The crowd watched me cross the ten-inch gap from the dock onto the shiny white boat… all 18 feet and 4 inches of her, from the bow to the propeller of her 115-horsepower motor. She had a beam of 8 feet, a draft of 13 inches, a 50-gallon fuel tank, and weighed 2,625 pounds.

Before a captivated audience, I stood on the bow like I was ready to announce I was running for President. I pulled out my credit card. I held it up for all to see. Samuel Martinez shined in silver letters over the blue card. I didn't care if it was protocol, classy, or tasteless amongst this boating community.

My eyes looked to hers, laser-focused, certain, bold, and damn determined.

"Is she taken?"

She laughed with those watching. "No, sir."

"She is now!"

The Return

"What the fuck is that?"

That was the final transmission heard by the men aboard Coast Guard Cutter Valiant. Captain Daniel Douglas made repeated replies to no avail. The 30-foot twin 300 horsepower outboard center console, 'Tits Up,' was later found capsized twenty miles offshore, between Hollywood Beach and Bimini.

The weather was clear. There were no reported storms. It was a calm day. The Coast Guard, local authorities, and volunteers conducted a search spanning one thousand square miles the next five days. Patrol boats cruised by the many small uninhabited islands. A HC-130J flew overhead with thermals scanning for signs of life. Its passengers were never seen or heard from again.

The search concluded after the fifth day as Tropical Storm Fay made its approach. Fay's erratic pattern managed to hit the state of Florida four times. It crossed in an odd zigzag pattern. It impacted the Florida Keys, Naples, New Smyrna Beach, and finally the St. Augustine and Jacksonville areas.

Months passed. The families had markers placed in memorial at the cemetery in Islamorada to find closure. Six simple white marble markers stood next to each other a foot apart, one foot above the green grass.

The inscriptions read:

Trey "the Tractor" McCoy, 1.14.1974 - 8.13.2008
Chandra "Princess" Jenkins, 12.10.1975 – 8.13.2008
Bo Jim "Boss" Dunkin, 10.29.1954 – 8.13.2008
Shay "Shake-E" Evans, 4.20.1981 – 8.13.2008
Cory "CK" Kendall, 3.16.1984 – 8.13.2008
Kendra "Cheeks" Kendall, 6.22.1986 – 8.13.2008

There was a large turnout for the memorial. A procession of eighteen bikers led an empty white hearse. Seven pickup trucks followed, three with tires as tall as a man. Four colorful pimped out rides followed with bouncing hydraulics. Behind them was a car club. Each small sports car made aggressive fart sounds you could hear across the island.

Following them were two black Crown Victoria's with blacked out windows. Neither Crown Victoria appeared to be with the other. Both kept farther distances once they noticed one another. Eventually, the occupants began watching each other, while watching the funeral party.

Behind them was a black suburban with mammoth bumpers typical for a government agency anxious to ram someone. A white suburban followed it following the Crown Victoria following the other Crown Victoria following the procession of fart-sounding sports cars, bouncing cars, and redneck pickups following the empty hearse following the bikers. Everyone saw everyone. No formal introductions were made and, in some cases, not needed. No nods of acknowledgment. Only cold stares beneath dark sunglasses. It was just as well.

In a single procession was the full circle; from machete-happy drug dealers in the white suburban, to the low-level gang bangers in the car club, to the mid-management bikers, redneck enforcers in the pickups, the strippers that kept the products moving to the customers, to the fishermen in the regular pickups that collected the airdropped drugs from the machete guys. All were in view to an assortment of authorities. No one knew who had the black suburban.

After the ceremony, family and friends returned to the trailer park. Three of the four families resided there. The bikers rallied in Bo Jim Dunkin's honor at Chi Chi's Gentlemen's Club. They ended the night with a massive shit-kicking brawl against the outnumbered fishermen.

The party at the Seahorse Shore Trailer Park ended in a fight shortly after midnight. The cops quickly broke it up. No shots were fired. It was relatively civil for such a gathering.

A few imagined that the six missing persons had staged their disappearance. Each had "commitments" to people you do not want to ever have commitments to. In this business, a few successful runs established good, mutual expectations. But when law enforcement got lucky, expectations crumbled with blame. When expectations were not met, machetes came into play to sever liabilities.

Officer Orlando Ortega watched the memorial from a distance. He sat in his gray County Marine Patrol pickup, chewing his cigar. He was not an assigned investigator. Curiosity made him skip fishing on his day off and sit outside the cemetery.

He knew Trey "the Tractor" McCoy for years, even before Trey became a frequent flyer with law enforcement. Trey played running back for the local high school. Ortega's son blocked for four of Trey's six years. They and his daughter all went to school with Chandra.

Trey and Chandra dated on and off. Years after high school, Trey rolled back into town on his Indian motorcycle. He saw Chandra, forever known as "Princess" in these parts and on stage at Chi Chi's, and they rekindled their romance. It was not exclusive. Princess maintained many romances. She was also an entrepreneur in the entertainment and male morale industry, offering many explicit, personal online and in-person services.

Bo Jim was a long-time local fishing captain well-known for his run-ins with the law. Some offenses were spectacular, requiring significant time behind bars. The bigger the offense, the harder the prison. But each time, Bo Jim "the Boss" emerged stronger, meaner, and more powerful.

Boss said he was "all but certain" he was Princess' father. He wanted to help her get a new life, beyond lap dancing the same ten bozos every night at Chi Chi's. So, he took her man Tractor under his wings.

Tractor's accomplice was Shake-E. He too had a long and impressive rap sheet he wanted to leave behind on the mainland. He brought with him his former cell mate CK and CK's little sister, Cheeks. The three shared a double wide at the marina where Boss kept his boats.

Shake-E was a charismatic leader. Like Boss, many gravitated to him. He was fearless. In only four months, Shake-E became the leader of the feared Cicadas Car Club of the lower Keys. They were known throughout these parts as the Triple C's.

<u>August 20, 2008. 3:20 pm ET</u>

"Any luck?" Officer Thompson asked Ortega. Thompson sat underneath the palm-topped gazebo outside the marine patrol station.

"I spoke with the two captains I knew were out in that area that day," said Officer Ortega. "They both joined the search, at least for the first day, after the distress call."

"How do they explain it?"

Ortega wiped the sweat from his thick black mustache. He glanced at the two gray 29-foot rigid-hull inflatable boats nested in their dock spaces. "They saw flashes in the clouds nearby."

"You mean lightning."

Ortega plopped onto the bench across from Thompson. He removed his olive Marine Patrol baseball cap and dusted it off, setting it beside him. "They swear it was different."

"How?"

Ortega cupped his hand to light the saved half-smoked maduro. "One said red. The other blue. Very horizontal... more than usual."

"Horizontal happens," Thompson said. "Red and blue they say? Sounds like purple to me. Very colorful recollections from the marina crowd." Thompson rose from the bench and stretched his arms into the incoming salty breeze. He watched the seagulls glide above the baitfish stirring along the seawall. A manatee popped his nose out of the water in the middle of the canal.

"Nine different boats described the same navigation problems that day," Ortega said. He watched the wind ruffle the American flag on the stern of his patrol boat. "I got another captain telling me he got home to port more than three hours faster than he should have. Nothing made sense."

"You sound like one of those Bermuda Triangle nuts," Thompson said. "Besides, you shouldn't stick your nose out any further. You're not a detective and you're not assigned to this."

"Aren't you curious?" Ortega asked.

"No," Thompson said. "And those captains should lay off the shit they're moving."

Ortega puffed his cigar. "Your navigation was all jacked up that day too, wasn't it?"

Thompson looked down at the rotting gazebo deck. "It was."

September 3, 2035. 08:20 am ET

"What the fuck is that?" Captain Jamal G. Jackson shouted down to his men from the open window on the bridge. The transport ship, the SS Marlino, was miles off the Florida Keys. It was heading north to Miami to deliver their boatload of boats. Its cargo included center consoles, dual consoles, cabin cruisers, flat boats, outboard motors, and their many spare parts.

The men inside ran out to the deck. They joined the others to witness the spectacle in the distance. Horizontal lines of lighting sprung out from the clear sunny day and stretched as far as the eye could see. The sky lit in shades of blue and then red, like God's patrol car was pulling the world over.

The men ran back inside the ship for cover. The storm's energy rang out like an explosion of sound and light. Rolling dark purple clouds emerged from the center. A giant beam of bright white light came down onto an island of black rock and thick mangroves in front of them. A flash of solid black darkness, not light, overcame them. It looked like night dropped right on top of them, across all the Atlantic. It lasted a long, frightening twenty seconds.

Mayday, mayday, Captain Jackson called out on the radio. He watched his console's instrumentation spin, flip, and flicker. By the time he contacted the nearest vessel by radio, it was over. The waters calmed. The wind died. The sun was bright. The clouds vanished.

"Everyone okay?" he shouted down from the bridge overlooking the loaded deck of containers. His men crept out. "All clear," one of them replied.

"What was that?" a deckhand shouted up.

"Just a storm," the captain answered. "Back to business."

Captain Jackson turned to the two men beside him. "Do either of you know what the fuck that was?"

"Well, you just said it was a storm," one of the men replied.

"I know what I said and that was no fucking storm," the captain said rubbing his shaved head. "If you said that was the start of the apocalypse, I'd buy that. But I've never seen bullshit like that."

The captain took his seat in his worn, black leather captain's chair and stared at the horizon. He sipped his cold coffee hoping it would jolt something in his throbbing head. He noticed the ship's instruments were normal again.

The island was no longer in his front view. "Did we get turned?" he softly asked First Mate Pearcy. The captain grabbed his binoculars and slowly stepped out to the observation platform. Pearcy hunched over and squinted into the radar screen.

"Still on the same heading, sir," Pearcy said. "Due North."

The captain ran his binoculars across the one hundred and eighty degrees of blue horizon. He scanned from the bow, across the port side, to the stern. "Then how did that island wind up behind us?"

Pearcy stepped out and grabbed the binoculars offered by the captain. "Lots of islands, Captain. You sure it's the same one?"

The captain ran back inside to check the radar for himself. There were no islands in front of them all the way to Miami.

"Captain," Pearcy shouted while staring into the binoculars. "There's people on that island waving for help."

<u>September 3, 2035. 4:15 pm ET</u>

Detective Marisol Ortega was starting another long day. Her small feet ached from standing in the riot the day before. Her ears rang from the shouts of protestors. It was getting harder to show up each day for her job. It was day 736 of the Miami riots.

Most rioters were paid, full-time, professionals. Some were trying to earn a spot to get paid. Others were there to take advantage of the chaos. They hoped to steal anything left, despite the great business exodus of 2034.

After enough time passed, the unrest became a part of the daily routine, a part of the culture. Most Miami rioters knew the detective and she knew them, at least the regulars.

Detective Ortega had nothing to do with the stability of the World Cyber-coin. She could care less who was WEF Premiere, U.S. President, Governor, or Mayor. She had no opinion of the ruling corrupt geriatrics the world was mad at.

She was only thankful the riots were not as bad as elsewhere. Miami always seemed half as pissed as the other cities. There were still things to enjoy and divert attention. Despite predictions, Miami was still happily above water, the beaches were still nice, but the cocaine shark epidemic deterred most swimmers. You would know that if you caught the Nature Channel's hit documentary series *Cocaine Chompers*.

But Miami's heat and humidity was never conducive to fiery crowds. And as Florida's long history has shown, the rest of the sunshine state could not care less what Miami did.

Detective Ortega was not even sure where she was to be any more. Regular police eventually became full-time riot control. People slept in the day. At dark, the chaos began, like punching in for a job. Monday through Wednesday was the new weekend, always a three-day window for protestors to rest.

Mayor Hector Venezia tried to withhold food rations from those with matching facial recognition to the riots. That caused a separate, more intense riot at *the party's* food distribution center. *The Party* quickly made him retract his threat and apologize.

Detective Marisol Ortega unexpectedly became a rising superstar. Her former runner-up status as Miss Florida, comfort with four languages and martial arts, and her tough attitude all packed into a petite 5'2" frame made her the network's top choice. She was quickly volun-told by her police department and assigned a two-person camera crew.

They were on location to shoot live for the full time Riot Channel, channel 57 on your local cable network. It was the channel for those needing a break from the live war coverage on News Channels 8, 13, 61, 68, 101 (in Portuguese), 130 (in Chinese), 201 and 175 (in Russian), and 169-174 en espanol. The

War Channel (366) had live feeds from towers, tall buildings, drones, and satellites… until destroyed and replaced by other towers, buildings, drones, and satellites.

The Dare Channel (channel 18) was dedicated to game shows daring people to do stupid, even illegal, acts for money. Sometimes, they collaborated with the Riot Channel, as people accepted challenges in the middle of the riots.

The Surgery Channel (Channel 88) broadcasted the Government Health Panels adjudicating who was entitled to various surgeries. Those over age 60 rarely had a chance unless they were significant donors to *the party*. At 5pm there was a live drawing for one lucky person on the "expiring list" to win a paid lifesaving surgery. In the evenings, they showed some of the actual surgeries for those with a strong stomach.

Surprisingly, the government-sponsored channels (Channels 2, 3, 15, and 66) were challenging the Riot Channel for ratings. Congressman Buck Davis (U, FL) performed a table-smashing suplex on Congressman Barry Creedy (D, NY). Smaller skirmishes broke out daily between *the party* members, *democrats*, and the remnants of the former republican party, referred to as the *unaffiliated*. Ratings quickly went through the roof. Americans watching at home tolerated boring legislative procedures in hopes of catching their elected representatives kick the loving shit out of each other. Congressman Creedy spent the remaining six months to his term in rehabilitation on a treadmill, sipping protein shakes with a straw through his wired jaw. In the election that followed, Creedy was replaced in the primary by retired wrestler Gary "Ground Pounder" Paulson (D, NY). He vowed to "pound some serious DC ass." Civility was dead. It made wonderful television.

But if you needed to wind down after a long day supervising artificial intelligence doing your former job, you could always catch a good old fashion riot. Everyone had their favorite rioters. Val the Vegan, Crying Caleb, roller-skating Pervy Pete, Naked "Hairless" Harry, and Coke-head Carol were crowd favorites. On the cop side, millions loved watching Detective Marisol Ortega in her signature blue jeans and black body armor controlling the chaos that was Miami. She was especially popular amongst the Hispanic community, hailing from the 46th state of Puerto Rico.

Detective Ortega hated playing babysitter to a television crew. Later, she appreciated their presence. In most cases, the cameras became added protection, recording future evidence. Other times she knew the cameras only escalated the situation.

Other cities across the country often got more attention. They were less predictable and much louder. But Detective Ortega's fearless attitude won her fans. Millions grabbed the popcorn, sat back, and watched it unfold live each night.

That night, she jumped at the offer to head in. She assumed there was a need for actual detective work. She gladly left the film crew to Sergeant Thorn, Jr.

<u>September 3, 2035. 8:45 pm ET</u>

Detective Ortega stepped inside the cold dark room, deep inside the Miami Regional Operations Center (MROC). She greeted Sheriff Ridder.

"I got the message to get here," she said.

"Not from me, Hollywood," Sheriff Ridder said. "But since you're here."

"I didn't ask to be on TV," Detective Ortega said.

"I know, I know," the sheriff said. He waved for her to stand beside him at the mirrored window. Four individuals waited in interrogation room three.

"Detective, these are certifiably the dumbest people I've ever met."

"What are they in for?"

"Nothing," he said. He fanned himself with the dark brown Stetson the press knew him for, even though he was the sheriff of Miami Beach. "Cargo ship rescued them, stranded on an island a few miles out," he said. "Coast Guard took them in, checked them out. They're fine and got handed to me. They refuse to give their names or answer any of my questions."

Detective Ortega watched them fidgeting, looking around. The bald one with the white wife-beater tank top walked up to the mirrored glass to check his gold teeth. He stuck his tongue out, making obscene licking faces, unaware of anyone watching.

"Do I need to be here for this?" Ortega asked. "I feel like I'm missing a really good riot or something."

"I didn't call you here, remember?" the sheriff laughed.

She looked at the other male, sitting quietly in a John Deere cap, scratching his straggly red beard. "They from a drug deal gone bad?" she asked. "Did they sink their boat? Somebody leave them to die on the island?"

She watched one of the women play with her blue-flamed tattooed breasts. It looked like she was weighing two pomelos. The other woman in burgundy, low rise, micro mini shorts leaned over. She grabbed and bounced the woman's pomelos, giggling.

"I don't know," the sheriff said. He tried to keep his Christian eyes off the woman in the shorts. She was stretching her long tanned legs out on the table after putting the other woman's breasts down. He turned away, toward the detective. "I checked those things… them… those people," he said coming to a pause. "I checked them out."

"I see," she said trying not to laugh at the boss.

"We ran DNA scans," he said collecting his thoughts. The woman in the packed shorts pulled her legs back down as she sat up. She flung her long black hair and adjusted her full pink tank top. Every motion interfered with the sheriff's ability to speak. He took a drink of water and cleared his throat.

"Oddly enough," he continued as Ortega tried not to laugh at him, "FDLE said to hold them with no further information."

"For who?" she asked. She watched the one in front of the mirror try to suck food stuck in his gold teeth. The girl with the blue-flamed tattooed breasts finished adjusting them and began filing her nails. She chewed her gum like it was a source of oxygen, like a fish flapping its gills.

"No idea, but our orders are clear that no one is to touch those… touch them," said the sheriff. He kept taking his cowboy hat off and rubbing his head. "The folks."

"I got you," Ortega said. "Nothing stopping me from saying hi and ensuring our guests are comfortable."

"Hopefully the room is clear," the Sheriff said. He grabbed the doorknob, staring back at her with a face of stone. "In their boredom, the two boys had quite the fart contest going on, much to the protest of the young ladies."

Detective Ortega pretends she is intrigued, staring into the window. "Much better than a riot."

"It was all fun and games until the brainiacs realized they're in a contained space," the sheriff said. "All I can say, detective, is you're going to feel dumber when this is over."

Detective Ortega followed the sheriff into the interrogation room. The man sitting down picked up his head and scooted out his chair. "Yo, Hoss, I had enough of this bullshit. Get us outta here!"

Ortega stood over him and stared him down, cluing him in not to get up and do anything stupid.

"We're finalizing papers," said the sheriff. "We'll get you all on your way. I'm sure you got family wanting to know you're safe. Like I said, we'll call them if you cooperate."

"How long were you out there?" Ortega asked. She walked around to take the free chair at the table.

"What up, Mama?" the gold-toothed- man said. He stretched his white tank top, showing off his tattooed arms over the metal table. He scanned her up and down, making it known by all that he was deeply focused on her jeans. He patted the seat of the vacant chair next to him. He left his hand on the chair, palm facing up, grinning. Ortega walked over with a flirtatious smile. She placed her right combat boot on his hand, crushing it against the metal chair as she leaned in toward him. "I'm fine, honey."

She released his hand as she stepped away. She moved the chair a few more feet further from him. He lifted his hand with the other, like a dead fish and massaged it smiling at her.

"How long were you all stranded?" she asked again.

"What's the date?" the flame-breasted woman asked filing her blue nails.

"Saturday," the sheriff said.

"Date!" she snapped back.

"3ʳᵈ of September."

"Yo, dawg, like what year?" the gold-toothed guy said to the sheriff, tilting back in the metal chair. The redneck in the straggly red beard gave him a stern grin.

"You weren't gone that long, son," the sheriff chuckled. "Still 2035."

The young man's eyes bulged at the sound of 2035. The other coughed and sat up, folding his arms tighter. Ortega leaned in toward the redneck. She spotted the tattoo across his right bicep and got closer to examine it. "Your cute little tractor with the Confederate Flag says what?"

"Death before dishonor," he said.

"Yeah, but you spelled it dishoner," Ortega laughed. "You were first out in every spelling bee as a kid, weren't you?"

"I fixed it," he said. He showed where he used a knife to gouge out a line, making the "e" closer to an "o."

"If you say so," Ortega said. "And the tractor?"

"Show me something of yours first, little mama."

Sheriff Ridder startled him, kicking his chair with his boot.

"The tractor?" she asked again.

"Football," he said glaring at the sheriff. "I plowed through defenses like a tractor."

"Damn straight," the other male said. They high fived each other and made little pistol fingers, shooting in the air. "Run 'em over, Cowboys!"

"Cowboys?" Ortega replied. "Funny, that was my school's mascot. My brother blocked for a guy who called himself Tractor."

"Different school," he said.

"My brother was his classmate and blocked only four of the six years that dumbass was at high school."

The man stared at the nametape across her black tactical vest. He folded his arms. "Good for him."

Ortega turned her attention to the blue-flamed breasted woman twirling her long pink hair.

"Bitch," the woman said shaking her head. She threw up her hand in the detective's face. "Get your damn grille out of my face or I'll tear your ass up."

"Yeah, you will, girl," the other girl in the shorts laughed. They started dancing in their chairs, hands up in the air, snapping fingers, clapping. The two guys gave each other high fives and shouted, "You know it" and "Ah yeah." The one with the tractor tattoo got up to adjust his long cargo shorts, scratching his crotch.

"You're all dressed weird," Ortega said. "Where are you all from?"

Tractor man leaned back in his chair and lit a cigarette. "A magical place called none of your fucking business, Mama. I don't have to tell you shit."

"You sure?" she asked.

"Yeah," he said resting his hands on his head, puffing the cigarette in his mouth. "I know my Generic rights."

"Are you trying to say Geneva rights?" Ortega asked smiling.

"Yeah," he said. "Pretty sure keeping us is against the Declaration of Independents too."

"Brotherman speaks for all of us," the gold-toothed male affirmed.

Ortega snorted aloud laughing.

"I told you," Sheriff Ridder said.

"Damn," she said. She turned as the door began to open.

An old man strolled in with Deputy Ramos. His neatly pressed charcoal slacks matched his long goatee. He wore a black Hawaiian shirt featuring orange hibiscus flowers.

"Howdy, I guess," the old man said admiring Sheriff Ridder's cowboy hat.

"Who are you?" Sheriff Ridder walked up to the stranger.

"I'm the guy you're holding them for," he said handing the sheriff a piece of paper. "I do appreciate it."

"Sir," Deputy Ramos interrupted, "you have an urgent phone call."

"That's for you, Sheriff," the old man said. "And please hold off any visitors. I am first."

"Visitors?" the sheriff asked.

"Lots and lots of visitors," he said. "DEA, FBI, ATF, CIA, FDLE, DHS… every three and four-letter agency you can think of. Hell, you might learn a few new ones too." He smiled pointing at the four detainees. "Yep, our guests here are going to be rather popular as the day goes. So, I appreciate you telling whoever does show to grab a sandwich or something and wait their turn."

"Wait a minute."

"That little piece of paper, Sheriff, says they're mine until I deem otherwise."

"Sheriff," the deputy popped his head back in and pleaded, "they really want you on the phone right now."

"The detective can stay," the old man said looking to Ortega.

She nodded to the sheriff. "I got this."

"Hold your horses," the sheriff shouted. Walking out, he asked Deputy Ramos, "Who's they?"

The deputy shrugged his shoulders, holding the door, and following the sheriff out.

As the door closed, the old man grinned at the four sitting at the table. He then looked to the detective. "Detective Ortega!" he said taking a seat at the head of the table. "There's a place not too far that makes the best Cuban sandwich. Why don't you grab us seven or eight of them and we'll all get to know each other. I'm sure these folks are hungry."

"Kiss my ass," she said standing over him.

He laughed and set his ashen fedora neatly on the table. "I'm not here to measure my whatever to yours," he said. "Besides, I'm messing with you. You obviously got my text." He showed enjoyment staring into her round, tan, face. "It's so nice to finally meet you, Marisol."

"You know me?"

"Please sit," he said. She stared at him for a minute before giving in to curiosity and taking a seat. He crossed his left leg over his right and folded his hands in his lap. He waited for each of the four at the table to acknowledge him. Three looked up. He waited for the final acknowledgement. The redneck in the cap turned his head toward him.

"Trey!" he shouted. The young man lifted his eyes.

The old man tapped his black sneakers onto the white floor in excitement. Ortega froze staring at Trey, examining his face.

"It's so exciting," the old man said, bouncing his head like he was listening to a happy song. "I've waited so long to meet you."

"You don't know us for shit," Trey said clenching his fist above the table.

"I do," he said with a smile. "I'm finally meeting the infamous drug-running clan of Islamorada missing since 2008." He threw his hands up in the air laughing. "You're celebrities to me." The man then leaned in close, toward Trey. "What's funny is *when* you all returned." He leaned back, looking to Ortega, laughing, "I think it's random."

Trey refused to reply. The old man turned his attention to the end of the table. He raised his eyebrows at the young lady sitting in her super short shorts. Her slender legs rested up on the table, showing a thin rose vine tattoo, from her ankles up to the tight shorts. "I know here, I must have… Cheeks!"

Cheeks couldn't contain her happiness over someone knowing her. She smiled back. "Hey, baby."

"Hey, girl," he said to her with a wink.

He pointed at the young man in the white tank top next to her. "And here I've got CK, yes?"

CK showed his gold teeth at the mention of his name. Trey slapped him in the arm. CK quickly stared down.

The old man turned to the pomelo woman with the gold nose ring, long pink hair, sitting in black spandex leggings. "And the famous strip teasing, you-name-it she-do-anything, online and ahead of her time, ruler of the trailer park, Chandra McCoy." The woman extended her middle finger as she filed the others. "Oh, come on," he laughed. "Don't be that way, Princess."

She replied, "You jealous I'm famous?"

"I always say… it's easy to be famous," the old man said staring down at his watch. "It's what you're famous for that matters." He looked to the detective.

"Now where are the other two?" he asked, rolling his fingers on the metal table. He made a loud clicking sound with his fingernails. "You killed them, didn't you?" he asked Trey with a smile. "Maybe left them behind?"

The old man's smile dropped. He softly asked, "Did *they*… kill them?"

"Who are *they*?" Detective Ortega asked.

"Ain't us, fool," Trey said. His legs kept shaking, occasionally tapping on the tile floor.

The old man waved to Trey looking away. "Did you know you folks are on the long historical list of disappearances off the Florida coast? They had a TV special about the legend of the Bermuda Triangle. You're all famous."

"Shut up, baby," Cheeks said to the old man.

"It's true, girl," he said with a wink. "They mentioned a few lost galleons with Spanish gold. Then some civilian and military planes lost between Miami, Fort Lauderdale, Palm Beach, Bermuda, and the Bahamas. Tons of sunk ships, never seen again. Then there's the mighty 'Tits Up' found capsized August 13, the year 2008."

"Not us, Jack."

"It is," the old man laughed. "It so really is!"

Detective Ortega thought back to all the years her father researched each of the missing aboard that capsized vessel. He didn't get out in time to rescue them. He took part in the search until it was halted by Tropical Storm Fay. He spent the years after busting newer, inexperienced boats trying to pick up the airdropped drugs. Local law enforcement saw growing turf battles as new teams tried to fill the gap made by the disappearance of Bo Jim "Boss" Dunkin's crew.

A grumpy fisherman by day, Boss secretly commanded an army. He coordinated with the cartel planes to drop the product. His fishing boats picked up the product. The strip clubs laundered the money and pushed the product. Motorcycle gangs secured highway dominance. They threatened any cops asking too many questions. Monster pickups and airboats traversed the swamps to remote stash houses in the Everglades. The car clubs and truckers raced everything up A1A and I-95. Bo Jim was boss from the international crossing to the local collection... from the Florida chain of custody to a distribution system across North America. Product could be picked up five miles off the Keys on a Saturday night and on the streets of Chicago by Wednesday.

According to Detective Ortega's father, Bo Jim Dunkin was a dangerously talented leader. "Boss made even the dumbest sons of bitches useful," he once told her. She thought about that long and hard, staring at the four soulless twits in front of her.

"You're all dead," she said.

"You called that, fool," Trey said. The four laughed at her.

"DNA matches all four," the old man said. "That's 27 years and you all haven't aged a bit. How long were you really gone?"

"Got the wrong folks," Trey said.

"I'm just jealous," the old man said smiling at Cheeks. "I mean, 27 years and everyone's looking young… looking good."

"Thank you, baby," Cheeks said.

"You're welcome, girl," he beamed winking back.

"How long were you gone?" he asked again.

"I think three years," Cheeks said. The others glared at her.

"I'm still wondering where Boss and your buddy, Shake-E are," he said. The old man straightened the edge of his fedora with his hands and set it back on the table taking a deep breath. He looked to Trey. "As much fun as this is, I don't know how much time I have to work any serious matters. God only knows how much you Florida hillbilly assclowns left things."

"Fuck you, Holmes," Trey said.

"Ok," the old man shouted. "Let's try a different approach," the old man said, leaning in, staring into Trey's eyes. "I'm going to tell you, son, and you better listen," he said with a frightening serious tone. "I… am… the man."

Trey's head sprung up, attentive to every word.

"You know it too," the old man said. "It's not my dear detective here, the nice cowboy sheriff, or anyone in the Coast Guard, the Army, Border Patrol, DHS, or Marine Patrol. It's not FDLE, Miami PD, DEA, FBI, or any of the other folks on their way. They're going right up your ass when they see your DNA match all you left behind. You haven't said a thing and I get it. I wouldn't be happy to be back either."

"What does that mean?" Trey asked.

"Detective," the old man said, "You are looking at a crew wanted by every three-letter agency there is. From running drugs to guns, extortion, insurance fraud, murder, even down to Princess scamming old folks out of their social security. Didn't matter if it was tied down or not, this crew ran the gauntlet."

He smiled at Trey. "You know the Columbians and Cubans had contracts out on you all? Technically, they're still active."

"Bullshit," Trey said.

"And then there's Yarg Bonsetti," the old man laughed. "Yarg's a mean motherfucker and he knows all about you ditching his son Oleg and five of his best men in the Atlantic for a late-night feeding frenzy. That was your modus operandi, my friend. I know. Boss handed you the folks. You took them out, all tied up, and watch them sink or let a shark finish them."

"Know nothing about it," CK said.

"Yarg Bonsetti's going to be so thrilled to see you alive." The agent wiped his forehead with a white handkerchief. "Dream come true, kid."

"Fuck you," Trey said.

The old man turned to the detective. "These guys were the only charter that returned with *less* people than they left with. At least, purposely."

The detective shook her head. "Yarg Bonsetti's the most ruthless crime boss in North America."

CK laughed. "Since when?"

"Since you all disappeared twenty-seven years ago," the old man said. "Yarg's been a busy man… and cursing you all those years, thinking about what he'd do if he ever got a hold of you. I know it's only three years to you, but… yeah."

Trey folded his arms and looked up to the ceiling. CK's legs began to shake loudly under the table.

"Fuck, man," CK whispered to Trey.

Trey pulled CK in by his shirt. "Don't matter. I'll settle whatever needs to be settled on my time! I'm back, motherfucker."

"That's the spirit!" the old man said.

Trey let go of CK's shirt. "Why we even listening to Pops?"

The old man leaned in toward Trey. "This is nice, but I really need you kids to hear me. The only thing that matters, right now, is that I am *THE MAN*. I am. Sooner you get that, you help the whole world."

Trey looked to the others. They remained silent, nodding no.

"Trey, I have lost more sleep than I care to admit, thinking how bad you all could mess things up. I mean, of all the people in the entire world!" The old man rubbed his burned palm along his dark, wrinkled face and ran it through his black licorice hair. "You know, we think you are their first. That's history, son."

They sat in silence. Their looks grew more worrisome by the second. The old man then took a deep breath and shouted.

"GReeEEEEE ZiiiPPPPPALANNNNNIIIII FaFa FaFa UNKTO KNUCKTU WAAAA PINANIIIIIIIIIIIIIIIIII!"

Detective Ortega jumped from her chair, her back to the wall. "What the hell?" she shouted at the old man, her hand over her heart. "You're too weird for me, dude." She yelled for the sheriff through the mirrored glass, hoping for a sign of life from the other side. There was only silence. "Hey, open up!" she shouted.

"They said you'd say that," Trey softly told the old man.

The others nodded. "Yeah, baby's cool," Cheeks said.
"Thank you, girl," the old man said.
"You're the man," Trey laughed, relieved.
"I am," the old man said.
"What is happening?" Detective Ortega asked.
"Tell you later, dear. You'll love it." The old man asked her to take her seat. She slowly eased back down into the metal chair. She stared down, into the table, in defeat. "My dad looked for you all. He was marine patrol and always wondered what happened. I saw the markers commemorating your deaths when I was kid."
"They nice?" Cheeks asked.
"I guess," Detective Ortega said. "But as time went on, my dad learned about each of you... your operation, who you were,

who you worked for, and what you did." She looked them in the eyes. "You're all the WORST human beings in the entire world!"

"Say what, bitch?" Princess jumped from her chair and lunged toward the detective. The old man quickly got between them, surprising them both with his speed. "Sit!" he shouted at the two of them.

Cheeks sighed and rolled her eyes. "A little judgmental, aren't we, honey?"

Arguing and shouting continued between the detective and the four detainees. The old man held up his hands as the referee, asking them all to shut up. "Thank you," he said. "Now, I don't disagree with the detective, folks." He placed his elbows on the table, leaning in, staring at Trey. "But right now, I need to know if they're staying, going, or got something else in mind."

Trey sat quietly, thinking. "I don't know."

"You were with them for how long?" the old man pleaded.

"We thought three years, but you're saying twenty-seven," Trey said.

"That's just when they dropped you off," the old man said. His eyebrows pressed down on his sad eyes. "You really can't guess what they are going to do, son? Think hard dammit!"

Trey put both hands deep into his pants, feeling around, with his eyes closed.

"Not that hard, son," the old man said looking away.

Trey continued digging around until he pulled a small object from inside his pants. It looked like a small crystal river rock the size of a golf ball with glowing neon blue lines.

"You kept that thing with your junk?" CK asked.

"I did," Trey laughed to CK sliding it across the table to the agent. "They said to give it to the man."

"And that'd be me," the old man said, staring at it.

"Who's they?" Ortega asked. Everyone ignored her.

"The clouds, the horizontal lightning, the problems with the instrumentation…" the detective said to herself.

"Like today when they found them," the agent said. "I feel like you're almost getting it, detective. Let me know when you've caught up."

Detective Ortega's heart raced to memories of her dad and his obsession about the Bermuda Triangle, the famous territory that claimed the lives of many traveling by boat and plane, to never be heard from or seen again, possibly sunk by an eruption of gases from under the surface of the Atlantic Ocean, or rogue waves and random vortexes swatting down the vessels and planes, or an electrical phenomenon, a time warp, a random skip in time and space witnesses spoke of… the lights, the colors, the horizontal lightning emitting from a source not of this planet…

"You're from one of those government agencies that track UFOs and aliens," Ortega said to the old man.

He snapped his fingers at her with a smile. "Nicely done. Now there's a few these days," the agent said. "But only one matters and I'm from it. Call me Agent… Joe."

"That's it? That sounds totally made up."

"Alright, you got me. I'm really Agent… Burt," the old man said. "Better?"

"Not at all, Burt," she said. "I thought you guys wore suits?" Ortega glanced over his hibiscus Hawaiian shirt. His right arm looked like lizard skin from burns, radiation, or some combination. His left arm had long, winding, faded black tattoos and he wore a triangular, unpolished metal watch.

"Honey, it's Florida," he pleaded. "I'm not wearing a suit in this humidity. If it makes you feel better, I have a suit at home. Kind of a dark gray number. My third wife said it matched my soul or something. She should talk."

"Where's the sheriff?" Ortega got up from her chair.

"I don't *need* you, detective," he said. "I only *asked* for you out of respect for your dad."

"You knew my dad?"

"I did," the agent said softly. "I ran across Officer Orlando Ortega quite a few times. Or really, he ran across me. An incredibly kind man… and smart, smart enough to know no one would ever believe him. He was *always* so proud of you." Marisol Ortega was, for once, speechless.

"That's so sweet," Cheeks said, trying not to cry.

Agent Burt nodded to her with his eyes closed.

"Stay, please," he said to Ortega. He leaned forward in his chair toward the table and tapped the crystal stone seven times. "And watch this!"

The stone spun like a top into a fiery gold blur of light, hovering a foot above the table. Ortega could not take her eyes off it, feeling its warmth. It emitted a white light followed by a softer blue light.

"What is happening?" she asked.

"I liked your dad better," Agent Burt said. "You talk too much." He continued to smile at the presentation. The brilliant light emitted a model of the universe across the room. CK, Princess, Cheeks, and Tractor appeared less impressed. Moving stars, planets, and galaxies, all seemed at their fingertips. A scratchy, robotic voice began to speak. Large letters in a golden light appeared, like English subtitles before them.

HUMAN BITCHES! WE CAME FROM A LONG ASS RIDE, NOT WANTING TO STIR ANY SHIT. OUR WAY IS LEGIT, TO NOT KILL HOMIES AND NOT HARM SHIT, TO SEEK BROTHERHOOD ACROSS OUR UNIVERSE. SO, PEACE, HOLMES.

TO BETTER DIG WHAT MAKES Y'ALL YOU, WE SNATCHED AND GRABBED A SIXER OF YOUR PEEPS THROUGH THE UNIVERSAL PORTAL TO YOUR PLANET.

"It's funny they all chose to put the portal right off Florida," Agent Burt said to Ortega. "I guess they heard everyone visits Florida and went with that."

"In the Bermuda Triangle?" Ortega asked.

"Yes," he said. "They put it somewhere in there."

"Who's they?"

"All of them," he said. "Eight species, ten planets, best guess."

"Eleven," CK said. Agent Burt nodded at CK finally saying something useful.

OUR WORLDS ARE LIGHTYEARS AWAY, TOO LONG TO TRAVEL WITHOUT MAKING A WORMHOLE IN THE PORTAL. IT WAS OUR FIRST TIME USING IT. WE SPENT THE NEXT 3 HUMAN YEARS MAD TRYING TO GET THE BITCH BACK UP TO RETURN THESE PLAYERS AND COMMUNICATE TO EARTH AS WE BE DOING TODAY.

"Took them bitches forever," Trey said.

"Again, they didn't build the highway," Agent Burt said. "They just jumped in it."

"I liked their place," Cheeks said. "It was pretty."

"That's nice," said Agent Burt. "I've heard that."

WE'VE BEEN HOSTING, WATCHING YOUR WAYS. WE CHRONICLED YOUR LANGUAGE, YOUR BEHAVIORS, AND KNOWLEDGE.

"Now my nightmares come to life," Agent Burt said to himself.

WE ACCEPTED YOUR HUMANS KNOWN AS BOSS, CK, CHEEKS, PRINCESS, TRACTOR, AND SHAKE-E AS EARTH'S AMBASSADORS.

"No, no, no, no, no," Agent Burt said staring at Trey. He closed his eyes and grabbed his forehead with both hands.

Detective Ortega's eyes never blinked as she watched the conclusion to her father's later life of curiosity, wonder, and study.

CK ASKED A LOT ABOUT ANAL CAVITY SEARCHES.

"I only know of two species that do that, folks," said Agent Burt. "I am sure these guys don't." CK quickly looked away.

WE DON'T DO THAT. THOSE ARE THE OTHERS.

Agent Burt folded his arms. "Called it."

WE DIDN'T KNOW WHAT THEY WERE UNTIL CK SHOWED OUR PLANET'S LEAD SCIENTIST. ZYTMANTILI WILL NOT BE THE SAME.

Trey and CK snickered to themselves.

"What is wrong with you?" Agent Burt shouted. Ortega put her head on the table, suddenly wishing she was somewhere else, unable to look the laughing CK in the face.

WE REPLICATED ALL ORGANIC MATERIALS EXTRACTED FROM YOUR VESSEL, TITS UP. PROMISED ENLIGHTENMENT BY YOUR AMBASSADORS, THE WHITE SUBSTANCE WAS REPRODUCED IN LARGE QUANTITIES UNDER THE LEADERSHIP OF CK AND TRACTOR.

"Cocaine?" the agent shouted at Trey. "You had aliens producing and using cocaine?" Trey and CK looked away.

WE USED THE WHITE STUFF TOO MUCH. THINGS GOT MAD. MANY FOUGHT EACH OTHER FOR IT, SOMETHING WE HAVE NOT SEEN FOR CENTURIES AND IS AGAINST OUR PEACEFUL WAYS.

"That shit's on them, man!" Trey said looking to the ceiling, avoiding the agent's stare of burning judgement.

CK AND SHAKE-E SHOWED US HOW TO ACCESSORIZE OUR TERRAIN SPEEDERS.

"Super cool shit," CK explained to Agent Burt. "Shake-E pimped them speeders real dang sweet. They got shit like chrome, but it moves. So awesome."

The agent put up his hand, signaling CK to stop. "In the interest of time, son, you go put that in the W column and let's move on." The agent re-tapped the rock.

CHEEKS AND PRINCESS LEARNED MUCH ABOUT US...

Princess' face froze. "That's sweet," Cheeks giggled.

AND OUR ANATOMY. THEY SHOWED US THINGS WE ARE NOT PROUD OF BUT WON'T STOP DOING.

"Oh my God," Ortega shouted with her head still down on the table.

"They're not much different than us," Cheeks said. "Just stuff is in different places."

"Damn tired of you judging us, bitch," Princess said to the detective, twirling her pink hair. Detective Ortega picked up her head, rolled her eyes, and turned her attention back to the presentation.

TRACTOR INTRODUCED US TO BEER. WE DIG THAT SHIT, YO. TRACTOR, MAD LOVE FOR YOU, BRO.

Tractor nodded and pounded his heart with a fist.

"You showed them cocaine," Agent Burt said to Trey. "Might as well get a planet of superiorly more powerful extraterrestrials high AND drunk. Cause, well, why the hell not?"

SHAKE-E SHOWED US THE ROPES ON THE GREEN LEAVES. IT WAS GREAT UNTIL THE ZIETANS WIGGED OUT.

"Marijuana too," Agent Burt said, disgusted. "You just had it all."

"They snatched us," Trey laughed. "Don't forget that, bro."

"We needed the Zietan class," agent Burt shouted. "They were our only hope if the Gortellian masses turned."

"Zietans?" Detective Ortega asked.

"Zietans are their assigned thinkers… the scholars of the Gortellian race. It's just how they do things."

"Yeah, them bitches vegetables now," CK laughed with Trey. "Told them to take it easy on that shit."

"You were guests!" Agent Burt screamed. He stood up from his chair, pointing at all of them. "You were their guests!"

WE CANNOT BLAME THEM FOR WHAT BECAME THE WAR. WE WERE ANXIOUS TO LEARN THE WAYS OF YOUR SPECIES.

"Son of a bitch," the agent exhaled, sitting back down. "They're at war now?" All nodded yes.

BOSS WAS A STRONG LEADER.

"Finally!" The agent smacks his hand on the table. "Let's hear about the brains of the operation, wherever the hell he is!"

BOSS QUICKLY TAUGHT HALF OF OUR CIVILIZATION TO BE HATING ON THE OTHER HALF. HE LEADS A BAD REVOLUTION AND IS STILL WANTED. WE WANTED TO RETURN HIM MOST, BUT STILL CAN'T FIND HIS ASS.

"Let me get this straight," Agent Burt said. "We now have a South Florida drug boss leading an alien army in a civil war on another planet?"

Trey nodded yes. "He's a natural."

"Hey, what can you do?" Agent Burt said shrugging his shoulders, rolling his eyes. "Fuck!" he shouted to himself.

WE ARE SORRY SHAKE-E CAN'T RETURN. WE PLEAD, MAN; IT WAS NOT OUR FAULT. HE DIED IN THE BATTLE OF MOUNT TYUAKHHFJ FIGHTING THE FORCES OF BOSS. WE LEARNED MAD COURAGE BY HIS EXAMPLE. FOREVER BIG THANKS FOR SHAKE-E'S SACRIFICE.

"Rest in peace, Shake-E," Trey said aloud. "A righteous death," CK said. Trey looked to the agent. "Bro was ambushed. He took out a shit ton of Boss' bitches before some green laser shit finally incinerated his ass to mush."

"Well, that's one way to go out," the agent said.

"I know, right?" CK said smiling with his gold teeth.

WE CAN NOW TELL YOU.
PRINCESS SOLD SHAKE-E OUT.

"You liars!" Princess jumped up from the table shouting. "All of them! Lying ass little bitches!"

FOR CHEAP.

"You bitch! I knew it!" Trey shouted, reaching across for her hair. CK tried to restrain him. Trey managed past CK just long enough to rip off Chandra's long pink wig.

"Oh, you bastard!" she screamed.

Trey ran circles around the room with the wig on his head, dancing, and yelling, "Look at me! I'm a washed-up ho." He pressed his chest together like he was showing off boobs, mocking Princess. Ortega stuck out her boot and tripped him. His head slammed against the metal table. His body fell to the floor. Agent Burt grabbed the wig.

Trey laid on the floor as the other three exchanged obscenities and hand gestures.

"Boss was my dad!" Princess shouted.

"No, he wasn't, you dumb skank," Trey shouted getting up to his chair, holding his forehead.

"He really wasn't," Agent Burt said. All quietly stared at him. He handed Chandra her hair. "Put your hair on and sit."

"Whatever!" Princess said, taking her seat.

"Boss was really manipulative." Agent Burt smiled to Ortega. "Got to give it to him."

Agent Burt tapped the device again as everyone quieted.

LAST WORD… PRINCESS IS A HO FOR DOING SO.

"Obviously," the agent said folding his arms, staring down into the table, silent.

"Fuck y'all," Princess said turning away to the glass wall, continuing to file her nails.

Cheeks sat back down and cried into her hands for a minute before going back to twirling her hair. Detective Ortega continued to watch with her mouth open.

WE TRAVELED GREAT LENGTHS AND CRAZY TIME AND SPACE TO OBSERVE YOUR PEEPS, YOUR WAYS, AND CONSIDER BUILDING A BOND FOR PEACE, DROPPING KNOWLEDGE, SHARING OUR TECH AND OUR MOST ACCOMPLISHED ADVANCEMENTS TO YOUR KIND.

"But…" the agent said, pausing in front of them, holding his hands out, shrugging his shoulders.

UNFORTUNATELY, OUR TIME, ABILITY, AND DESIRE TO DO SO HAS ALTERED. OUR DESTINIES BE JACKED UP. IN THE WORDS OF PRINCESS, "IT ISN'T YOU, IT'S US."

"There it is, folks," the agent said.

WE DEFINITELY WON'T BE RETURNING.   EVER.

The room was silent. The rock spun faster. The galaxy of stars surrounding them in the room circled as the light faded. All avoided eye contact with each other and waited in silence, like a roller coaster coming to an end.

Detective Ortega was relieved to know her father's suspicions to what happened that day twenty-seven years ago were justified. All the years people called him odd, all the years he grew quiet, he kept his theories to himself. He didn't want his children to be seen as products of a crazy conspiracy theorist. He continued his job in the Marine Patrol despite his insatiable drive to find the truth. He had to save that for the off hours… to inquire if everything we knew about the universe and humanity's place in it was wrong, overestimated, or underestimated. Along the way, he made it far enough into the rabbit hole to get the attention of Agent Burt (or whatever his name is). In time and after enough run-ins, the two men became friendly acquaintances.

Her father, rest his soul, would have loved to have seen this, regardless of the mixed outcome.

The crew inside that cold interrogation room knew Yarg Bonsetti, the Cubans, the Russians, the Columbians, and most three-letter agencies were waiting for them somewhere outside in the Florida heat.

Earth was not getting invaded, blown up, pillaged, or molested today. No cavity searches. Not even a quick visit.

They came to Florida and learned it's not for everyone.

"Well, that wasn't so bad," Agent Burt said as the rock made its final spin.

LATER, BITCHES.

<u>Acknowledgments</u>

This book is dedicated to Betty and Jim. These stories were written with the greatest love and gratitude. I hope and pray to see you again.

Thank you to my love, Jeanette. You have heard my stories a million times. A few are finally in a book.

And to my dear Florida:
Please don't ever listen to the other forty-nine.
I love you the way you are!

Jeddie.net